MORE MYSTERIES FROM THE
BERKLEY PUBLISHING GROUP . . .

THE
CROSSWORD
MURDER

NERO BLANC

BERKLEY PRIME CRIME, NEW YORK

THE CROSSWORD MURDER

A Berkley Prime Crime Book / published by arrangement with
the authors

PRINTING HISTORY
Berkley Prime Crime trade edition / August 1999
Berkley Prime Crime mass-market edition / October 2000

The Penguin Putnam Inc. World Wide Web site address is
http://www.penguinputnam.com

ISBN: 0-425-17701-7

Berkley Prime Crime Books are published
by The Berkley Publishing Group,
a division of Penguin Putnam Inc.,
375 Hudson Street, New York, New York 10014.
The name BERKLEY PRIME CRIME and the BERKLEY PRIME CRIME
design are trademarks belonging to Penguin Putnam Inc.

PRINTED IN THE UNITED STATES OF AMERICA

10 9 8 7 6 5 4 3 2

Dedicated to
Livingston L. Biddle, Jr.
For his unparalleled contribution to
the state of the arts in America

THE
CROSSWORD
MURDER

CHAPTER

1

"**H**OLD MY CALLS!" Thompson Briephs flicked the lock in his office door as he barked out the command. At ten-thirty A.M. the temperature in the Massachusetts coastal town had already reached a brutal 94 degrees and the despairing throb of the antiquated window air conditioner did nothing to alleviate the problem. The brass doorknob twisted greasily in Briephs' hand; the heat wave that had gripped New England for a relentless two weeks had begun to feel like his personal demon. He shook his head as if trying to expunge his sense of frenzy and oppression, but there was no escape. The heat followed him everywhere, clogging his lungs and nostrils and swelling his eyelids until they ached. Beneath the urbane lines of a navy blazer and knife-pressed khaki trousers, his middle-aged but athletic body railed at man's impotence when confronting the forces of nature.

Briephs ran damp fingers across his well-formed lips, then tested the lock again. Through the door's frosted glass panel, he watched the blurred outline of his secretary move across the outer room: a tall and hopelessly angular female physique topped by an aging, toothy face and hair the color of dirty sand. JaneAlice Miller's single display of femininity was a bold slash of fuchsia lipstick. Briephs stared through the glass at the repellent color; the door panel illuminated and enhanced the purplish-red shade like a rainy night magnifying the glare of oncoming car lights.

"Are you all right, Mr. B? It sure is hot out . . ."

JaneAlice idolized her boss; she'd been his willing slave for thirteen years and so abject and fawning in her attentions that her fellow employees at the Newcastle *Herald* were convinced she had masochistic tendencies. That and the fact that her sole source of solace seemed to be an obsession with aging or dead movie stars and their life works. She could rattle off the name of any film, its cast and director as well as recite salient lines of dialogue. It was a trick she was not encouraged to perform.

"Mr. B? Are you okay?"

Briephs didn't respond. Instead, he automatically repeated his previous gesture, passing a perspiring hand across his mouth and then wincing as if in physical pain.

"Maybe you need a bicarb, Mr. B . . . You probably didn't get enough sleep last night after that *lavish* fund-raiser . . . Oh, speaking of lavish, Mrs. Housemann phoned to thank you . . . She said the affair went *very* well . . ." JaneAlice's gawky form bobbed about as she spoke. She was so close to the door's far side that Briephs could hear her palpitating breaths. She sounded like a gaffed sea bass, the thought of which immediately produced a spasm of nausea. Thompson was forced to gasp and shut his eyes; sweat covered his scalp and the backs of his legs.

"Did you hear me, Mr. B? . . . This heat sure is something, isn't it? The meteorologist says we can't expect any relief for at least another week . . . Oh, Mrs. Housemann also said she's lunching with the mister today and mentioned she'd stop by to show her gratitude in person—sort of like when Adolphe Menjou . . ."

Briephs leaned his head into his palms and groaned aloud. The last person he wanted to think about was his editor in chief's newest wife, the flame-haired, aggressively voluptuous Betsey Housemann—née Grumpilski.

"Mr. B?"

"I heard you!" The words flared out of Briephs' mouth. He groaned again, but more softly. "Mrs. Housemann already telephoned my residence to thank me for last night. She neglected to mention she'd be lunching with her good husband."

The former Betsey Grumpilski's husband, Steven, was a quick-tempered septuagenarian who'd clawed his way up through the *Herald*'s ranks. Ever conscious of having been denied a prep school and Ivy League education like Thompson's, Housemann's response to any adversarial situation was sudden and ruthless anger. His feuds and vendettas were as legendary as his rages over misprints and errata. Heads could roll over misspellings; careers were threatened by sloppy reportage. Steven carried this business doctrine into personal life, becoming a vengeful and often mendacious opponent in the many competitive sports he played. There were few golfing partners he didn't outlast, few squash and tennis courts that hadn't echoed with his outraged shouts. Housemann also believed he could outmaneuver Father Time if he picked a younger bride as soon as the previous model began to show wear; he married frequently, with the fervor some men reserve for purchasing automobiles.

"Now, JaneAlice, as you're well aware, I require privacy to sort through the day's submissions." Briephs sighed noisily as if to express how beleaguered he felt. "I don't wish to see or converse with anyone . . . Betsey Housemann, included. Is that clear, Miss Miller?"

The sudden use of her surname sent chills of self-pity up and down JaneAlice's spine. "Oh, Mr. B! Don't be cross with me! I'd never do anything to hurt you! Not in a *billion* years. I'm your *Girl Friday*, you know." She paused at the door briefly, then skittered away, a praying mantis changing color and shape.

Returned to silence, Thompson Crane Briephs, the Newcastle *Herald's* renowned crossword editor, pushed aside the latest offerings from his many contributors as well as an envelope bearing the logo of his crusty literary agent, and another from the New York publisher who compiled his annual puzzle collection. Those messages would wait—but the hand-delivered envelope, the one that had been slipped surreptitiously into the pile of incoming mail, would not. Briephs found himself breathing irregularly. His mouth was as dry as baked mud.

He stared at the cheap white paper; it was smudged with grime as if the fingers that had carried it to the *Herald*'s offices had never encountered soap. "This has gone on far too long," he announced. "I've been reasonable until now, but the entire situation has become absurd. Farcical, really . . . If one were given to dramatic allusions . . ." Despite the brave words, he was sweating profusely. The starched collar of his pima cotton shirt felt sodden and oily around his neck. "Dammit!" he muttered more loudly.

Briephs' public persona—his impeccably tailored jackets, the discreet silk neckties and regal mane of silver hair—were all part of a carefully constructed façade. As a member of the illustrious Crane family, the clan who'd first settled Newcastle's rocky shores, he wasn't permitted to appear in any guise other than exemplary blueblood and model citizen. At fifty-one, Thompson had had plenty of practice.

"Dammit," he repeated, then slit open the grimy envelope. Inside was the usual word game—or more accurately, a piece of a word game cut from the *Herald*'s daily crossword. But whoever had developed the habit of hacking apart Thompson's puzzles had created new sets of clues that even the most slack-jawed, nose-ringed teenager would have found embarrassingly inadequate. Only infrequently did the format vary or a clue contain a sophisticated etymological riddle, leading Briephs to suspect his tormentor might be more than one person—or a single being so verbally adept that he, or she, could afford to play the idiot. Thompson guessed he was being toyed with; if not, his elusive correspondent would have demanded more money. Everyone in Newcastle knew Thompson Crane Briephs was a wealthy man. A very wealthy man.

The present message contained the usual threat of "exposure" if "Thompson Briephs" didn't "ante up." This time the amount was a paltry two hundred dollars.

"Eleven hundred last time . . . five hundred before that . . . three thousand four months ago . . . A year of being nickel-and-dimed to death," Briephs groaned. "What is this creature waiting for? Where is the method to this madness?"

Briephs dropped the letter and envelope into his calf-skin attaché case. By now, his handsome shirt was thoroughly soaked; the monogrammed pocket clung to his skin like ancient adhesive tape. Reflexively, he tucked his hand back into the attaché case, fingering a loose-leaf notebook that contained the beginnings of his latest and as yet unfinished collection of puzzles. This "bible" was never far from his reach; touching it gave him momentary solace.

"Bartholomew Kerr's on the line, sir." JaneAlice's tenuous voice broke into Briephs' reverie. "He says he won't take a moment. It's about the society column. He wanted to mention the theatre piece you're backing, but didn't have time to discuss it last night . . . He said you must have slipped away before he realized it . . ."

Briephs' hand jerked away from the notebook, ripping a manicured fingernail on the hard edge. "Dammit, Jane-Alice! I distinctly said 'no interruptions'!" His voice rattled the glass.

The secretary again retreated from the entrance to her boss's forbidden sanctuary. "But he said—"

"I don't care what that sniveling snoop told you!"

"Yes, sir." A faint sound of weeping followed this exchange. Briephs raised impatient eyebrows but stifled an additional tirade.

"I'm going home," he said instead. "I can't operate under these appalling conditions. Tell Mr. Housemann I'll fax the Saturday and Sunday puzzles."

"Oh, Mr. B, I hope it wasn't anything I did!"

But Briephs had already slammed out of his office and strode through JaneAlice's. The attaché case was clenched in his fist.

Briephs watched the doors of the *Herald*'s elevator snap shut. Its sculpted bronze façade to the contrary, the car's interior was airless and stank of old shoes, unwashed hair and too many layers of yellowing floor wax. He wrinkled his patrician nose in distaste, then jabbed the button for the garage level. The elevator began rumbling through the brick building, coming to a halt on the third and second floors, although the halls remained mercifully empty. Briephs could hear voices arguing, doors slamming and a cacophony of unanswered telephones—the customary panic to meet Friday's deadline. "Dammit," he swore, stabbing the garage button again. The minutes were ticking away, and he was stuck in an elevator from hell. He could feel sweat prickling his scalp and the palms of his hands. "This is ludicrous," he muttered between clenched teeth. "I'm Thompson Briephs. I should not be subjected to this type of abuse."

Finally he reached the *Herald*'s cavernous underground parking garage. An inadequate number of fluorescent lights cast putrid green shadows that intensified the humidity while failing to fully illuminate the area. Involuntarily, Briephs combed his fingers through his silver hair as he peered through the murky gloom, searching for signs of life. When he was certain there were no witnesses, he opened his attaché case, pulled out the letter and envelope, shredded them and dropped the pieces into a Dumpster. Then he walked to an adjoining arched alcove and his waiting canary-yellow Jaguar XJS convertible—a toy purchased with the advance from his tenth annual collection of puzzles.

Briephs pushed the Jag's black canvas top into its boot, tossed in the calfskin case, jumped into the driver's seat, and was about to turn the key in the ignition when he heard the unmistakable sound of high heels tapping across poured concrete. He jerked around and stared through the darkness, gradually recognizing Betsey Housemann sashaying slowly toward him. A statuesque woman who claimed to be thirty-seven, she was dressed to kill in a tight black silk blouse and short blue leather skirt that barely covered what it had been designed to cover. Her hair billowed around her face like mounds of crinkled red cellophane.

"Sneaking out on me, are you, Tommy-Boy?"

"I wasn't aware you were coming so soon, Betsey."

"I'm 'coming' to see Steven, honeybunch . . . Besides, I thought you didn't approve of inelegant speech in public."

"The verb is a common one, Betsey . . . Old English *cuman*, meaning to approach . . ."

"You know that lingo stuff bores the you-know-what out of me . . ."

"Perhaps you shouldn't have espoused yourself to a newspaperman. Words, I believe, are Steven's stock in trade . . ." Briephs made an instinctive grab for his brief-case.

"My lord and master isn't expecting me till lunchtime. Maybe I could make a quick detour . . . Come out to your hideaway for a little warm-up exercise . . . We could pick up where we left off last night . . ."

"Not today." Briephs turned the key in the ignition.

"You can be a real creep, Thompson."

" 'So is this great and wide sea, wherein all things creeping innumerable . . . ' I'm a man, dear girl, in case your memory doesn't span a mere twelve hours. I don't slither on my belly. I walk on two feet. Now, I'm afraid I must go. I'm regrettably late."

Betsey's tall form swayed over the driver's-side door. For a moment Briephs imagined she was going to grab his keys and heave them toward the garage's inaccessible recesses. Or swallow them. Betsey was capable of almost anything.

"You know, Tommy, sometimes I think I hate you," she cooed in a husky voice.

CHAPTER

2

BRIEPHS GUNNED HIS car up the garage ramp, wincing at the sudden glare as he entered Thomas Paine Boulevard. Lining the broad pavement, shrubberies, trees and pots of geranium, verbena and dusty miller wilted and withered while heat waves shimmered from the rows of handsome Greek Revival– and Colonial-era buildings that housed the city's financial and commercial hub.

He stared at the stone and clapboard structures and at the shops and banking institutions nestled discreetly within them. Many of the buildings dated from the glory days of the clipper ship and whaling trade; they were an understated but affluent compendium of fresh white paint, gold lettering, Doric columns and scrubbed brick sidewalks. At another time, Thompson would have been grateful for the town fathers' foresight in maintaining

Newcastle's architectural heritage. Today the refurbished façades seemed the epitome of venality and deceit: elegance concealing corrupt and moneygrubbing souls.

Briephs turned right on Nathaniel Hawthorne Place and headed for the former customs house, now converted into a transportation depot. There, he bypassed a Peter Pan bus discharging passengers from Springfield, parked his car, entered the restored stone building and went through the same procedure he'd followed for the past twelve months. When he'd deposited the payment in its customary locker and hidden the key in its usual nook, he walked slowly out the main entrance, circled back to his car and sped off again, following a circuitous route of waterfront lanes that skirted the pristine base of Liberty Hill.

Thompson needed to avoid the denizens of the exclusive neighborhood. His mother's house sat among the gracious, pillared Revolutionary War–era mansions, only a stone's throw from that of her brother—Briephs' uncle, the senior United States Senator Hal Crane. White Caps and Gull's Way had been Crane family properties since they were built; not one had been sold, nor a foot of their spacious lawns and gardens altered. Long-dead Cranes, descending on Newcastle from their homes in heaven or in hell, would have found their former domiciles undefiled.

Briephs left Liberty Hill and turned onto the harbor road, pushing his foot to the accelerator as the lanes widened and flattened. He flicked on the Jag's CD player; the Pavarotti recording of *Turandot* rang out at full volume but Puccini's arias of dominion and power were of no avail. Thompson Briephs didn't feel capable of conquering anything.

As he approached the posh Patriot Yacht Club and its marina, he slowed and came to a halt beside the security gate, affixing his customary, noncommittal smile.

"Good afternoon, Mr. Briephs, sure is a hot one, ain't it? Weatherman says New England's breaking all kinds of records this year." The guard's face bore the grin of a peace-filled man. "You're home early today."

"You're most observant, Daniel." Briephs hedged. "I assumed I'd be more comfortable at home. Sea breezes are generally considered cooler than those on land."

"Hope you're right . . . No end in sight, neither . . . Not even a drop of rain, the paper says . . . My wife's tomato plants . . . well, they're a right mess, that's all—"

"Difficult times all around," Briephs interrupted, then gunned the Jag again, passing scores of multimillion-dollar yachts bobbing serenely in their berths. At the far end of the parking area stood a row of garages disguised as the boat sheds of an earlier era. The door to Thompson's garage opened in response to the click of a remote control wand, and he slipped inside. From there, he proceeded on foot down a walkway until he reached a floating dock and his new seventeen-foot Boston Whaler. Boarding, he let out a sigh that was partly relief and partly joy.

Briephs steered the Whaler past the marina and into open water. Less than a mile from shore, he spotted the three rocky outcroppings that comprised his island home. He'd purchased the clumps of land fifteen years earlier, then hired the minimalist architect Isham Walker Dae to design a dwelling that would span the islands and serve as a showcase for Briephs' one true passion—his extraordinary collection of Minoan antiquities.

Dae's creation was a labyrinthine structure worthy of King Minos and his fabled man-eating Minotaur. Room twisted upon room in a convoluted mazelike design while the signature bloodred and ebony of the ancient civilization imparted to the stuccoed walls, floor tiles, even the lighting fixtures and custom-crafted furniture, a primitive, unearthly feel that was at once erotic and spare. To say that the crossword editor reveled in this peculiar construction would be an understatement. It was his haven and refuge, his fortress and obsession. In homage to his trade and to the mythical Aeolus, a Greek demigod believed to be ruler of the winds, Briephs had christened the singular structure Windword Islands; no man or woman set foot on its shores without receiving a prior commandment from its dictatorial owner.

"Daddy's home," Thompson murmured while the Whaler made land. "Your daddy's come home to his baby."

CHAPTER

3

AFTER LASHING THE Whaler's bowline to the dock at the western side of Windword Islands, Briephs followed a winding, wooden walkway, traversing rocks and tidal pools before reaching his home. He breathed another sigh of relief as he opened the door. Once inside, the summertime world of seagulls and beach scenes and hot-weather temper tantrums vanished. Briephs was embraced by his home's cool and shadowy presence as if by a long-lost lover. He passed deeper and deeper into the secret corridors, smiling to himself as he traced pathways only he had memorized. Finally, he reached the kitchen, a mundane but necessary staple of modern life. In accordance with Briephs' instructions and I. W. Dae's fanciful invention, the room's walls and ceiling had been drenched with a primordial red and so arranged that nothing electronic or functional intruded. The cabinets' surfaces mimicked lath and stucco; the countertops had been carved of ancient oak; the sink was a rough-hewn bowl of stone, the faucet an amphora neck of curving bronze.

Briephs opened a Sub-Zero refrigerator, whose double doors had been disguised with rows of trompe l'oeil funerary urns, pulled out a chilled bottle of Puligny Montrachet, poured a glassful into a goblet re-created from an ancient Attic design, took a long and healthy swig, then strolled another passage, ascending a staircase constructed of sea stones, and emerging at last in his bedroom overlooking the ocean. It was here that the real jewels of the editor's collection of antiquities were kept: pieces so rare most were believed to be unique.

"Daddy's home," he whispered again. He was feeling better—definitely better. "Your loving daddy's home." With a smug laugh, Thompson shucked off his clothes and entered the bathroom. Every inch of this retreat had been mirrored, allowing him to become a hundred nude men in the blink of an eye. He regarded the reflections fondly. Except for his silver hair, he was as fit as he'd been in his student days at Andover and Yale. " 'Mourn ye Graces and loves,' " Briephs quoted, then chuckled again. "Oh, I think no mourning today . . . We'll welcome those lovely folk instead . . ."

Thompson gazed at the mirrors a second more, then stepped into the shower, permitting the hot water to roll over his welcoming skin. In less than a minute, however, the peaceful mood was broken by the sound of a motorboat approaching the island.

He switched off the water—soap still clinging to his body—and listened. It wasn't unusual for tourists to let their vessels drift close to Windword for a look, but this visitor was clearly no stranger, nearing the island's eastern shore. Briephs had a keen ear for outboard engines; whoever was maneuvering the boat was sailing from the west— and closing in quickly on the dock.

He waited for the familiar sound of Fiberglas meeting wood piling. When the bump came, he returned to the shower and hurriedly rinsed away the remaining soap. Then he dressed in a burgundy-colored silk robe and descended to the living room. He held the wineglass like a scepter or a cudgel. Curiously, his other hand gripped his calfskin attaché case. Briephs didn't stop to consider how ludicrous this object might appear as an accessory to a dressing gown.

When he saw who his visitor was, his laugh rang out, half joyous and half hysterical. "Oh my God, you gave me such a scare! You mustn't do that, pumpkin . . . arriving without phoning first . . . That's really very naughty!"

Briephs shook his finger playfully at the visitor, then threw himself on a banquette covered with tapestried pillows. "This hellish heat . . . The meteorologist at the *Herald* insists we're not due for a break until late next week . . . if then . . ." He took a leisurely sip of wine, laughed again, then fell silent when he realized his guest didn't share his mirth. The attaché case now rested on a pillow beside him. "Can I get you a glass of wine? Or something stronger? As you know, my liquor cabinet's full of nasty spirits."

"The money wasn't there, Tommy-Boy."

Briephs sat erect. "Excuse me? . . . Money . . . ?"

"You heard me."

"Money . . ." Briephs repeated. "Money?" He toyed with his dressing gown's lapels as if they were the ermine trim on a royal mantle. "What money?"

Then a sudden revelation shot into his brain. "Incredible! So, *you* are the one . . . the person who's been sending those dreadful letters. My little hunch was correct, after all . . . Well, well, well . . . What do you know about that? Daddy *was* right . . ." Automatically, his hand stroked the calfskin case, then withdrew with a display of excessive calm. "The payment was there," he continued blithely. "I left it in the locker as always . . . and the key in its customary place."

"Oh, the key was there all right. But no cash. You stiffed me, Thompson!" The name was spoken with an unmistakable sneer, although an undercurrent of sham bravado shaded the rest of the words.

Briephs gauged the speaker's unease, and his expression turned secretive and sly; he wasn't cowed in the slightest. "You ought to be ashamed of yourself," he scolded. "Running me around like a perfect lunatic. I was frantic when those letters arrived . . ." All earlier apprehensions allayed, Briephs laughed again, then sipped languidly at his wine. "One piece of advice, though: never play word games with a master; I just might have a few tricks of my own—"

"It's no joke, Tom-Boy . . . I'm deadly serious."

"Are you? Well, in the future perhaps you might consider consulting your *O.E.D.* a bit more rigorously . . . Most of those puzzles you sent were laughable."

Startled at Briephs' apparent unconcern, the visitor returned to the previous demand. "The money, Tommy. Now!"

"You're not getting another penny . . . In fact, I might consider asking you to repay what you've already pilfered from me . . . I recently happened upon some rather unsavory stories making the rounds down on Congress Street. Many of those 'ladies' are more than casual acquaintances, as we both know . . . They tell me you have a predilection for underripe flesh, and that you're not too particular whether the child is a boy or a girl. I must say I was surprised . . . Impressed, but surprised . . . So there you are, my dear . . . Tit for tat, as they say . . ." Briephs' eyes glowed; he downed the remaining swallow of wine. "Are you sure I can't fix you a libation? This Puligny Montrachet is quite lovely—"

"That's a lie, and you know it."

"Are you referring to my cellar or my reference to Congress Street?" When the visitor failed to respond, Thompson continued in the same commanding tone: "What a nasty, backbiting town this is! So, you've never heard of the Lily Club . . . ?"

A stony glance greeted this question, but the answer was determinedly nonchalant. "I want that money, Tommy-Boy."

Briephs chuckled. "This is fun!" Then he abruptly changed tack. "Listen, pumpkin, you'd better scurry away home if you don't wish the details of your 'love life'—or this pathetic blackmail business—made public."

The visitor seemed to mull over this information. "What do you mean?"

"I've got my own form of life insurance right here."

Briephs calmly patted the attaché case. "Your name is revealed in my newest collection of puzzles. It's a little game I've been playing with myself—trying to surmise your identity . . ."

"That's a lie!"

"Another lie! You really do seem to be suffering from a persecution complex—"

"I want that money . . ."

"You're not getting it, dear friend. Now, I suggest you vacate the premises. You may not be the most enlightened of souls, but I do believe we can attain a modicum of civilized behavior. Besides, this little frisson should add some spice to our relationship, don't you think . . . ?"

In answer, the intruder lunged for the attaché case and yanked out the loose-leaf notebook. The covers flew open, revealing several pages of quarter-inch draftsman's graph paper and nothing more. Briephs gasped while the black-mailer flung the notebook onto the floor, where it slid beneath the divan.

"You lying twit!"

"The puzzles were there this morning. I swear they were." Briephs looked as horrified as his unwanted guest. "I'd never let them out of my sight . . . Oh my God, Jane-Alice must have . . ."

"Ante up, Tom-Boy!"

Finally pushed to the limit, Briephs stood. "Absolutely not!" His guise of bemused indifference had evaporated, supplanted by the indignant wrath of his forebears. "I insist you leave Windword Islands immediately. This entire charade is an outrage."

"What if I don't want to leave? I can be a dangerous person when I'm angry, Tommy-Boy."

"Really! This discussion has degenerated into something unbelievably common and unpleasant. Now, I suggest we repair to the kitchen, decant the wine and ponder our joint future. I'd say we both have some . . . ah . . . *interesting* secrets."

"You're not running out on me, Tommy-Boy."

"I decry that ridiculous soubriquet."

"I can give you a lot more to cry about."

Briephs considered explaining the linguistic differences between the two verbs, but instead marched into the kitchen, where he attempted to revive his jesting attitude. "You're not going to tie me up? Or get rough? Isn't that what usually happens in these circumstances?"

"Can the chitchat, Thompson."

" 'The lady doth protest too much, methinks' . . . or words to that effect . . . You really should try reading Shakespeare some time, dear friend . . . His style and use of metaphor does wonders for elevating one's personal lexicon . . . That particular reference is from *Hamlet* . . . apt, don't you think, given the young Dane's oedipal leanings and your proclivities . . . ?"

"Dare I say that's all Greek to me?"

Thompson chuckled serenely. "Now, you're catching on. Very good." He turned his back on the interloper and began pouring himself a second glass of wine. "Now, my suggestion is that you climb into whatever vessel you've got docked out there and leave . . . We'll pretend this shabby little scene never occurred . . . *Plus*, I want you to promise to desist from sending those threatening missives."

"I'm afraid that isn't possible, Thompson."

"Of course it is. Or haven't you heard of gentlemen's honor? Morality? Probity? Rectitude? You're familiar with those ideals, are you not? Besides, you can't need money that badly. No one I know does. But, alas, this isn't about money, is it, pumpkin?"

Briephs felt two hands touch his shoulders. "Really! This psychodrama is unnecessary. Unless, of course, you enjoy it. In which case, you must permit me to join the party."

The hands were withdrawn, but Briephs' body trembled. His heart raced while a severe tightness assaulted his throat. At first he imagined it was a reaction to the wine—perhaps a bad bottle or one with too many sulfites. His throat burned and his eyes bulged. He lifted his head, but the movement increased his agony. He reached toward the source of the pain, clutching at his neck and encountering what seemed to be a woman's stocking twisting around his throat, cutting off his air supply.

"Have you gone mad . . . ?" he squeezed out in a raspy cough. He tried to work his thumbs under the nylon tourniquet as it tightened around his throat.

He made another attempt to speak, but no sound came. He clawed at the strangulating nylon and then at the oaken countertop. As the peril of the situation finally hit home, he grasped the kitchen faucet, trying frantically to dislodge it. But the fixture was solid bronze; it held fast. In a frenzy of despair and rage, Briephs' arms flailed across the counter, knocking his wineglass and a hidden microwave oven crashing to the floor. Finally, he dropped to his knees, gurgled a long and liquid rattle and collapsed in a lifeless heap.

The visitor withdrew the nylon stocking and, staring at the prone body, murmured, " 'Good night, sweet prince'— or words to that effect. *Hamlet*, by the way . . . Act V," then proceeded to clean up the mess.

CHAPTER

4

ARA CRANE BRIEPHS' maid opened the door for Rosco Polycrates. As she permitted him entry into White Caps' marble-tiled foyer, she looked him over, her stiff black dress, organza apron and lacy cap rustling and creaking with an air of distinct disapproval. Rosco guessed the illustrious residence had never required the services of a private detective before.

"Wait here, Mr. Polycrates. I'll see if madam is ready to receive you."

Her uniformed figure stalked stiffly away, disappearing into a hushed realm of antique mahogany furniture, silver bowls and picture frames, Oriental Export vases and burnished, paneled walls. Even the crystal chandelier remained aloof and unlit, and the densely curtained windows regally somber while the heat wave, as if denied access for social reasons, clung to the door frame, leaving the foyer surprisingly chill and dank. Rosco shifted from foot to foot and silently cursed himself. I should have worn socks, he thought. At least today.

Rosco Polycrates was third generation Greek-American; he'd been in the private investigation business for a little over six years. Before that, he'd spent eight years as a detective with the Newcastle P.D. Cited five times for bravery, and once more for simply being a good cop, he'd finally decided he was too much of a free spirit for the bureaucracy of law enforcement. He didn't like filling out paperwork. He didn't like jouncing around in the department's unmarked cars; he preferred his rusting Jeep. He hated carrying a gun, *and* he refused to wear socks. He was now thirty-eight; the business was doing reasonably well; he was trim and healthy, and by most accounts a pretty good-looking guy—albeit a trifle unkempt.

"Mrs. Briephs will see you now."

The maid led the way through the foyer, turning right into an even darker corridor and finally opening a door to a sitting room so large it contained several distinct groupings of couches and chairs. The place reminded Rosco of photographs he'd seen of swanky hotels—or maybe the White House.

"Mr. Polycrates, ma'am," the maid announced. "Will you be requiring anything further?"

"Thank you, no, Emma."

Whatever grief-stricken, maternal hysteria Rosco had expected, when he'd been telephoned at eight that morning, wasn't to be found in Thompson Briephs' mother. Erect and snowy-haired with a patrician angularity and penetrating, violet eyes, Sara Crane Briephs was ensconced in a high, straight-backed chair whose sole concession to human comfort was a thin cushion of crimson velvet. To her right and slightly behind her—as befitting a dowager empress—stood a middle-aged man in a perfectly cut charcoal suit. He had a powerful chest and jutting jaw. Rosco had the impression he'd seen him before.

"Thank you for arriving promptly, Mr. Polycrates. I despise tardiness. If we're to work together, I must insist that you conform to my wishes."

Rosco wasn't asked to sit; so he stood, aware that the lady was scrutinizing him from head to toe. The maid's examination paled in comparison to that of her mistress.

"Do you have something against haberdashery, Mr. Polycrates?"

"Pardon?" Rosco added a hurried, somewhat tentative, "Ma'am?"

"You have no hosiery, Mr. Polycrates . . . No stockings . . . Did you forget them?"

"No . . . ma'am. I-I don't really like them."

"Ah . . . youth . . . youth . . ." Sara graced Rosco with a brief but glowing smile. "Never permit yourself to grow old and dreary, Mr. Polycrates. Age is merely a state of mind."

"I was sorry to hear about your son, Mrs. Briephs."

"So was I." This was the first hint of sorrow Rosco had heard in her voice. Clearly, Sara Crane Briephs wasn't a person who believed in wallowing in emotion. "That's why I telephoned you . . . Please take a seat, Mr. Polycrates."

Rosco did as he was told, finding himself rigidly upright

in a chair as stiff and formal as Sara's. This one resembled the carved wood thrones that wealthy churches reserved for visiting bishops. He wasn't certain if he should feel honored or switch to another seat.

"The newspapers stated that your son died of heart failure, Mrs. Briephs. As I said on the telephone, there's not much I can investigate . . . It sounded to me as if the M.E.—the medical examiner—had already made his ruling."

"My son was fifty-one years old, Mr. Polycrates. He was in excellent health—as am I. We are an indefatigable family. My father hunted tigers in Siberia when he was well into his eighties; I am now eighty myself, yet I continue to play tennis regularly, and each winter I revel in cross-country skiing at my cabin in the Berkshires. Last year, I trekked the Himalayas. My son came from very solid New England stock; he was an excellent athlete, and he had no history of coronary disease."

Rosco remained silent following this blistering speech, but the man beside Sara's chair murmured a quiet, but emphatic: "You have to trust the doctors, Sara."

"I don't *have* to do anything, *Mr.* Roth." If Sara's gaze had been capable of hurling flame, Roth would have turned to ash. "You are in my brother's employ, not mine. Familiarity may suit him and his rabble-rousing colleagues down in Washington; it does not wash with me . . . Now, when did you tell me he was planning to return?"

"In seven days, Mrs. Briephs."

Sara sighed dramatically. "And you can't convince him to curtail his journey earlier than that?"

"The Senator's in Southeast Asia . . . on a mission to explore financial incentives and renewed political ties . . ."

"Typical!" Sara snorted. "The usual liberal mishmash! Of course, he was dead-set against the region when there was a war on. Fickle alliances, faulty judgment . . . My brother has always been drawn to inappropriate causes—and ties." Then, resuming her level tone she said, "We will delay Thompson's funeral until Hal's return, but my decision is not based on your request, Mr. Roth. It is founded on my belief in family solidarity. Now, leave us, please."

"I think I should stay, Sara . . . Mrs. Briephs." Roth's modulated tone had become a low but definite growl. "Your brother would wish it. Besides, I still see no need—"

"Hal is not here, Mr. Roth—as you have so meticulously noted. Do I need to ask a second time, or will you leave pleasantly?"

When Roth had reluctantly closed the sitting-room door behind him, Sara gave Rosco a conspiratorial smile. "Is there any wonder that man is nicknamed Bulldog?" Then she resumed her businesslike mode, changing demeanors with a speed and agility Rosco found disconcerting.

"I didn't ask how much you charge, Mr. Polycrates. As you may have surmised, our family has never before required services such as yours."

"Three hundred a day, plus expenses . . . But look, Mrs. Briephs . . . ma'am . . . You may want to listen to what Mr. Roth is saying and trust the doctor's examination. It's not often they'll go back on their initial findings."

"I will never accede to that man's demands. He is an uncouth and evil creature, and I fail to understood why my brother insists on maintaining him as an associate. Roth is an *arriviste*, besides being an immoral, money-grubbing politico. I've always believed him to be a bad influence, and I've known him for many, many years, and it's only a matter of time before my brother arrives at that same conclusion . . . Three hundred a day, you said?"

But Rosco felt he couldn't permit the conversation to continue. Sara Briephs had obviously idolized her son; it was typical of a woman of her generation and breeding to refuse to face the fact that he might have been less physically robust than she. "Mrs. Briephs, sometimes these fatalities can be attributed to other causes . . . interruptions in electrical impulses from the brain for instance . . . Have you asked the police to conduct an autopsy?"

"I will not have my son cut up like a piece of calf's liver," was the stormy response. "Thompson swam back and forth to his island on a regular basis. He played tennis with me weekly and worked out at a private gymnasium. He did not die of a heart attack . . . or some bogus electrical impulse. He wasn't a machine, Mr. Polycrates . . . Now, will you take the case or not, because if your response is negative, I must bid you good day."

"Why me, Mrs. Briephs?"

Sara's keen glance regarded him. "You don't miss much, do you, young man?"

"That's my job."

"I like quick-witted men. I always have . . . To answer your question, Roth disapproved of you. In fact, he went out of his way to disparage you . . . insisting you only worked on cases involving infidelity or insurance 'scams'—whatever they are . . ."

Rosco winced, but Sara either didn't notice or graciously overlooked his reaction.

"But the main reason," she continued, "was your surname. It would have pleased Thompson's quixotic sense of humor to see the name of a sixth-century Greek tyrant in the Newcastle phone book . . . It's a family appellation, I take it?"

"Yes, ma'am."

"The Greeks and Portuguese have added immeasurably to our community in recent years, Mr. Polycrates. And I speak from a vast reservoir of experience. My great-great-great-great grandfather built this house."

"My family was still back in the homeland then. I'm only third generation."

"So I would have surmised, Mr. Polycrates. That doesn't prevent you—or your grandparents—from contributing to Newcastle society."

"I suppose not, ma'am—if that's how you put it." Rosco's brain was spinning, yearning to ask the standard questions but guessing Sara would sidestep them with the same deftness she'd applied to the rest of the interview. She was a woman accustomed to running her own show. "Can you tell me anything you might consider helpful, Mrs. Briephs?"

"Such as?"

"Your son's habits, his associates, history . . ."

"My son attended Andover preparatory school, then

continued on to Yale—as did all his forebears. He was a fine athlete, dressed impeccably and was an extraordinarily facile wordsmith. He accepted a position at the Newcastle *Herald* the same year he graduated from college. I had assumed he would turn his talents to more serious literature, but he was a lover of innuendo and wordplay. Cryptics suited his quixotic tastes.

"As he matured, he became interested in collecting antiquities—from the Greek Minoan period, specifically. The ancient Cretans worship of sport and of youth may have influenced his choice . . . He also served on the boards of several local arts institutions, and was vitally connected with the theatre here in town. At the time of his death, he was involved in financing a musical drama scheduled to move to Broadway . . . All this in addition to a wildly successful career . . . Thompson received accolades from every part of the country."

Rosco cleared his throat. This was the most difficult part of any investigation: questioning a blood relation. "Did your son have any enemies you might know of? . . . Or a lover he'd recently quarreled with?"

But Sara dodged the query with a quick: "Steven Housemann is the *Herald*'s editor in chief. He held that position when Thompson began working there."

"So he hired your son?"

Again the response was evasive: "Mr. Housemann has been editor in chief for a good many years . . . He recently remarried . . ."

"I see," Rosco said, although he didn't understand the connection between Housemann's personal life and

Briephs' career. "So there's nothing more you can tell me about his place of work?"

"I've been told his present bride is half her husband's age—the latest in a long line of inappropriate mates, I might add."

"Are you insinuating that Mr. Housemann is unstable?"

"Oh, my dear Mr. Polycrates!" Sara laughed in her girlish voice. "If I were to insinuate something you'd know it. Thompson always said I had a wit as sharp as a surgical scalpel." Then the violet eyes misted over. "You'll have to ask JaneAlice for information on the *Herald*'s inner workings."

"Was she your son's wife?"

"Oh, my dear!" Sara giggled again. "What an outlandish thought! . . . JaneAlice! . . . Wouldn't Thompson have found that a delicious suggestion." Sara slipped into sorrow again, and, as rapidly, pulled herself out. "You'll have to excuse me, Mr. Polycrates. I have a tennis lesson at ten sharp. We're working on my volley today. In all these years, I've never been comfortable with the position . . . I feel so . . . so vulnerable standing close to the net. An odd sensation since I fear nothing else—"

"May I visit your son's house?" Rosco interrupted. "See it for myself?"

"Oh, that awful place!" Sara burst out. "Thompson was determined to flout tradition; and there was nothing I could do to dissuade him. Collecting the art and artifacts of a dead civilization is one thing; re-creating it is quite another. But my son was a stubborn man . . . Of course, you may see Windword Islands. Emma will provide you with a key before you leave." Sara stood regally. "Three hundred dollars a day . . . plus expenses . . . ?"

"That's correct."

"I assume you're worth it, Mr. Polycrates."

"I do my best, ma'am . . . But please, call me Rosco . . ."

"I'll do nothing of the kind. I had a Boston terrier of that name when I was a child. He was ugly and you are not."

As Rosco crossed the circular gravel drive that spread before Sara's stately home he heard someone calling his name. He turned to watch John "Bulldog" Roth approach. The expensive suit didn't disguise a barrel-chested build a stevedore would have been proud of.

When Roth was within five feet of his prey, he smiled— an expression that didn't reassure Rosco in the slightest. "I'd like to have a word with you before you leave, Mr. Polycrates." Roth kept his back to the house as if fearing that his lips might be read.

"Shoot."

"Sara's not quite herself. I'm sure you can understand . . . Tommy was her only child . . . At any rate, the Senator feels that it would be best for all concerned if this entire matter was closed as quietly as possible."

"This comes from the Senator himself?"

Roth seemed to ponder his choices. "With Senator Crane abroad, I have a certain responsibility to see that no undue disturbances arise. And, as the Senator is running for reelection this year, I'm sure you can appreciate that any news items, no matter how trivial, are bound to attract unnecessary attention—especially from the Senator's opponent."

"In my neighborhood we don't consider death a trivial news item . . . What are you suggesting, Mr. Roth?"

Roth stiffened. "I believe the simplest solution is for you to take a few days' time, following which you report to Sara that you've found nothing unusual . . . I'll make certain you're reimbursed for a full week's employment . . . Then we simply let the issue pass without undue publicity or histrionics."

"I've always had a tremendous amount of respect for the Senator," Rosco responded. "In my opinion, he's one of the few honest men remaining in Washington." He pulled a business card from his wallet and handed it to Roth. "If the Senator wants to speak to me in person about this situation, ask him to give me a call—and tell him not to worry about the time difference. He can reach me at home if he'd like. The number's on the card."

Then, without giving Roth time to reply, Rosco turned on his heel, crossed to his Jeep and eased out of Sara's driveway and into traffic. He smiled and thought, I like her . . . She's one tough cookie. But the bulldog is another story altogether.

After that, Rosco began considering Thompson Briephs, the medical examiner's report and Sara's insistence that there was more to the tale. Rosco's last job had been far less complex; it had involved an enterprising fisherman who'd decided to send his boats into the Atlantic with a one-way ticket to Davy Jones' locker—thereby swindling

Shore Line Mutual out of a hefty sum, as well as causing a few unfortunate sailors some very hairy hours. But Briephs' story wasn't as simple as insurance fraud, and Roth's attempted interference only served to complicate it further. Rosco pulled his Jeep over and let the facts bounce around in his brain. Finally, he decided to make a few preliminary phone calls, then visit his former partner, Lieutenant Al Lever, down at the Newcastle P.D. If the official story held water, Rosco would report back to Sara without charging a fee. If he didn't like what he learned, he'd dig out the truth.

CHAPTER

5

THE STATION HOUSE hadn't changed one iota since Rosco had left the police force. Institutional green paint still clung to the plaster walls; air conditioners wheezed and grumbled; the hallways smelled of stale coffee and stale, prepackaged doughnuts, and the basement continued to serve as Newcastle's morgue. Rosco acknowledged greetings from several officers as he strolled past the duty desk and up to a door marked HOMICIDE. He tapped twice and walked in without waiting for a reply.

"Good to see you, Polly—Crates. Hot enough for ya?"

Originally from Boston, Lieutenant Lever affected a strong Southern twang with the words *Polly* and *Crates*. It was a feeble attempt at humor, but Rosco smiled for old times' sake; the mispronunciation of his name had always been a running joke.

Al Lever was only a year or two older than Rosco, but

those years had left their mark on his appearance. He was overweight, bald, pasty white, and had a constant smoker's cough.

"Still the 'barefoot boy with cheek of tan,' eh, Polly—Crates?" he chortled. "What did Mrs. Briephs say about your choice in footwear?"

"Mind if I sit, Al?"

"Go for it. We don't stand on ceremony here." Lever motioned to an ancient office chair on castors. "Did the old lady serve you tea and crumpets?"

Rosco wheeled the chair toward Lever's desk.

"Mrs. Briephs was very polite. She has a way about her. I can't say as much for the goon who was keeping her company. He looks like a former hit man."

Lever coughed. "Drop the case, Rosco." His voice was deadly serious.

"You know me better than that, Al. If someone tells me to drop a case, it's the last thing I'm going to do . . . What went down with her son?"

"The official line is heart attack. Do yourself a favor, tell the lady you can't help her, and go play some handball."

"That's from the M.E.? Heart attack?"

Lever pulled the coroner's report from a pending file on his desk and slid it toward Rosco.

Rosco looked the report over and dropped it on Al's blotter. "That's pretty ambiguous wording Carlyle's chosen. It sounds like he's covering something. I'd like to have a look at the body . . . if that's okay with you?"

"You'll have to go through channels."

"Oh, come on, Al," Rosco moaned. "You know I can pull

the paperwork. That's not going to stop me. I'm working for a relative. I have a need-to-know. You slow me up by a day, maybe two. That's it. Just walk down there with me. We save a little time. If everything's kosher, I go home . . . play handball with the gang like you said."

Lever stood, walked over to the office door and locked it. He lit a cigarette, then moved to the window, stared out at the harbor and inhaled deeply.

"You mind if I smoke?" he asked.

Rosco only smiled.

"Okay, I'll fill you in. But, dammit, Rosco, I want you to keep it between you and me. It doesn't leave this office. I'm on thin ice here."

"I'm going to find out anyway."

Lever recognized the truth in this. He took another drag. "Briephs was strangled."

"What . . . ?" Rosco sat up straight. "Al, come on, you guys can't cover something like that. That's not you. Thin ice is an understatement. You're a good cop. You're not going to—"

"Easy. Easy," Lever interrupted. "It's not what you think . . . We found Briephs' naked body spread-eagled and tied to his bed with nylon stockings. A fifth stocking around his neck. It was a sex game. You follow me? That's all it was. Accidental death . . . With a prossy, most likely . . . You know Briephs' uncle, the Senator, right?"

"Not personally, but I've met his right-hand man—as of today."

"Not ten minutes after we informed Mrs. Briephs of her son's death, the Senator's pit bull, John Roth himself, is walking through that door. How he got here that fast, I'll never know. The man's a piece of work."

"Mrs. Briephs didn't mention anything about this stocking business—"

"You're getting ahead of me. I never gave her a cause of death. We didn't have the M.E.'s report compiled yet. I just told her his body had been found . . . things were being 'handled' . . . the usual . . . Anyway, ol' Bulldog tells me the Senator doesn't want news of his nephew 'consorting' with 'unsavory characters' to hit the papers. It being an election year and all."

"But the Senator's not here; he's in Southeast Asia," Rosco began, then added, "Why are you so sure he was with a hooker?"

"You never worked Vice, my friend. We used to pick Tommy-Boy up on a regular basis when we'd do a sweep for girls and johns down on Congress Street. He liked the rough ones, I can tell you that. And it was getting kinkier all the time, from what I heard. We kept it quiet. He contributed big time to the Police Athletic League . . . And don't eye me like that. The League needs the money. You spent more time with the kids than anyone . . . Look, I know most of the girls on Congress. You want to poke around down there, go ahead. They can give you some freaky stories about Thompson C. Briephs and their 'confidential expeditions' to that little island of his. He was definitely getting into tough love."

"So Roth insists the Senator wants it hushed up and you agree?"

"Come on, Rosco, where's the harm? Briephs' mother is

an old lady. Ol' Bulldog's right when he says the shock would probably kill her . . . And who gets hurt in the end? Some fifty-dollar-a-night hooker. She gets two to five on accidental manslaughter and walks in six months. What's the point?"

"I don't like it."

"Leave it alone, Rosco."

"I want to see his body."

"Drop it."

"Not a chance."

Lever sighed in frustration. "I don't have time now and I mean that. Come back at three. I'll walk you into the morgue then."

"No funny business?"

"No funny business."

Rosco stood, crossed to the office door and unlocked it. "What do you know about a woman named Annabella Graham?"

"The crossword lady at the *Evening Crier*?"

"Yeah."

"You've never seen her around town . . . ?"

"Not that I know of."

Lever laughed, coughed violently, then lit another cigarette. "Of all the guys in Newcastle, I can't believe you've never set eyes on Annabella Graham." Another laugh erupted from Lever's chest—followed by another coughing fit.

"This damn heat wave!" he sputtered. "My allergies have been driving me crazy . . ."

Rosco didn't comment.

When Lever's attack subsided, he eyed Rosco with a good deal of secret delight. "Annabella Graham," he hummed. "What would you like to know about her?"

"I've got a meeting with her . . . Thought I should educate myself on this puzzle biz. Find out about the newspaper game before I start poking around the *Herald*." Rosco opened the door and stepped into the hall. Before he got ten feet, Lever called after him: "One bit of advice, before you make a fool of yourself . . ."

"What's that?"

"Annabella Graham is married."

CHAPTER

6

ROSCO HADN'T SET foot on Captain's Walk in years. He was surprised at how many of the old seafarers' residences lining the now malled-off street had gone through extensive renovations. Annabella Graham's petite but immaculate eighteenth-century home was no exception. The wood siding appeared to have just received a fresh coat of white paint; the glossy black shutters reflected the dappled sunlight peering through leaves of an elm resting in the tidy front garden, and the antique windowpanes sparkled with the old-fashioned glint of spirits of ammonia and elbow grease. Rosco could almost picture a captain's wife gazing out one of those parlor windows, patiently awaiting the return of her world-weary traveler.

"You must be Mr. Polycrates." Annabella opened the front door, and stood on the porch, where a wicker love seat and matching chairs provided a setting that Rosco imagined might have been lifted whole from a magazine on home design. "I somehow expected you to look more like that character who sells automotive tools on late-night television."

"Not Uncle Morty . . . Mr. Socket Wrench? Somebody should put that guy out of his misery."

She laughed lightly and asked him in, flipping the door closed behind her as if its carefully preserved history were of no particular importance. "Uncle Morty." She chuckled again. "The very one." Her tone had the same offhand ease as her manner—something Rosco noted with pleasure.

Lever had alluded to the fact that Annabella Graham was a good-looking woman, but she was more than that: slim and tall with vibrant, dark gray eyes and straight, fine hair the color of a baby duck's down. It was a striking shade, as bright as a halo; from the haphazard way it was pushed behind her ears, Rosco guessed she'd spent a good deal of her life trying to convince the world she wasn't just a pretty face. But it was her smile he liked best. It was honest and happy; it made him want to grin in return.

"Why don't we talk in my office?" she said as she led him through the house. "If I seem pushy, don't take it personally. I'm in the middle of lunch, and running late with a deadline."

"I can come back, if there's a better time."

"There's never a better time, I'm sorry to say. I'm one of those people who schedule an hour for a job that takes three—and never learn my lesson. Never. Don't worry, I'll tell you when to leave."

The interior of the house was as fastidiously restored as

the exterior; even the furnishings were appropriate to the period: a subtle blend of Queen Anne interspersed with more rustic pieces of Shaker design. Nothing was out of place—not a pewter pitcher, not a needlework footstool or bentwood box; Rosco began to feel as if he'd stumbled into a museum. Out of politeness, he commented, "You've done a great job here."

"Oh, it's all my husband's work. Garet was one of the vanguard in the Captain's Walk restoration. He bought the house seven years ago. I waited for him to finish fussing with rattail hinges, brass door latches, fabric swatches and paint chips before I married him." She paused and looked at the room as if assessing it with new eyes. "I guess you're right, though . . . The place *is* picture perfect." A wistfulness tinged the words, but was quickly expunged by the breeziness of her next comment. "I've never been adept at home decor. Scratch that statement . . . I'm truly *terrible* at interior design."

They stepped into her office with a timing that seemed to punctuate the remark. A small rear porch had been enclosed and transformed into a work space. It was an absolute disaster: papers strewn everywhere, on the desk, the window seat, the radiator cover and nearly every inch of the floor; what little space remained was crammed with books—French, German, Italian, Spanish and Latin dictionaries plus an enormous world atlas, an *Encyclopaedia Britannica* and an *O.E.D.*

Resting on the sole piece of unused furniture—a canvas deck chair—was a black-and-white dinner plate containing a dozen deviled eggs. Rosco looked at the plate, gradually realizing the design employed a crossword puzzle grid. Then he noticed the curtains followed the same motif: bold black letters marching up and down a white ground. Two empty coffee mugs sat on top of the atlas; they also sported a crossword theme—as did a lampshade tilted crookedly above the mugs. As Rosco continued to study the room, he realized the entire place was a symphony of black and white; even the cluttered floor had been painted to resemble a puzzle grid.

"You seem to take your work seriously," he said.

"They're mostly gifts," was the slightly embarrassed response. "You should see my bathroom . . . towels, shower curtain, even some of the tiles . . . Garet claims it's hideous . . . Have a seat, Mr. Polycrates— Wait. I'll take the eggs . . ." The crossword dinner plate was transferred to a prominent place on the desktop—beside a date book emblazoned with a word game. "Are you hungry?"

"I don't think so, thanks."

Annabella Graham sat at her desk while Rosco took the canvas deck chair. Sure enough, the fabric was black and the wood supports a shiny white.

"Do people actually call you Rosco?"

"Yes."

"That's a slang term for pistol, you know. Spelled R-O-S-C-O-E. I use it in my puzzle occasionally. Were you born with it or is it an assumed name to match your profession?"

"Born with it, I'm afraid. No *E* on the end, though."

"Your dad wanted you to go into law enforcement?"

"That, I'll never know. He died when I was a kid. I never knew him, really."

Annabella pursed her lips and frowned slightly; Rosco could see that she was berating herself for insensitivity. He recognized the emotion; he'd experienced it many times himself.

She hesitated, apparently pondering an appropriate reply, then decided to return to the safety of the business at hand. "So, Rosco, what can I do for you?"

"Well, Mrs. Graham—"

"No, no. No Mrs. Graham, please. And no Annabella. I'm Belle."

"Sorry. I assumed because you were in the word-game business, you'd be called Anna. You know like Annagra—"

"Stop!" She raised her hands in mock dismay. "Don't even say it. You have no idea how often I get that comment. I considered taking my husband's surname when we married, but it seemed unprofessional . . . As to why my parents chose to saddle me with such a name, what can I say? Quirky people, both of them . . . So what brings you here, Rosco? I'm not in the habit of being interviewed by private detectives . . ." She bit into a deviled egg. "Are you sure you don't want one? They're awfully good."

Rosco shook his head. "I guess you heard that Thompson Briephs passed away over the weekend?"

"Of course." Belle picked up a second egg.

"I've been asked to look into the possibility that he may not have died of natural causes."

"Wait," she said with obvious excitement. "You mean Thompson was murdered?"

"I've been asked to investigate the *possibility* of homicide."

"And you think I did it?" Belle's eyes positively glowed with pleasure. She looked like a kid at Christmastime.

"No, no. Let me step back here . . . explain how I work . . . Say, for instance, Uncle Morty, Mr. Late-Night Socket Wrench, turns up dead and I'm asked to look into it . . . Now, I don't know anything about the TV business, and less about automotive tools, so the first thing I do—before questioning Morty's associates—is to learn about his lifestyle from a disinterested source . . ." Rosco realized Belle was staring intently at him; she nibbled a third and then a fourth egg, slipping her teeth through the frothy yolk. He'd never seen anyone get so much enjoyment out of such a mundane object—and look so attractive in the process.

He pushed ahead. "In this case, it's a dead crossword puzzle editor from the Newcastle *Herald.* So, I go to the *Evening Crier* and interview Briephs' counterpart there, i.e., you—just to get a few pointers on the newspaper biz . . . Is that all you're having for lunch? A dozen eggs?"

"It isn't a dozen; it's only a *half* dozen—cut in half for deviling, naturally." Belle had obviously been queried about this peculiar habit before. "But I did eat an entire dozen once." Her smile became seraphic. "I'm very fond of deviled eggs . . . and anchovies and licorice. I'm not much of a cook when it comes to more complex recipes. I grew up in a household run by two professors; dinner was a haphazard event, to say the least."

"Fortunately, licorice isn't hard to whip up."

Belle cocked an amused eyebrow. "At least I wear anklets with heavy shoes."

"Pardon me?"

"Hosiery . . . footwear . . . haberdashery . . ."

"Oh, right . . . A bad habit left over from my days at U. Mass . . . Boston, not Amherst. No socks was a look some of us scholarship guys affected to make the girls think we went to Harvard . . . This is the second time today I've been taken to task with that *haberdashery* word."

Belle laughed. "You must be interviewing some rather elderly and starchy folk; it's not a word in common usage nowadays . . . To return to your question, I don't know how much help I can provide. I met Thompson only a few times—at the museum functions my husband attends when he's in town . . . From what I understand, Briephs and I had an entirely different approach to work. I edit at home. I loathe going into the *Crier* offices, whereas Thompson did most of his creating at the *Herald*. Although he never used a computer. I don't either; I hate them . . . What else? His house was his pleasure dome; I. W. Dae designed it, you know . . . Of course, you're aware Briephs had an extremely valuable collection of Greek and Mycenean artifacts? Minoan, I should say . . ."

Rosco nodded. "I'm scheduled to visit Windword Islands first thing tomorrow morning."

"I've never seen the place," Belle said. "Garet told me it's extraordinary."

"So your husband visited Briephs' home?"

"Yes."

Rosco heard something in her tone he could only categorize as guarded. "Could I question him?" he asked. "Your husband, I mean?"

"Not unless you buy an airline ticket to Egypt," Belle said. Again, the tone was vaguely distressed. "He's on an archaeological dig in the Valley of the Kings . . . one of the sons of Seti I—a recent and quite spectacular find . . . Garet's team only closes down the site for the rainy season, and resumes excavation as soon as it's dry." She paused while an emotion crossed her face that Rosco couldn't read. He decided to leave Belle's husband alone.

"Do many stressful situations come up in connection with your work?"

"Well, I have deadlines . . . and an editor in chief. I don't know how Briephs' editor, Steven Housemann, works, but mine's constantly berating me. Thompson turned out annual puzzle collections, as well. He had a publisher in New York . . . Then there are the letters—"

"Letters?"

"There's always someone accusing you of having the vocabulary of a fourth-grader. You'd be surprised how much hate mail I get. 'If you'd done your research you would have made a better connection between the verb *to auger* and the common tool you carelessly referred to as a *screw*' . . . That sort of thing . . ."

"You must be a walking dictionary."

Belle blushed; Rosco envisioned her scalp burning beneath her pale yellow hair. "I've always been fascinated with etymology," she mumbled softly. "Besides, I have help." She indicated the reference books with a vague wave of her hand.

"Foreign-language dictionaries, too? I hardly passed English Lit."

Again, the embarrassed blush. "Learning new languages is a kind of hobby with me. Once you know a couple, picking up a third or fourth is easy. You look for similarities in syntax and origin, derivation . . . bridges such as *lago, lac, loch, lakkos* and 'lake' . . . *kyriakon, kirk*, 'church,' and so on. It becomes a sort of game . . ." Belle stopped short when she realized Rosco was staring at her; she fled to safer ground. "So you think someone murdered Thompson?"

"I don't want to start any rumors. Let's just say I'm looking into it."

"Contributors," Belle stated suddenly. "You might find a clue there."

"Who are they?"

"The people who submit puzzles."

"You mean you don't make them up yourself?"

"I create most of my own; I'm addicted to solving riddles, but I understand Briephs didn't always share my enthusiasm. He prided himself on drawing from a more diversified base . . . Then he'd edit, adapt the clues, make them easier or harder, depending on the day of the week . . . Contributors can be possessive about their work, however—as well as a little psychotic. They live a life of the brain—and sometimes little else. I can imagine one of those types nursing a dangerous grudge against an editor he thought had altered his work—or rejected him once too often. Writers, you know, can be a peculiar lot."

CHAPTER
7

ROSCO RETURNED TO police headquarters half an hour before his three P.M. meeting with Lever. His intention was to duck into the morgue early and persuade Carlyle, the medical examiner, to show him Briephs' body—without the watchful presence of the lieutenant. But Lever was a step ahead. He'd given strict orders that the corpse couldn't be viewed until he arrived. The M.E. passed the message on and retreated stonily to his office.

At precisely three, the lieutenant stepped off the elevator and smiled. "Why doesn't it surprise me to find you here early?"

Rosco shrugged.

"I'll get Carlyle. He's got to open up for us."

• • •

The three men walked the length of a musty corridor, then passed through a set of double doors that swung heavily on their hinges.

Rosco had been in the morgue a hundred times before, but he never got used to it. The drop in temperature alone was enough to make his blood freeze. Everything was stainless steel: the four examination tables, cabinets, sinks, everything. The room had the threatening glint of a cutlery store. As they walked in, Carlyle's assistant, Estelle, was in the process of running a scalpel down the center of a dead woman's chest—throat to navel. The ash-blue skin peeled back like a sausage casing. The cadaver had been drained; there was no blood. Rosco thought Estelle looked disappointed.

Along the far wall were body bins. Four rows of twenty-five. A hundred drawers in all. Each was stainless steel, with a handle and a slot for the name of the current occupant. Rosco was amazed at how many bins were full. Over twenty of them had nametags.

"Why so busy?" Rosco asked Carlyle.

"We've got four unclaimed; other than that, no more than normal for a heat wave. Read the obits, Polly—Crates. People die all the time."

Rosco was surprised at Carlyle's surliness, but he guessed the M.E. didn't like people double-checking his work.

"Briephs is over here. Number eighteen." Carlyle slid the large drawer out and pulled back a pale blue sheet, revealing the deceased's head and chest. "You want to see the whole thing?"

Lever looked at Rosco. "Well?"

"You tell me, Al. I can see the marks on his neck." Rosco glanced at the M.E.

"I've got work to do. Let me know when you're finished here." Carlyle turned and headed back to his office, having no desire to discuss his sketchy report.

"Well, Al, anything below the waist?"

"These are the only marks."

"How'd you find him? Faceup? Or down?"

"Up."

"And tied?" Rosco lifted Thompson's arm. "Nothing on the wrists?"

"Carlyle says that type of abrasion wouldn't necessarily show . . . Especially if he was tied up voluntarily. Heart attack, like he says. This sort of thing happens quick. They don't struggle. It's his contention Briephs' heart stopped beating before the oxygen supply was cut off."

"What's with Carlyle, anyway? He's not usually so disagreeable."

"Maybe he doesn't like people second-guessing him."

Rosco lifted Briephs' head and took a closer look at his neck. " 'Respiratory and heart failure due to exertion and extenuating circumstances' leaves a lot of room for second-guessing . . . Estelle, could you come here for a minute?"

She left her cadaver and ambled toward the two men. In the cold glare her face looked ghoulish and gray. "Yes?"

"What's your read on this one?" Rosco asked.

"We try not to contradict one another here, Mr. Polycrates. You'll have to check the official report . . . You're no longer with the department." She strolled back to her work.

Rosco shook his head. "She's a big help . . . Al, look at his neck closely. Ten'll get you twenty this guy was nailed from behind."

"So."

"So . . . If he was strangled from behind, why'd you find him faceup?"

"The girl turns him over," Lever said as though he were talking to a five-year-old. "It doesn't take a genius to figure that out. She doesn't believe she actually killed the poor schmo and she turns him over for a look-see. Then she panics and reties him . . . Maybe it's not even a girl. Maybe it's a guy. Who knows what Briephs was into . . . ? Drop it, Rosco. Why drag the family through the gutter? You're making this out to be something it isn't."

"I don't like it. How much pull does this Bulldog Roth character have down here?"

This struck a nerve with the lieutenant. "Don't push your luck with me, fella. If I thought there was something to investigate, I'd be on it. Nobody tells my department what to do."

"I'm still going to check it out."

"Well, start down in the district, start with Congress Street. My money says you find your answers there . . . Unless it was a boy-boy thing. But, check on them, too. Have a ball."

"No," Rosco said as he slid Briephs' body back into the wall, "I'm going to look around his house first."

Lever began coughing. It seemed to go on for nearly a full minute. "I'll have one of my men take you on the police launch," he eventually squeezed out. "I don't like my crime scenes agitated."

Rosco smiled. "Don't bother, Al . . . I can get there on my own hook. Besides, you know what they say: If there ain't no crime . . . there ain't no crime scene."

CHAPTER

8

ROSCO REFUSED TO admit he was a landlubber—not after thirty-eight years as a native in a water-mad city like Newcastle. But the fact was he couldn't set foot on a boat without turning green and panting like a dying fish. Peter Kingsworth, Patriot Yacht Club's harbormaster, who was now ferrying Rosco to Windword Islands in the club launch, noticed his passenger's discomfort immediately. "Not feeling too slick, are you, Rosco?" he shouted above the staccato rap of salt waves attacking the Fiberglas hull. Peter was the square-shouldered, sunbronzed descendant of a long line of Massachusetts fishermen. He had no use for men who couldn't tie a sheepshank or half hitch. He revved the launch's engine; the boat lunged forward while Rosco lurched against the gunwale. "I'll have you there in no time." Peter beamed. To Rosco the smile looked less than consoling.

As the launch cut a wide rooster-plume of spray and circled toward Windword's pier, he had the sensation of being watched by a second pair of very amused eyes. He glanced at the pier as Belle Graham called down, "I hope you don't mind my joining you. I couldn't help myself." Her long tan legs dangled over the dock's side, and her hair blew white-gold in the sunlight.

"Tell me you didn't bring deviled eggs." Rosco wasn't certain if he was happy to see her or not.

"Not a one." Belle reached out and offered Rosco a surprisingly strong grasp that helped pull him to safety. "I see you're not accustomed to water travel."

"It shows?" The question contained more than a little wounded pride.

"I'm Peter," Kingsworth called out.

Rosco's nemesis leapt agilely onto the pier, securing the launch's twin lines with a quick, professional ease.

"Belle."

"Glad to meet you, Belle." The amperage in Peter's grin could have been used to signal battleships. "How come I've never seen you at the yacht club?"

"Because my little boat and I are much more comfortable at the public marina. Nothing personal, Peter, it's just closer to home."

Rosco decided that if the ocean's swells hadn't made him puke, the continued presence of the harbormaster might. "Since I'm here with professional jurisdiction," he announced more stiffly than he'd intended, "Peter, you'll have to wait with the official vehicle . . . launch . . . vessel . . . whatever . . . Belle . . . well . . ." Rosco watched humor playing in the shadows of her face, and was suddenly conscious of a genetic need to impress her. "You can accompany me. You may be able to supply answers about Briephs' business practices."

"Aye aye, sir." She smiled.

Rosco imagined the expression gracing Peter's sunny countenance as well. He studiously avoided glancing in the harbormaster's direction.

The inside of Windword came as a shock to both visitors.

"I had no idea . . ." Belle whispered. "I'd heard it was an almost exact replication, but not like this . . . Not—"

As their eyes grew accustomed to the dim and umbrous light, Rosco and Belle moved slowly forward into the foyer. High, curved walls stained a mottled bloodred gave the impression of entering a man-made cave, while variously shaped doorways lured the eye toward a murky, invisible interior. At the same time, the baked-in heat of the rocky exterior vanished completely, leaving the stone and stuccoed walls cool to the point of chilliness.

"Not like what?" Instinctively, Rosco moved close to Belle's side as if she needed protection.

"Well, look at these rounded surfaces . . . look at the variations of shading . . . as if ancient pigments were used, cinnabar, perhaps and annatto . . . and the bronze torchères . . . the chiseled stone floor . . . the ceiling." Belle gaped at the tall space above her head. "This must be an exact replica."

"A replica of what?"

"A royal residence built during the period of the Minoan

civilization." Rosco's blank gaze made her hurry to explain.
"A Bronze Age culture centered on the island of Crete . . .
It began in 3,000 B.C. or thereabouts, reaching its pinnacle
about the time of the Middle Kingdom in Egypt—that's
pre-ancient Greece . . . A favorite form of entertainment
focused on bulls frolicking with half-clothed athletes."
When Rosco continued to stare, she added, "Crete is in the
Aegean . . . near Greece."

"Thank you. My name's Polycrates, in case you'd forgotten."

"So, I'm to assume you have the rest of this information
at your fingertips? King Minos . . . the Minotaur . . .
Daedalus and the Labyrinth at Knossos . . . Theseus . . . ?"

Rosco's silence prompted a half-joking "Please spare me
any displays of the male ego."

"You're telling me this place is a scaled-down version of
one of those ancient castles?"

"That's what my husband told me . . . I found it hard to
believe anyone would—or could—replicate a Minoan
royal residence in Newcastle. But from what I've seen so
far, Garet was correct in his assessment."

They moved up a half flight of rough-hewn granite steps
and began traversing a dark, windowless passage. Open
doorways led into shadowed rooms. The pervasive crimson
and ebony color scheme reminded Rosco of an artist's con-
ception of hell. "But you've never been here before, correct? Your husband was invited, and you weren't . . . Why
is that?"

"Thompson's entertainments were strictly stag events."

"Lever told me he picked up prostitutes when he needed a special treat."

"Did he now?" was all Belle replied.

"I'm not insinuating your . . . I mean . . . Never mind."

Belle's lack of response further flustered Rosco. "I'm only repeating what Lever said. I didn't know Briephs, of course."

"Nor did I," Belle answered after a moment. "Not enough to count."

They pressed forward, following a corridor that twisted one way, then another, seemingly wrapping back on itself while floor tiles of the same *ombréd*, carnelian red echoed and enhanced the spiral. Rosco felt he was walking in circles and said so.

"That's the brilliance of the architect's vision," Belle told him. "It must be the Labyrinth—or a modern-day version."

"The Labyrinth's the place this Minotaur guy ruled?"

"No, Minos was the king. The Minotaur was a creature who was supposedly half-human and half-bull; he was reputed to be an offspring of King Minos' wife, Pasiphaë."

"That stuff's a little racy for me. I'm an old-fashioned kind of guy."

"And Greek, as I recall." Belle grinned in the pale light. "The tale gets worse . . . The Minotaur was confined in a mazelike, underground arena called the Labyrinth; the place was designed by an imprisoned Greek architect named Daedalus—the father of Icarus, the boy who flew too close to the sun. But that's another story . . . Anyway, this man-beast combination was periodically supplied with a selection of handsome Athenian youths and lovely maidens: tribute due the island kingdom following a war between Greece and Crete. Presumably, the young people who found an exit from the Labyrinth did so; the rest were never seen again."

"I'm not crazy about stories involving sexual abuse of minors. I never was."

"You must have made a squeamish cop."

Rosco looked at Belle. She wasn't smiling in the slightest.

"Some of us get out of the force with our morals intact."

Belle's expression remained pensive. After a moment, she continued: "Well, I don't believe the Minotaur myth revolves around sex. The monster was supposed to eat the youths."

"Ah, well." Rosco shrugged. "That's okay, then."

Belle touched his arm. "It's a myth, a fairy tale . . . But the legend does inform many of the ways archaeologists study the ancient culture. The Minoan civilization was fixated on bulls, as well as on beautiful young men sporting long ringlets—and their counterparts: voluptuous, barebreasted girls in gauzy skirts . . . I'm sure we can find an example of the type of artwork I'm referring to in Thompson's collection. I've heard he has several pieces that are downright lubricious . . . smutty."

"I know what 'lubricious' means."

Belle smiled but didn't speak.

They climbed the stone stairs to the master suite, where the sight of Briephs' recreational-sized bed, to which four nylon stockings were still tied, made Belle grimace in disgust. The indentation made by the body was still in evidence. Rosco moved cautiously around the scene, studying everything without disturbing a speck of dust. Belle kept her distance as though her feet had sprouted roots.

"I see why someone like Lever would arrive at his assessment," Rosco muttered.

His words jolted Belle into reacting. "Those are awfully thick stockings," she mumbled.

Rosco scrutinized one, without touching it. "What are you saying?"

"They're thick and they're ugly . . . Bargain-basement support hose . . . the kind old ladies buy."

"Well, maybe Briephs liked to be tied up extra tight."

Belle considered this; Rosco could see how repellent she found the suggestion—and the place. He began wondering if he'd been wise to allow her to join him. Death had a tendency to color the air long after the body had been removed. The scene wasn't for the uninitiated.

"Maybe . . ." she finally agreed. "But I don't think he would have bought hose like that . . . Not if he wanted to pretend a woman had tied him up."

Belle edged past the bed and entered the bathroom, from which Rosco heard a startled gasp. "You'd have to be a perfect physical specimen to face this house of horrors every morning."

Rosco joined her. "He was into looking at himself, that's for sure." Life-sized and miniature Belles and Roscos ricocheted across every flat surface, mirroring and distorting the pair until they stood backward, sideways and on their heads.

"The Thompson Briephs mutual admiration society," Belle murmured while Rosco studiously failed to respond. "There's something definitely odd about this place," she added. "Even you're beginning to look like a satyr."

Belle returned to the bedroom, creeping past the hose-tied bed to examine a cabinet containing Briephs' rarest treasures. The first artifact she spotted was a painted faience statuette of a woman whose tight bodice was pulled open to expose her large breasts. Her figure was hour-glass perfection, and her nipples jutted forward demandingly. Clenched in her outstretched hands were two writhing snakes that seemed to lunge toward the viewer. Belle had never seen such a perfect example of Minoan art before.

Beside the statuette was a steatite vase. Again, the applied colors were bold and bright, as if three thousand years since its creation hadn't intervened. The design depicted a boy with a tiny waist, broad shoulders and slim hips; a semi-smile was fixed on his face while his long, curly hair exposed his neck. The youth faced the backside of a kneeling bull.

"You should look at these, Rosco, if you want an idea of what I was talking about," Belle called.

Joining her, he was silent for several moments. "This is the kind of stuff your husband likes?" The question was tinged with a healthy dose of disapproval.

"He's an Egyptologist, but, yes, he admires this period, as well."

"I see." Another long pause. "Well, live and let live, I guess."

"Historically, the Minoan Age is a complex period," Belle said.

While Rosco prowled Windword's dining area and kitchen, muttering a thoughtful, "One wine goblet appears to be missing from the cabinet, assuming it was a set of twelve . . . shards of broken glass on the floor near the sink . . ." Belle paced the living room, marveling at the peculiar time-warp feel of the place. It was like stepping through an art historian's monograph and into the presence of a dead civilization. The fact that Newcastle's harbor remained hidden behind windowless red walls only heightened the sense of dislocation.

She stared at the built-in divans; they only seemed to be lacking royal personages and their naked slave retainers. She imagined Briephs reclining here in splendor, but the picture made her shudder as if she'd suddenly taken a chill. To clear her thoughts, she decided to study the furniture's construction, curious as to whether Briephs had continued his strange fantasy by ordering authentic timber framing for the pieces. Careful not to touch the fabric surface, she knelt in front of the longest divan and peered beneath it.

What she discovered weren't wooden pegs, however, but an empty loose-leaf notebook. Three sheets of blank quarter-inch draftsman's graph paper hung loosely from the three rings; they were the exact type she used to construct her crossword puzzles. Without thinking, she grabbed the

notebook. "Rosco, look at this. Thompson's workbook."
Hurrying toward the kitchen, she met Rosco halfway.

"We should be careful about what we touch. In case the
police decide to dust."

"I completely forgot . . . I'm sorry. I was being so careful
before."

"Where did you find it?"

Belle gestured sheepishly. "Under the large divan . . ."

"I guess there's no harm done. But in case the police do
come out to dust for prints . . ." Rosco shrugged. "Well, we
know whose not to take seriously." He studied the notebook. "Just blank pages."

"I know. Isn't that weird?"

"What do you mean?"

"Well, if he was anything like me, he would've had some
work in progress. I think something's missing."

Back at home, Belle was tempted to take the rest of the
day off. Her jaunt with Rosco had left her restless and
vaguely dissatisfied with life. Her existence seemed pat
and ordinary, and she felt momentary dismay as she
walked through the front door and stared at the perfect
harmony of the entry hall and living room. The rooms
looked like a layout for a Martha Stewart photo-shoot:
"How to restore and renovate your charming period
home."

Belle silently cursed her absent husband for his impeccable taste, but that sentiment only aroused more complex
emotions. Garet had seemed such a wonderful match
when they'd wed: An intellect to challenge hers, comple-

mentary interests; she'd imagined a cozy future spent solving philosophical conundrums, a circle of fascinating and witty friends, long, convivial dinners pondering themes of earth-shattering relevance. But somewhere along the way their dual personalities had begun to drift irretrievably apart, leaving Garet to increasingly withdraw into his work while Belle "played" at making word games. Even her prowess at language had ceased to impress and charm him. It seemed to Belle that he somehow felt she had failed to meet her potential.

Belle sighed and wandered toward her office, snagging a plate of deviled eggs from the fridge on the way. She compulsively gulped down two, then lifted the copy of the morning *Herald* from the floor.

"Well, let's see what the competition's up to." Until she'd said the words aloud, Belle hadn't considered that it would be necessary for the *Herald* to replace Thompson Briephs. She flipped through the entertainment section of the rival paper, wondering who had edited the daily puzzle.

When she found the crossword on page 16, she was startled at its unconventional form; letters had been left dangling and the shape was erratic. Nevertheless, she scanned the clues for one of Briephs' trademarks, and at 9-Down, discovered what she was looking for. *Ref. work* . . . three letters, abbreviation starting with an "O" . . . She concluded that the puzzle must have been an uncompleted work on file at the *Herald,* then picked up her red Bic pen and casually began filling in the blanks. Belle prided herself on working in ink—although she was never ashamed to cross out one answer in favor of another—or another.

Naturally, Garet considered this behavior "reckless"—and naturally, she made a point of writing *everything* in ink.

She muttered to herself as she worked, *"Theatre folk . . . six letters . . .* Hmm, I've used that one . . . *In a jam . . . ?* Good . . . typical Briephs' pun . . . 31-Across: *Bacall to Bogie . . .* Darn, what was his nickname for her . . . ?"

Momentarily stumped on 52-Across, she worked the Down columns until she discovered the answer, then sat bolt upright in her chair. She grabbed the telephone and called Rosco. "You're not going to believe this," she announced without waiting for the customary exchange of pleasantries.

Rosco let out a heavy sigh. "Belle, I'm working on a case here—"

"I know, but I think I've found the answer." Without giving him time to respond, she hurried ahead. "I just finished today's crossword in the *Herald*. Its form was peculiar, but you can't imagine what words showed up."

"Belle—" His voice softened a little.

"TRAP, MAIL, BLACK and HOSE—"

"You called to play a game of twenty questions?"

Belle ignored his irritability. "It's obviously Briephs' puzzle, Rosco. And I think he's trying to tell us something."

"Like what . . . ? He was trapped and killed by a black male with a garden hose?"

Across

1. "I want ___ just like . . ."
5. DHL competitor
9. African witchcraft
14. Produce
15. Hit
16. It's north of Mexico
17. Sailor's order
19. ___Ray
20. Mr. and Asner
21. Gross home? abbr.
23. Honker
26. Top grade
28. Snare
29. Polish
31. Bacall to Bogie
32. Highway no-no: abbr.
33. Lift
35. Indisputable genius
36. Russian gelt
37. Actress Charlotte
38. Manitoban
39. Hosp. rooms
40. Doctrines
42. Morrison group
43. Picnic pests
44. End games for short?
46. ___Schwarz
48. Cape move
52. El toro's karma?
57. Italian Olympian's goal?
58. Stir up
59. Type of hound
60. Free
61. Fashion mag
62. It's pointless?

Down

1. Charleses' dog
2. "Georgie___," Redgrave film
3. Dry
4. "Un-cola"
5. Theatre folk?
6. Rosebud, e.g.
7. Antes up
8. Retreat
9. Ref. work
10. "Let the devil wear ___," Hamlet
11. Falter
12. Ready, ___, fire
13. Socks
18. Flightless one
22. October toothless one
23. Pay-off
24. In a jam?
25. Cleans
26. High and dry
27. Lands
28. Fish
29. Cleaner
30. Dead wives?
32. Frosh rooms
34. CA industry
35. Not down, but out
41. Daze
42. Aimless jotting
43. Mimes
45. Send
46. Cordelia's father's sidekick
47. Indigo
49. Above
50. Gum ___
51. Serf
53. ___Ziegfeld
54. Also
55. Caviar
56. 57-Across, e.g.

PUZZLE #1

CHAPTER

9

"N O, NO, NO," Belle nearly shouted into the telephone, her excitement escalating in response to Rosco's obvious lack of enthusiasm. "MAIL, mail, M-A-I-L, not M-A-L-E. Not a black male, but blackmail. I think Briephs was being blackmailed. My guess is that's what he was trying to tell us."

"I have the name of a good psychiatrist, Belle. She works for the police department."

"So . . . ?"

"I think you should be seeing her."

"I'm serious, Rosco. I think Briephs knew he was in danger. And this puzzle was his life insurance. First of all, guess what 35-Across is?"

"Belle, I appreciate your enthusiasm here, but—"

"Just guess."

Rosco let out an elongated sigh, though in reality her excitement was catching. Besides, he liked the sound of her voice. "Okay, I give up—what's 35-Across?"

"THOMPSON BRIEPHS."

"And . . . ?"

"Well, it's unheard of. You don't insert your own name in a puzzle. Plus, it's intriguing that his name just happens to have fifteen letters, don't you think? It fits quite neatly."

Rosco opened his mouth, but never had an chance to speak. Belle was on a roll.

"Wait. There's more. 52-Across . . . I couldn't get it at first, but it turned out to be AFTERNOON DEATHS. A wordplay on Hemingway. How about that? Hold on, don't say anything. Listen to these words: BRIBE, PAYS and TRAP . . . Another thing, as I mentioned, there are form problems with this puzzle. Briephs left single letters hanging. He'd never do that . . . Never! No one would. Not even a rank novice. But when you add the dangling letters to the fact that he was strangled with HOSE, the picture becomes frighteningly clear, doesn't it? Well . . . ? What do you think? You're not saying anything."

"You told me not to."

"I can't believe you're not accepting this supposition as fact. We're definitely dealing with a message from Briephs."

"Come on, Belle, how could anyone predict they were going to be strangled with a nylon stocking?"

"If it had been a sex game, why not? Why wouldn't Briephs have surmised how his blackmailer would kill him? They'd probably played their bizarre little roles many times before."

"Previous experience tells me that most men don't have sex with people who are blackmailing them. Besides, there's absolutely *nothing* that points to Briephs being blackmailed . . . No, my guess is, the folks at the *Herald* have just come up with some form of testimonial for Mr. Thompson C. Briephs and they weren't clever enough to get the form correct."

"Well, there's one way to find out if I'm right about all this."

"How's that?"

"We'll go over to the *Herald* and ask the editorial staff who created today's puzzle."

"Well, believe it or not, except for the *we* part, that's exactly what I have planned for this afternoon—a trip to the *Herald*."

"I'll come with you."

Rosco said, "I don't think so," in a tone that illustrated he could be a force to be reckoned with. "Listen, from where I stand, this is a criminal investigation, it's not a word game. I'll handle this on my own."

"I wish I could see your face right now. I'll bet you look incredibly hard-boiled."

"You don't know."

Belle resisted the temptation to laugh. "JaneAlice Miller," she said quickly instead.

"What?"

"That's who you want to talk to at the *Herald*, JaneAlice Miller. She was Briephs' secretary. My guess is she knows more about Tommy than his own mother."

Remembering his fumbling conversation with the redoubtable Sara, Rosco laughed. "I don't imagine Mrs. Briephs would like to hear you say that . . . especially about a secretary."

"JaneAlice Miller," Belle insisted. "I met her a few times at Press Club luncheons. She trailed Briephs as if he were the Lord Almighty. Start with her."

"If I have time."

"Ask her who created today's puzzle. She'll know, if anyone does."

"*If* I run into her."

"I could phone her for you . . . Professional courtesy, that type of thing . . . Sympathize about Thompson's untimely demise, and then worm the puzzle information out of her."

"Belle, drop it, okay? I'll keep you posted."

CHAPTER

10

Rosco's Jeep didn't like the scorchingly hot weather better than anyone else. It was prone to overheat at speeds in excess of fifty miles per hour—or when stalled during Newcastle's afternoon log-jam. He guessed it had something to do with the radiator, but a total disinterest in the finer points of vehicular maintenance was another of Rosco's private quirks.

As he worked his way toward the *Herald* building, the downtown traffic slowed to its habitual crawl, then eventually halted altogether. Rosco maneuvered the Jeep into a bus stop, flipped the windshield visor down and slipped an official police parking permit between two rubber bands. He'd walk the remaining five blocks to the newspaper offices.

Once inside, he scanned the building's registry. Thompson Briephs' name had not yet been removed—room 427.

Before moving toward the elevator, Rosco made note of the editor in chief, Steven Housemann—room 401.

The *Herald*'s elevator was an art deco masterpiece, albeit one that had seen happier days. The doors were embellished with two sinuous women cast in bronze; they brandished copper lightning bolts behind their backs while gazing loftily at pewter-hued moons; their metallic clothing was draped to give an illusion of sensual transparency—a nudge and a wink to the hard-bitten newspapermen of an earlier era. The interior was crafted of teak and walnut; brass handrails in serious need of a dose of polish served as accents. It also had a peculiar, musky odor, like the home of an elderly person with fading eyesight and a diminished sense of cleanliness.

Rosco pushed number four and the elevator ascended with a groaning rattle. Exiting, he found room 427 toward the end of the hallway and tapped three times on the glass-paneled door.

JaneAlice Miller was pretty much what he'd expected—except for the fuchsia lipstick. She was equine and lanky, and her hair resembled the frizzled mane of an overworked horse. Despite her height, she seemed weak and shaken, and her eyes were so red and puffy, she looked as though she'd been crying for a week.

"Miss Miller?" Rosco asked, assuming the likelihood of her being *Mrs.* Miller was slim to say the least.

"Yes?"

"My name is Rosco Polycrates. Mr. Briephs' mother has asked me to help with the funeral arrangements, and since she's fairly unfamiliar with his workplace, I was hoping you'd be able to give me an idea whom we should invite to the memorial service . . . ? And of course anyone who should be discouraged from attending."

JaneAlice's lips trembled, but no words came from her fiercely painted pink mouth. Rosco noticed the lipstick was decidedly crooked.

He pressed on: "You can call Mrs. Briephs if you'd like." He reached for his wallet. "I have her number right here."

"Oh, that's all right," she sniffled. "I'm just upset."

"Of course . . . May I come in?"

JaneAlice retreated into her outer work area, leading the way toward Briephs' inner office without another word. Rosco closed both doors as he passed through.

Alone with Rosco in her boss's sealed haven, JaneAlice was instantly aware of how good-looking this stranger was, and she struggled to be flirtatious through her swollen eyes. "You can examine his Rolodex if you wish." She forced a pitiful smile. "I'm sure no one will mind . . . I was his *confidential* secretary, you know, just like—"

"Well, JaneAlice . . . You don't mind if I call you Jane-Alice, do you?"

"Oh, please," she fluttered.

"Well, I'm sure the people in Mr. Briephs' Rolodex must be aware of his death by now. What his mother is most concerned about are the folks who may have had a . . . shall we say . . . a strained relationship with your boss? Unless, of course, this is something you have no knowledge of."

"Oh, I know a great deal . . . I was the only person who truly understood Mr. Briephs. I was the only person who knew how to care for him. The others were all after something for themselves. I thought only of him. Did you ever see Jean Simmons in—?"

"Were you romantically involved with Mr. Briephs?"

JaneAlice blushed until even her pallid hair glowed red, and her eyes welled up with a fresh batch of tears. "Please, Mr. Polycrates, I've never . . . I've never . . . Oh, I wouldn't even . . . Not in a million years."

"I'm sorry. It's none of my business."

"He was a great man. A genius! An exemplary journalist . . . I would never have been worthy to . . . Well, to do anything more than he asked me to."

Rosco gave her a minute or two to regain her composure, then pressed forward with an adjusted line of questions. But JaneAlice's responses made little sense. Her scattered monologue produced such a confusion of names and telephone numbers, Rosco didn't bother taking notes.

"Why don't we slow down a little here, JaneAlice? Let's start off with this. Has the *Herald* hired a replacement for Mr. Briephs?"

"Oh, that woman . . . that . . . floozy . . . that charlatan . . . After all the trouble this newspaper had with her, I can't believe she's now been hired to take over for Mr. Briephs. It'll be the death of me. You wait."

"Who might that be?"

"Shannon McArthur, that's who! She's a liar, a cheat, a fraud, and a potential vote for Communism, if you want my opinion . . . And it was Mr. Briephs who exposed her plagiarism. He had her name dragged through the mud and she deserved it. And now she's coming to the *Herald* to take his place. It's not right. It simply isn't! She's a vile person!"

"And that's who made up today's puzzle?"

"My goodness, no! She wouldn't have the brains for today's offering. That was one of Mr. Briephs' creations! And a most unusual one, too! Mr. Briephs prided himself on his progressive and interconnecting cryptics, you see. Something I'm sure Shannon McArthur will be incapable of. My boss was always five puzzles ahead. Thank heaven I removed them from his attaché case, or we wouldn't have any puzzles this week. Although he left none of the solutions. Mr. Housemann will kill me when he finds that out . . . Anyway, I won't have to see or talk to this *woman* until she takes over next Monday . . . I don't know how long I'll last. Why, she isn't even as intelligent as that blonde *thing* at the *Evening Crier*."

This brought a slight smile to Rosco's lips. "I understand she's rather attractive," he said almost unconsciously.

"Well, that's the opinion of some! Men may think she's lovely to look at, but external appearance is no test for the beauty of the soul . . . I'm sure she's happier than a clam at high tide with Mr. Briephs' passing—"

"So, aside from this unintelligent *blond*—"

"Annabella Graham." JaneAlice fairly spat out the name. "Miss Graham—"

"It would be *Mrs.*, if she had any decency! She's a veritable *Jezebel*, just like in the movie—!"

"I see," Rosco interrupted. "So, aside from this Graham woman and Miss McArthur, is there anyone else you feel

Mrs. Briephs should dissuade from attending her son's memorial?"

"Betsey Housemann," was the immediate response.

"She would be Steven Housemann's wife?"

"That's what he likes to believe!"

"I see . . . Now, a while ago you mentioned some names that confused me slightly. Were those coworkers by any chance?"

"I suppose . . . I'm not sure . . ."

"Let's go back to those folks, shall we? You mentioned a Bartholomew Kerr, I believe?"

"Oh, my goodness—" JaneAlice began, but a knock at the outside door interrupted what promised to become another lengthy soliloquy. The secretary nearly leapt out of her skin at the sound; when she heard her name called by a commanding male voice, her bony chest drew in three consecutive sighs that sounded like air being forced out of a plastic bag.

"Gracious! It's Mr. Housemann!"

Terror caused her to rush from the room, leaving Rosco to wonder if JaneAlice believed the editor in chief to be an ogre—or if something more sinister were gnawing at her brain.

"Oh, Mr. Housemann! I'm so sorry . . . I didn't hear you knock . . . and I always have the door on automatic lock. Women can't be too careful with all the crime around . . . even in an office building as well-maintained as yours."

Rosco couldn't discern actual words in Housemann's reply, but the sound seemed soothing, even kind.

Nonetheless, JaneAlice still seemed upset as she conducted the editor in chief to Briephs' inner sanctum.

"This man has been hired by Mrs. Briephs to help with funeral arrangements," was all JaneAlice said before bolting from the room and leaving the two men in surprised silence.

Housemann turned his tall, spare frame toward the visitor. Only an abundance of ice-white hair betrayed his years. In musculature and bearing, he resembled a man half his age. Rosco extended his hand in what he intended as a somber gesture of sympathy.

"May I express my condolences, sir?" he said. "You must be greatly saddened at Mr. Briephs' passing."

A hint of something like glee passed behind Housemann's eyes, but disappeared before Rosco had time to characterize the emotion. Instead, the editor in chief's expression turned thoughtful. "Indeed," he said gravely, then tacked on a quick, faintly impatient, "And you are?"

"Rosco Polycrates, sir."

Rosco felt the use of *sir* made him sound classier. Mrs. Briephs would never hire an average guy to organize her son's funeral.

"Greek, are you?"

"Greek descent, yes, sir."

"I wouldn't have imagined Sara knew any Greeks." The observation didn't sound like a slur, simply a newspaperman's attempt to get to the heart of the story. "Well . . . and what is it you need to know?"

Rosco repeated the lie about Thompson's mother requiring assistance with her son's memorial service, to which Housemann answered, "Still doesn't trust Bulldog

Roth, does she?" then cannily added, "You wouldn't be connected to the Polycrates Detective Agency, would you?"

Rosco studied Housemann's face. It was calm, perceptive and clever, a masterful, even commanding face. There'd be no fooling Steven Housemann. "Yes, sir, I am. Although my capacity here is purely as an assistant to the lady. As you can imagine, she's in a state of shock, and, as you noted, there's no love lost between the Senator's chief of staff and Mrs. Briephs."

"So you're not involved in a criminal investigation?"

"Should I be, sir? The cause of death was listed as heart failure."

"Quite right," Housemann answered, then smiled with a show of magnanimity. "Please extend my deepest sympathies and those of my wife to dear Sara. Although Betsey knew Thompson only marginally, she is as deeply saddened as I."

After that short speech, Housemann called JaneAlice and instructed her to "aid Mr. Polycrates in every way possible," then suddenly interrupted his own order with a brisk: "Tomorrow would be more convenient for conversation, Mr. Polycrates. As I'm sure you can appreciate, the staff is struggling to fill Thompson's shoes before his replacement arrives. You may not be a crossword-puzzle addict, but believe me, this town is filled with them, and Tom-Boy was their god."

When JaneAlice produced another spate of sobbing at this homage to her dead lord, Rosco decided to take Housemann's advice and return the following day.

• • •

The elevator had scarcely begun its descent from the fourth floor when Steven Housemann slammed Briephs' inner office door with such force that the frosted glass panel appeared in danger of shattering. "What in heaven's name are you thinking of, JaneAlice! What makes you think you should give information to a private detective! This is a newspaper."

JaneAlice's tears rose to a wail.

"Get hold of yourself, woman! Don't you have any brains! What do we want someone like Polycrates snooping around for? And a Greek, on top of it!" Housemann's rage was so great that his face had turned an ominous shade of purple; every vestige of serene authority had disappeared. His white hair now looked wild and his powerful physique tense and threatening. Rosco would have been astonished at the transformation.

"Really, JaneAlice; you have less sense than a garden slug! You could have argued that as a public journal we must preserve our First Amendment rights; you could have stalled for time; you could have done anything but help that . . . that . . . guinea-dago!"

JaneAlice quavered with each new attack. "Please don't shout at me like that, sir—"

"I'll shout at whomever I please! This is a newspaper, not a ladies' club! And speaking of social events," Housemann sneered, "how is it that our reigning blueblood queen hired some wop?"

"He's Greek, sir."

"Greek, guinea, dago, mick, whatever. He's a foreigner!

A lowlife foreigner with entrée to those snooty paragons of virtue on Liberty Hill! He's just a crawling cretin, that's what he is!"

JaneAlice gnawed on her lip until the fuchsia lipstick vanished. For a moment she considered fighting back, and attacking Steven Housemann at his weakest spot: his less-than-faithful wife, Betsey, but in the end decided to save that trump card for another day. "What should I tell Mr. Polycrates when he returns tomorrow?"

"Tell him to see me. I'll put an end to this pseudo investigation!"

CHAPTER

11

PACING BACK AND forth from her office to the kitchen, Belle was a bundle of kinetic energy. She simply could not sit still and concentrate on anything as mundane as work. "MAIL . . . HOSE . . . BLACK . . . TRAP . . ." she muttered to herself. "Why does he think my ideas are so brainless?" Catching sight of her reflected image in the toaster's chrome surface, she made a face of resigned dismay. "But Rosco's not the first male to judge me on appearance alone. Garet has him beat by a mile."

She compulsively wolfed down half-a-dozen gooey licorice drops, followed by her last remaining deviled egg, then turned the corners of her mouth down in an even more sour expression. "Yuck! What a wretched combination . . . I've got to learn to cook something decent." By now, she was beside her desk and telephone. She snagged up the receiver in the same impatient manner, rapidly punching in numbers, then banging the instrument back in place.

"He should be back by now . . . How long does it take to interview one skittish secretary?" But even as the words were out of her mouth, Belle realized how futile her complaints were. She was a crossword editor, not a private investigator. Thompson Briephs' alleged murder had nothing to do with her.

"So it's back to the boring paper and pencil," she groused. But before seating herself, she made one last stab at calling Rosco. This time he picked up.

"Well, what did she say? Especially about those clues I found."

"Didn't anyone ever tell you how to conduct a telephone call? I say hello, you announce your name." Indulgent humor was evident in Rosco's tone.

"This is Belle Graham calling . . ."

"So I gathered."

"I'm being serious, Rosco."

"I know you are, but this isn't your case, Belle . . . I appreciate your advice, but as I told you, this is a criminal investigation—"

"What did JaneAlice say about Briephs' name being one of the clues?"

"How do you know I even talked to her?"

"You mean you didn't?"

"Well, yes . . . But that's not the point—"

"Well, what did she say? AFTERNOON DEATHS! And THOMPSON BRIEPHS spelled out . . . I mean, what could be more obvious?"

"To tell the truth, that theory never came up."

"What! Why not?"

Rosco shifted tack, becoming all business. "Belle, I'm grateful for your enthusiasm, and I apologize if I sound patronizing, but this is a job for professionals."

But Belle was made of tougher stuff than he realized. "Did JaneAlice admit that Thompson was the author of today's puzzle?"

"Look, Belle, you've been a big help, and I've enjoyed your input—"

"Did she?"

Rosco paused. Obviously, this lady wouldn't take no for an answer.

"Briephs was an 'exemplary journalist,' according to his secretary. He always kept five puzzles ahead—a 'progressive and interconnected' group, according to JaneAlice."

Belle's glee was evident in the quick intake of breath that echoed through the receiver, but she resisted the temptation to add, I told you so. "That makes four remaining cryptics . . ." she muttered to herself. "What about those puzzles, Rosco? I'll bet you anything your murderer's name turns up in those puzzles. I'll bet his name even has fifteen letters. If you find someone with fifteen letters in his name, your case is solved! So, where is our tenacious Miss Miller hiding them?"

"In the first place, Belle, what makes you suspect she's hiding anything? And in the second—"

"I know, I know . . . It's none of my business."

Rattled by their sudden intensity, both Belle and Rosco backed off.

"I don't mean to scrap your efforts, Belle, but this needs to be handled a certain way."

She was quiet for a moment and eventually yielded, "You're right, this has nothing to do with me . . ."

"No, you've been very helpful . . . I mean it."

"But it's dumb . . . Briephs planting information within his puzzles . . . like messages from the grave."

They paused again, unwilling to relinquish their incipient mutual attraction. This time it was Rosco who took the lead. "You were correct about JaneAlice, Belle . . . Scared of her own shadow . . . She insisted Briephs was a 'genius.' I got the feeling she would have crawled over live coals if he'd asked her."

"And that doesn't seem remotely kinky to you?" Belle wisecracked.

"Not coming from her," Rosco retorted. "Thompson Briephs was a handsome man; JaneAlice may have been secretly in love with him, but I can't imagine it went further than that."

"It takes all kinds. Some men feed on slavish devotion."

Again, this struck them both as dangerous territory. "Not me, I'm happy to say," Rosco answered after a moment's silence.

Now it was Belle's turn to offer up a small summation of the situation. "So, JaneAlice has four remaining puzzles," she thought out loud. "Did you get copies?"

Rosco's response was a curt "No" that he softened by adding, "JaneAlice and I discussed her boss, and his replacement, a Shannon McArthur, who, incidentally, JaneAlice despises. She doesn't think much of you, either . . . Called you a *blonde thing*, if I remember correctly."

"Feminine jealousy." Belle chuckled.

"I don't know . . ." Rosco hedged. "She made some fairly catty comments about how lovely you are to 'look at.' "

Ordinarily, a remark like that would have made Belle see red, but all at once she found herself hoping Rosco agreed.

"What did you say to that?"

Again, sensing shaky ground, Rosco sidestepped the question. "Look, Belle, you've got to understand I didn't go to Briephs' office as a private eye . . . Past experience has taught me there are better ways to collect information."

Impressed by the sureness of his tone, Belle didn't speak for a moment. "So, what did you use as a cover story?"

"I said I was an assistant hired by Mrs. Briephs to help with the funeral arrangements . . . In order to differentiate between her son's friends and business acquaintances, the deceased's mother had suggested a conversation with Thompson's secretary. Naturally, the bereaved parent was incapable of making the call herself—"

"Wow," Belle interrupted. "That's very sneaky."

"That's what I'm paid for." Recognizing the manipulative spin this put on his character, Rosco added a quick "Of course, I'm Honest Abe in real life." Belle's pensive silence made him hurry ahead. "But before JaneAlice could supply me with a complete list of names, Steven Housemann appeared . . . He's an impressive guy. Very bright. And graciousness personified—"

"Steven Housemann! You've got to be joking! I've never met a more cantankerous cuss!"

"Perhaps that's because you work for a rival newspaper."

"Perhaps it's because he insists on marrying women half his age, and can't keep up with them!"

Rosco didn't speak for a minute. "You mean Betsey?" he finally asked.

"Who else? A piece of fluff from Congress Street whose 'retirement'—if you wish to call it that—appears hardly ended. Housemann becomes jealous as all hell if he thinks she's batting her eyelids at a former 'client' . . . Don't tell me JaneAlice endowed her with some phony social pedigree!"

"I wouldn't exactly call it that," Rosco answered evasively.

"That's precisely what JaneAlice did, isn't it? That woman must be positively loco . . . Under that sullen brow is a genuine lunatic . . . Did she accuse me of trying to get Briephs' job, perchance?"

"Belle, why don't we get together and talk this stuff over. It seems you have information that conflicts with Jane-Alice's and Housemann's."

"I'm home," Belle answered, calming down.

"I'd thought maybe dinner . . ."

"Dinner out? At a restaurant?"

Rosco's impulse was to backtrack. *Mrs.*, he kept remembering JaneAlice snapping. " . . . If you'd rather not, I certainly understand. Newcastle's a small town in many ways. I don't want to put you in a difficult position . . . We could meet at your office . . . This is business, after all."

But Belle had leapt ahead of him. "Dinner out . . ." she murmured in a dreamy voice. "I haven't done that in ages . . . soft music and candlelight . . ."

"Do you like Greek food?"

"I love anything I don't have to cook myself."

CHAPTER

12

JANEALICE HAD JUST doused the office lights when the telephone rang. It was six-fifteen and well past quitting time. She was tempted to let it ring and have the call shunted to voice mail, but she resisted, groaning aloud as she picked up the receiver. Her throat and head still ached after her dressing-down from Steven Housemann; she felt she'd never cease crying as long as she lived. "Newcastle *Herald*—crossword editor's office," she managed to croak.

"Thompson C. Briephs, please."

The voice was muffled and otherworldly, almost as though it had been computer-generated. JaneAlice had difficulty determining whether the caller was a soft-spoken male or a gravelly voiced female. The request was repeated.

"Thompson C. Briephs, please."

JaneAlice forced a teary "Mr. Briephs is no longer with us."

"Ah, yes. Well, we all know that, don't we? Perhaps I better than anyone."

"Who is this?"

"Just call me an ancient admirer, JaneAlice. This is JaneAlice Miller, isn't it?"

"Yes . . ."

"Good. One question, JaneAlice; today's *Herald* crossword puzzle? Where did it come from?"

"Who is this? You're frightening me. What do you want?"

"I don't mean to frighten you. Unless of course that's absolutely necessary. Today's puzzle, it was one of Briephs', wasn't it?"

JaneAlice remained speechless.

"All right, no need to answer. Obviously, it was. Tommy-Boy told me he'd left a few cryptics behind . . . But I was foolish. I didn't believe him. Tell me, JaneAlice, how many were there in all?"

"F-F-Five," JaneAlice stuttered, fearing the voice was capable of discerning the truth through the telephone lines.

"Five? Well, that's an intriguing number. And, where might the other four be?"

"Who is this?" she whispered again.

"I want those puzzles, JaneAlice."

"I . . . I . . ."

"Let me explain the situation, my dear. Whatever you may have heard, Thompson C. Briephs did not die of natural causes. I'm sure you know the *gentleman* had a number of enemies. He won't be missed by too many people. And I'm also sure I performed a great service in putting him to rest . . . Now, where are the other puzzles?"

"They're . . . They're gone."

"Gone? Gone where?" The voice became slightly louder and more insistent. "JaneAlice . . . ? Are you still there?"

JaneAlice's mind was racing. A second puzzle had already been sent down to the pressroom. It would appear in the early edition and be on the newsstands by six A.M. The other three cryptics sat in a file folder in her top left-hand desk drawer—where she'd squirreled them away for safekeeping on the very day of Mr. Briephs' unfortunate demise.

"JaneAlice?" the voice demanded sharply.

"Yes . . . ?"

"Where are those puzzles?"

"They're gone," she lied again. "They're being typeset. I don't have them. I—"

"You must retrieve them, JaneAlice. Do you understand what I'm saying?"

"They're gone. Besides, there are no answers. What can I do?"

The voice on the other end became enraged, "Answers! How long do you think it takes the average person to figure out those puzzles? Now, you listen to me; I know my way around that building as well as you do, JaneAlice. Those office doors are never locked. You must locate those puzzles. Now!"

"I . . . I . . . can try."

"Don't try. Do it. Then I want you to put all four puzzles into an envelope and take it to the Peter Pan bus terminal. Do you know where that is?"

"Yes."

"Good. This isn't so hard, is it? Now, when you get to the terminal, go directly to the lockers on the lower level. Find locker number 139 and place the envelope in it. Remove the key and take it to the trash receptacle that's located to the right of the flower shop—it's also on the lower level. It will be to your right as you face the bank of lockers. Behind that receptacle you'll find a small magnetized metal box— the kind people use to hide their car keys. Place the locker key into the box and return it to the back of the trash can. Do you understand all of this . . . ? JaneAlice? We cannot waste any more time."

Again JaneAlice remained silent.

"JaneAlice, I feel a certain desperation creeping into my voice, and I'm sure you're astute enough to hear it as well. If you cannot follow these simple directions, I'm afraid I'll have to resort to more drastic measures. Neither one of us wants that, now do we?"

"No . . ."

"So, you *will* put the puzzles in the locker?"

"Yes . . ."

"Good. Do it before midnight tonight. And JaneAlice?"

"Yes?"

"If you speak to anyone about this or fail for any reason to deliver the puzzles, I'm afraid you'll be joining your dear Tommy sooner than you expected."

"But—"

"By midnight, JaneAlice."

The caller hung up, leaving JaneAlice a trembling haystack of frayed nerves. She sat in her chair and dropped her head while her hand instinctively slid into the top left drawer and removed the manila folder containing the three remaining puzzles. They were Thompson's creations, his babies. She'd spent so many years safeguarding her boss's work—even from his own hands, sometimes—that she couldn't conceive of allowing the lunatic creature on the other end of the telephone to so much as touch the puzzles. But what to do with them? What to do? For a moment, she considered ripping them up, but then recoiled at the notion.

Minutes ticked past while her jittery mind struggled to find a solution. I can't contact the police, she decided. The killer was very clear on that point, plus the police would only laugh at me, and in doing so, mock Mr. Briephs' sacred memory. She reached up and switched on her desk lamp. The glare was harsh in the semidarkened office. Combined with the greenish fluorescent light seeping in through the glass panel on the door, it gave her the appearance of a woman possessed. You'll be joining dear Tommy much sooner than you expected, a demonic interior voice warned, oddly reminding JaneAlice of the crazed woman caller in Clint Eastwood's *Play Misty for Me*.

Suddenly a smile affixed itself to her thin lips. Of course! She'd separate Thompson's remaining children and scatter them in three directions, by mailing them to other parties. That way she'd be blameless; she could tell this revolting individual—if he or she called again—that the cryptics had vanished. It wouldn't be a lie, just a slight stretching of the truth . . . While the recipients of dear Thompson's handiwork would be equally safe from threatening phone calls. It was an admirable plan! Something one might find in a Bette Davis movie. JaneAlice was thrilled with her achievement.

She pulled three business-sized envelopes from her desk, folded the puzzles into thirds, carefully inserting one into each envelope. She then put her mind to the task of deciding who should receive the puzzles. After a minute, another thin and slightly crooked smile found its way to her lips. "Yes," she said aloud, "Mr. Briephs would have loved this connection—*The Good, the Bad, and the Ugly.*" She carefully printed the names and addresses of her choices on the three envelopes, positively beaming at her own cleverness.

Then she walked to the hallway and dropped her dispatches into the *Herald*'s mail slot. A tremendous sense of accomplishment swept over her. She returned to her office, snatched up her purse and said aloud, "Tonight I'll stop and have dinner out . . . Go to the movies . . . To blazes with the Peter Pan bus terminal and its dingy lockers."

CHAPTER

13

THE ATHENA RESTAURANT boasted a bold and garish façade. Plaster columns fronted stuccoed cinder blocks, giving the place an aura of flimsy impermanence better suited to a movie set than a venerable New England city. The area was two blocks from the resuscitated City Pier, a spot that found more favor with tourists than with local residents. Nearby was the double-storied Fish House, boasting a red neon lobster in each of the ground-floor windows, an Italian trattoria of dubious culinary intent, and an outdoor Mexican cantina whose decor sported posters advertising beer and tequila. A gigantic cardboard mouse laboring under a vast sombrero stood guard by the front entrance. On this sultry summer evening, the street was packed with vacationing would-be diners; video cams were the accessories of choice.

"I haven't been down here since the pier was rehabilitated," Belle said. She hoped her voice didn't betray her disappointment. She couldn't understand why she felt so absurdly let down. This is nothing more than a business meeting, she told herself. What did I expect?

But Rosco was too perceptive not to intuit her dismay. "It's a lot better than it looks from the street. You'll see. Besides . . ." He couldn't bring himself to mention that a quieter eatery might have provoked unnecessary gossip.

"Besides what?"

"Besides, they've got the best *avgolemono*—lemon soup—around."

"I'm sure it's fabulous," Belle answered with a prepasted smile as he opened the door and ushered her into the Athena.

Inside, the false notes of the exterior vanished. The tables were simple, covered with red-and-white-checked tablecloths and an abundance of glistening white napkins. Candles flickered in the discreet shadows while a quiet buzz of conversation kept time with the soft plink of silverware meeting china and the gentle rhythm of bouzouki music that reminded Belle of sunlight spilling over the sea.

But it was the restaurant's walls that most entranced her. Divided into intimate alcoves, each was expertly painted with a mural, a modern-day view—or so she imagined—of Greece: an olive-tree-lined mountaintop overlooking a seductively blue Aegean, a grassy valley dotted with fallen columns, an island village whose ancient and crooked houses were daubed in a white so pure it looked like frosting.

"I feel as if I'm on vacation," Belle said. This time her smile was genuine.

"Have you ever been there? To Greece, I mean."

"No . . . Prior to meeting you, my only introduction to the Greeks was reading Aeschylus and Sophocles—although his statement, 'Silence gives the proper grace to women' rather turned me off."

Rosco laughed.

"And you? Have you visited there? Your homeland, I should say."

"Third generation, and I've never made it back. Neither did my folks . . . A widow struggling to raise four young kids doesn't zip around on transatlantic flights."

Belle and Rosco gazed at the painted scenes. A wistful yearning passed between them that served to heighten their sense of isolation from Newcastle and their very separate lives.

"Are you married?" Belle asked without knowing why she did.

"I was. For a short time . . . a high-school romance that didn't stand the test of time. The usual thing . . . I was warned against it by my friends; she was, too."

"I know all about the test of time," Belle said, then fell silent.

Conversation halted until the waiter appeared with a wine list that Rosco ignored and a menu he also dispensed with. Instead, he ordered a bottle of Achaia, then rattled off a list of specialties. "The *taramosalata*'s great, ditto the *avgolemono, dolmades* and *kebab*."

"Those seem like perfect choices."

"But you can order anything you want," he added quickly. "I didn't intend to make the choice for you."

Belle grinned. "It sounds to me as if marriage made you gun-shy."

"I'm just trying not to be . . . overbearing . . . I think that's a word that popped up in my divorce papers."

"I'm a pretty independent person. It would take more than 'overbearing' dinner suggestions to put me in my place."

" 'Once burned' . . ."

"I know. 'Twice shy' . . . I'm not a kid, Rosco."

When the apron-clad waiter returned bearing the wine, corkscrew and glasses Greek-style in one hand, Rosco became suddenly businesslike. "So tell me what you know about Steven Housemann."

Belle parried with her own no-nonsense question. "Not until you tell me what kind of stockings JaneAlice was wearing."

"What . . . ?!"

"JaneAlice Miller . . . It's a hunch I've been playing with: unrequited love becomes lethal—a perfect film scenario . . . Maybe she caught Thompson in a compromising position, and her mind snapped. If you tell me she favors support hose, I'll know I'm right. Plus . . . Have you noticed that her name has fifteen letters?"

"That sounds like too much late-night TV, Belle."

Belle drew herself up indignantly. "I never watch television!"

Rosco laughed. "Not even Uncle Morty?"

"Okay, once, but other than that, never."

"Oh, I believe you. It's just that you looked so . . . authoritative . . . like Thompson's mother, Sara. She must have been quite a firecracker in her day. I don't imagine there were many men in this town who could resist her."

"Except her brother, the Senator."

Rosco studied Belle, looking beyond the shining eyes and smiling lips. As JaneAlice had said, she was "lovely to look at," but Belle also possessed a keen and perceptive brain, and she liked to laugh—all qualities he found disconcertingly attractive.

"You have a lot more background on this situation than I do," he said to cover his lapse of professionalism. "Can we return to Housemann?"

"Steven Housemann takes a new bride almost as often as he purchases a new Mercedes Benz. His current 'lady' is Betsey; my guess is that she may outlast him—"

"This doesn't sound like the man I met."

Belle thought for a moment. "Steven's a very wily gentleman. He carved his career the hard way. There's nothing 'old school' about him—although he'd like the world to believe there is. Briephs epitomized Steven's blueblood ideal: expensively educated . . . a certain lassitude of morals cloaked in courtliness—laissez-faire as the French put it. I never understood the relationship between the two men—not that it was any of my business—but Steven was definitely jealous of Briephs. Jealous and fascinated . . . 'The desire of the moth for the star,' to quote Shelley."

"But Housemann referred to Thompson's mother as 'Sara.' I gathered they were close."

"That's typical of Steven. He wouldn't call her that to her face. In fact, I doubt he's ever invited to her home unless it's with a horde of guests—a fund-raising benefit or such."

"He seemed aware of her feelings toward Bulldog Roth, too."

"He's a newspaperman. He's done his research. There's no love lost between Sara and Roth. Roth is a political hatchet man—one of the best in the trade. He's been with Hal Crane since his freshman days in office; Roth won't permit anything—I repeat *anything*—to come between the Senator and his bid for reelection."

"He sounds more like a thug than a politico."

Belle merely raised her eyebrows. "The obvious assumption would be that it's Roth's influence that strained the relationship between Sara and her brother . . . You met her; what was your impression of the doyenne of Newcastle?"

"Regal, but no-nonsense . . . I got the feeling she was quite a flirt in her day . . . She still is."

"And politically?"

"Well, her brother's one of the most powerful Democrats in the Senate, so I suppose she's a— You don't mind if I use the L word?"

Belle shook her head.

"A liberal."

Belle grinned. "You have a lot to learn about the denizens of Liberty Hill. They'd commit communal hari-kari rather than renounce allegiance to the Republican Party. They believe Hal Crane 'betrayed his class.' Sara, as his older sister, leads the charge . . . I'm sure you've read that the Senator is in Vietnam at the moment, reestablishing cordial ties between our nations . . . Not the type of effort the country club set applauds."

"Publicly, maybe . . . But don't forget, that's all about trade. There's oil in them-thar hills. I'd bet money on it."

The *taramosalata* occupied them for the next few minutes. It was creamy and rich with the tang of the ocean and an aftertaste of salt that reminded Belle of diving through an ocean wave. She found herself licking the last traces from her fingers while Rosco watched wonderingly.

"My mother would have swatted me and my brother and sisters for doing that," he said.

Belle laughed. "And my mother *insisted* I eat certain foods with my fingers . . . asparagus, for instance. That was how the *intelligenzia* in Italy did it. She and my father liked fashioning themselves after fallen European nobility . . . We even had a samovar."

"That sounds like a demanding childhood."

" 'Eccentric' might be a better word. Tenured professors can be like that . . . I won't bore you with the arcane subjects of their intellectual quests except to say they were happiest when engrossed in research—especially of long-dead cultures . . . I used to yearn for a bunch of noisy siblings to break the silence . . . or at least have supper with."

"Where are they now, your parents?" Rosco said as he finished off his *taramosalata*.

"When Mother died, Father decamped to Florida. I didn't understand his choice then, and I still don't—which just proves the quirkiness of the human soul. Anyway, Father rarely journeys north, and I'm ashamed to admit I don't make the trek south as often as I should."

Rosco didn't ask what had brought Belle to Newcastle; he guessed it had been her husband, but didn't want to pry. And Belle was just as happy to leave Garet out of their conversation; she shifted the focus away from her own history. "What about your family . . . ? I'm sorry if I was insensitive in bringing up your father when you first interviewed me."

"You don't have to be sorry. Dad died young—like I said, and I really don't remember him. He was a commercial fisherman. Like his father before him . . . My mom toughed out the early days of widowhood. Not much money but plenty of neighborly support—immigrants like to stick together. She never remarried. That wasn't the way of her 'people.' She's still living. And still very much in charge—even of my older sisters and younger brother. She's also a great cook."

Belle laughed gently. "Ah . . . But can she concoct the perfect deviled egg?" Then, as if their shared histories were too intimate to handle, she abruptly changed tack. "I forgot to mention that Housemann prides himself on his physical prowess. He's a health nut devoted to all forms of athletics—besides being highly competitive. I wouldn't be surprised if he challenged you to some kind of game the next time you meet."

"Handball doesn't exactly rank as an exclusive sport— not where I come from, anyway."

"That's how he grew up, too, Rosco—and he doesn't take kindly to people who demean him."

"What about Betsey?"

Belle fiddled with what remained of the grape leaves on her plate. "There were rumors . . . Of course, they're so often the product of bored minds. Newcastle does adore gossip."

"Well?"

"I told you Betsey has a wandering eye?"

Rosco grinned, remembering exactly what she'd said. "I don't recall you using such a ladylike term."

Belle continued studying her plate. "People said she was having an affair with Thompson . . . There were hints . . . little things, such as the two of them leaving a function almost simultaneously . . . Then there was her sudden interest in his theatre project."

"Theatre project?"

"You've been to Plays and Players?"

"Sorry, that stuff's too highbrow for me."

"*Pretentious* would be the word I'd use." Belle laughed. "Anyway, Thompson got all his cronies involved and I mean *all*." Rosco read Belle's husband into this remark, but didn't interrupt. "The artistic director persuaded Tommy to angel an experimental production—a musical version of the life of Mary Todd Lincoln."

Rosco's astonished "Of what!" made Belle laugh so hard, her eyes filled with inadvertent tears.

"Replete with a singing, dancing John Wilkes Booth!"

"The idle rich certainly know how to waste their money," Rosco marveled while Belle commenced another infectious peal of laughter.

"If your parents were professors, why didn't you go for an academic career?" Rosco's question surprised Belle. She thought for a moment, although it wasn't an answer she was pondering but Rosco's motivation. The query seemed peculiarly personal, the kind of exploration a dating couple might engage in; and she wasn't altogether certain how to proceed.

"Rebellion, I suppose . . . I've always been fairly pigheaded, although I do love noodling around with words. My upbringing, as you might imagine, was *highly* cerebral. At one point, I considered becoming a poet, but then I discovered H. D.—Hilda Doolittle—she wrote about the Greek islands, coincidentally. Her imagist verse completely knocked the wind from my sails—no reference to mythology intended. That was the end of poetry for Belle Graham." She turned her wry comment into a semi-serious jest. "I can't believe you didn't get the remaining puzzles from JaneAlice."

"Well, it just didn't come up. And honestly, I'm just not buying this concept of yours . . . A lot of coincidences that—"

"Thompson Briephs didn't believe in coincidence. You've seen his house. Does it look like the creation of a scattered brain?"

Rosco didn't answer.

"So you're not going to pursue my puzzle theory?"

"No. Not right off the top. I work better if I pursue my own hunches. Besides, I'm not fully convinced the situation wasn't more or less what Lever described."

Belle remained silent, although Rosco could see her mind was whirring. "Lever's scenario has a 'hired companion' cavorting around Briephs' home, right?"

"I don't think he'd use the term 'cavorting,' but for lack of a good mixed-company word, yes."

"Well, I'm only thinking aloud . . . but perhaps Peter Kingsworth saw her—or him—arrive or leave."

"What makes you think the prostitute might be a male?"

"I don't know . . . a hunch . . . Anyway, I think we should talk to Peter."

"It's on my agenda. But if he'd seen anything, I imagine he would have opened his mouth by now."

"Well, perhaps he might remember a strange boat or something . . ." Belle's gray eyes were luminous, and her lips parted with a glowing smile. Rosco had a terrible desire to chuck the investigatory conversation and tell her how beautiful she was. Instead he scraped a fork across his empty plate, an action Belle completely misinterpreted.

"Ah, the male ego! You didn't like our bronzed yachtsman very much, as I recall!"

In answer, Rosco blurted out, "What's the skinny on Bartholomew Kerr?"

But Belle only laughed. "I think Peter is very pleasant . . . Maybe I should be the one to question him." Then a playful grin settled on her face. "Bartholomew's the society columnist at the *Herald*. He knows everything about everyone, but I doubt he'll talk to you."

"Where there's a will there's a way."

"I wouldn't be so certain . . . Bartholomew loves affecting a British accent and lexicon; he looks pasty and pathetic—a mole minus the fur—but hidden beneath his striped bow ties and seersucker suits is Newcastle's version of J. Edgar Hoover. I'll bet Bartholomew has a secret file on everyone in town."

Inadvertently, Rosco gazed into Belle's eyes. The urge to change the conversation was becoming alarming. "And Shannon McArthur?"

Belle returned Rosco's glance. "I'll make a pact with you: I tell you everything you want to know in exchange for JaneAlice's puzzles."

"You don't give up, do you?"

"What about it?"

"I'll tell you what I *will* do; I have a nine-thirty date with Steven Housemann tomorrow morning. I'll pick you up at eight and we'll stop in and see JaneAlice first. I wouldn't count on her giving up those puzzles too easily, though."

Belle's pleasure at this concession made her skin grow rosy and warm, and on the way home in Rosco's car, she talked almost nonstop about her childhood "rattling around the ivory towers of academia." Her descriptions of the brainy but pathologically forgetful folk who'd peopled her childhood made them both laugh.

It was at her door that the spell was broken.

"I'd ask you in, but—"

Rosco's response was too brisk by half. "I can't anyway. I've still got work to do. I'm always Mr. Business when I'm on a case."

Both reacted to the unfortunate choice of words, Belle, by assuming a taut, professional smile, Rosco by turning needlessly gruff. "You can't expect to question the hookers on Congress Street if you don't keep their hours."

Belle's smile grew so rigid it looked chiseled in place.

"The hookers on Congress Street . . . of course." After a moment, she added a forced, "Thank you for dinner. I enjoyed myself."

"Let's do it again sometime."

"Of course."

Rosco recognized the evasiveness in her tone. "Belle," he began, then amended the effort by substituting, "I'll pick you up at eight tomorrow morning."

Another lifeless smile. "I'll be ready."

CHAPTER

14

AT SEVEN A.M. Rosco's clock radio woke him with twenty seconds of blaring electronic buzz and then switched over to *Imus in the Morning*. The I-Man was just a little too cheery for Rosco, so he flipped it off and headed for the bathroom and a hasty shower and shave. After downing a quick cup of coffee, he found himself in the front seat of his Jeep and on his way over to Captain's Walk to meet Belle.

Last night's dinner had left him with a good deal of energy, but the journey to the red-light district had proved exhausting and he'd managed only four hours sleep because of it. Trips to Congress Street and the Newcastle Strip had always been unpleasant for Rosco, and the previous evening's excursion had been no exception. The thought that women, and men, found it necessary to sell their bodies to sustain themselves never failed to leave him in a funk. A funk that would ultimately wear at him for a day or two.

In most of his other cases—cases involving Congress Street or the Strip—it had been simply a matter of checking on some husband who'd been unfaithful, or a child suspected of drug abuse by a concerned parent, or a disappearance. In these situations he'd merely observe. It was rare that he'd have to talk to the women and men who earned a living there. But last night had been different. For over three hours he'd talked to every girl who worked the street. Some had been more helpful than others. Some he remembered from his days with the Newcastle police. Everyone had been aware of Thompson Briephs, his lifestyle and his death.

Briephs had apparently become quite a regular in the district within the past few years. At least eight women had been guests at his island home. The talkative ones told Rosco it wasn't unusual for them to go out to Windword in groups of two or more; typically there would be "party boys" from the Strip there as well. Often Briephs would structure weekend-long orgies where his visitors would romp through his mazelike house, indulging in the kinkiest sexual practices with whomever they happened to meet. Rosco also learned that not all Briephs' guests were professionals. Some of Newcastle's more prominent citizens, men and women, would show up at these gatherings, but the streetwalkers refused to name names. As expected, all the ladies of the night had strong alibis for the evening in question.

Rosco had opted not to check with the party boys on the

Strip. By the time he'd finished with the girls it was close to three A.M. He was tired, and he'd doubted many men would be left on the street. Most would have headed off to the Lily Club—a place Rosco didn't relish exploring. He'd do it another time.

As he waited for a traffic signal to turn green he found his mind returning to his dinner with Belle, and a warm, somewhat crooked smile formed on his lips. His time on Congress Street had only served to make him feel empty and lonely, and he was looking forward to seeing her again. Her energy and spirit were contagious.

Dammit, he thought, why are all the good ones married?

He shook his head, watched the light turn green and said aloud, "Such is life, Bucko."

When he reached Captain's Walk he was ten minutes early. He double-parked in front of Belle's house, put on his emergency flashers and pulled yesterday's edition of the *Herald* out from under the Jeep's small rear seat. He went directly to the blank crossword puzzle and filled in two of the answers Belle had given him the day before: THOMPSON BRIEPHS, number 35 across the middle, and AFTERNOON DEATHS, 52 across the bottom. It was only then that he realized that all the daily puzzles must be fifteen letters square. Rosco stared at the puzzle for nearly five minutes but only managed to fill in one other answer: AGAL, for 1-Across, "*I want ____ just like . . .*" He shook his head, tossed the paper onto the backseat, strolled up the walk and knocked on Belle's door.

"You're early," she said in an overly businesslike tone.

"And a good morning to you, too."

"You said you'd be here at eight. It's seven fifty-five . . . Did you pick up this morning's *Herald* on your way?"

"Was I supposed to? I mean, we're going to their offices, aren't we? They have them free in the lobby."

Belle let out a sigh.

"I somehow feel I've missed something here. Can I come in? Or should I wait in the Jeep?"

"Perhaps that's best."

"Okey-dokey." Rosco walked back to the Jeep, and Belle joined him ten minutes later.

"How was last night?" she asked after fastening her seat belt.

"I had a great time, Belle. I was glad to get to know you a little better. However, I'm still not convinced the answer to this case will be found in a dead man's puzzles . . . Sorry."

"I'm not talking about that, and you know it." Her words sounded oddly strangled. She hated to admit how uncomfortable she felt knowing that Rosco had spent the better part of the night with the women of Congress Street.

"What are you talking about?"

"I'm talking about *after* dinner. How did you *fare* with the ladies of the evening?" Belle most definitely stressed *fare* and then silently cursed herself for doing so.

But Rosco was unaware of her self-criticism. "I *fared* extremely well, thanks. Saw a lot of old friends. Kind of like a party down there the more I think on it."

Belle crossed her arms over her chest and looked straight ahead.

Rosco U-turned into traffic and continued, "Anyway—and I don't know why I'm telling you this—I guess it's because I like you, because by rights none of it is any of your business, but it seems that Briephs spent a lot of time cruising Congress Street . . . Also the Strip."

"You went to the Strip last night, too?"

"No, the girls wore me out. I'll check on the boys tonight."

"Well, have fun. That's all I can say."

Rosco was silent for a minute, then finally said, "Actually it's depressing, Belle." He cleared his throat. "It's depressing and exhausting, and the worst part of this job. Believe it or not, it's worse than going to the morgue—at least it's over for them . . . You never want to have to visit Congress, believe me. The people down there are in trouble, and there's not a soul in the world who's going to help them out."

He was quiet again, and Belle was tempted to put her hand on his as it rested on the Jeep's gearshift. But she didn't.

"Well," he said, clearing his throat once more, "the point is, I didn't find out much of anything . . . Some of the girls have been on the street since I was with the department. And I think they'd confide in me if they knew something . . . So, I'm no longer buying Lever's hooker scenario. These girls wouldn't have the first idea how to get off that island on their own. That became obvious last night. Whoever killed Briephs has a boat. It's the only answer."

"Or Peter Kingsworth ferried them."

Rosco gave her a sideways glance that caused the Jeep to veer toward oncoming traffic.

"All right," Belle said, "Scratch Peter. Charon, the boatman bearing souls across the River Styx."

"Greek mythology . . . I know. I'm not as dumb as I look."

"The expression is 'I'm not as dumb as *you* look.'"

"If you're ten years old, it is."

"I didn't learn it until I was fifteen!"

"Too much ivory tower."

They both laughed, the ice broken. Belle was the first to resume the discussion. "But your assumption eliminates no one. Everyone in Newcastle has a boat. I have a boat. The mayor has a boat. Even the Senator has a boat."

"I don't."

"Yes, but you're odd."

Rosco looked at Belle. The full force of the rising sun flooded her face, and she was forced to squint to return his glance. Her smile seemed warmer than the sunlight; it made her appear angelic.

"You're odd," she repeated.

He smiled back and said, "Thank you."

After five or six minutes Rosco eased the Jeep into a parking spot around the corner from the *Herald*'s front entrance. As Belle searched through her purse for meter change Rosco reached under the front seat and removed a small red canvas bag.

"I'll get this," he said, hopping out and placing the canvas bag over the meter. On it was printed: *Meter out of order. Your parking courtesy of the Newcastle P.D. Have a nice day*.

"Where did you get that?" Belle asked with obvious envy in her voice. "I want one."

"Actually the city hasn't used them in years, but I don't think the meter readers have caught on yet."

As they began walking toward the corner an ambulance raced through the traffic signal, lights flashing, and siren shrieking at a level intended to wake people in Boston or even Albany.

"Jeez," Belle said as she moved her hands to her ears. "You wouldn't think that much noise was necessary, would you?"

From reflex, Rosco stopped and watched the ambulance pass. About three-quarters of the way down the block it slowed and ducked into the *Herald*'s underground parking structure. Rosco stood silently for a moment.

"What?" Belle asked.

"I'm debating whether to go see what's up. Old police habits don't die easy."

The sound of another siren pulled their attention back to the intersection. It came from a tan four-door sedan, obviously an unmarked police car, with a red flasher slapped onto its roof. As it sped by, Rosco recognized a familiar face behind the wheel.

"Al," he muttered.

"Lever?"

"That's right . . . Look, Belle, I'll meet you in the *Herald* lobby. I'm going to check this out." Rosco sprinted off toward the garage entrance, leaving Belle alone on the sidewalk.

CHAPTER
15

ROSCO REACHED THE garage ramp at the same moment Lever's car made its turn. The vehicle was traveling slowly enough for Rosco to open the door and jump in alongside the detective; the leap from asphalt to rubberized floor mat was so seamless it looked like a circus routine.

"What the deuce are you doing here?" was Lever's none-too-gracious greeting.

"Just visiting. What's going on?"

"My wife tells me, 'Lock the doors when you drive through the city. Anyone could jump into your car.' I should listen to her more often." Lever worked the sedan through the poorly lit underground parking area, searching for the ambulance.

"What's this all about, Al?"

"Well, you figure it out, Rosco, you're a smart guy. Who do I work for?"

"Homicide."

"Bingo."

"Who got it?"

"Caucasian female's all I have."

"*Herald* employee?"

"Beats me."

Lever spotted the ambulance at the far end of the cavernous garage, wedged into one of the many hidden alcoves. He raced to a skidding stop beside it. Both men jumped from the car simultaneously.

"Hey," Lever shouted. "Who told you to move that body?"

A uniformed officer stepped out from a parked car and said, "Good morning, Lieutenant. The paramedics say she isn't dead. They're getting a slight pulse. Might be able to save her."

"Who the hell is she?"

"No positive ID yet. The night watchman was getting ready to leave, heard a scream and ran back down."

"He see anything?"

"He's over there." The cop pointed to a man in a blue guard's uniform leaning against the trunk of a dark green Chevy. "He didn't get a look at anyone. Says he was more concerned about getting an ambulance down here."

Rosco eased his way to where the paramedics were strapping the unconscious woman to the gurney. She was severely beaten around the face and neck with what was obviously a dull instrument of some kind. Her flesh was pulpy and purple, and her eyes completely swollen shut. But even with the way her face had been rearranged, Rosco knew he'd seen her before.

After the paramedics closed up the ambulance and hustled off, Rosco ambled back toward the lieutenant, who was now questioning the security guard.

"So, you didn't see anything then?" Lever pressed.

"No, sir. Usually I get off at eight." The guard glanced reflexively at his watch. "But my replacement was late. So I was waiting for him at the top of the ramp . . . At about eight-o-five, eight-ten, I heard this scream and ran down. It took me almost three minutes to find her. All these alcoves—I didn't know where to look first. I'm surprised this doesn't happen more often down here. They need a gate up top. Anyway, by the time I found her, whoever did it was long gone. So I radioed for an ambulance and police."

"And you've never seen her before?"

"Nope. But I work the midnight to eight shift. There's a lot of folks I don't know. People who come to work after eight, I usually never see."

"Okay, thanks. I want you to stick around until we're done here."

"Yes, sir."

Lever watched Rosco approach. "You still here?"

"Yep."

"Well, I've got to get a forensic crew in here, so don't touch anything."

"What did the guard see?"

"Nothing."

"Do you know who she was?"

"Not yet. Her purse is still here, but it's missing any form of identification."

"Money?"

"Gone. Someone cleaned her out."

"I guess she was mugged, then," Rosco suggested.

"Looks that way . . . Armed robbery, she resists—they never learn, do they?"

"Nope," Rosco agreed. "Tough way to save twenty bucks." Then he put his hands into his pockets, turned and walked the length of the parking structure. It was damp and sticky and gave off an odor that was typical of every seeping, ancient brick-and-stone basement. At the end, Rosco hustled up the exit ramp and onto the street. He was surprised to find Belle waiting in the shade of an elm tree.

"I know you said to meet in the *Herald* lobby—" she began. "Actually, I was going to come down and find you, but I have a phobia about those places. Maybe it's because I have such a rotten sense of direction . . . I'm afraid I'll get lost and never see the light of day again . . . *So*, what happened?"

"Someone tried to kill JaneAlice Miller."

CHAPTER

16

L AWSON'S, THE COFFEE shop across from the *Herald* had become a Newcastle institution. It had been enthralling or infuriating customers for the past forty-odd years and its waitresses looked as if they'd been on duty since day one. So did its green-flecked Formica countertop and the booths whose banquettes were covered in cracked pink plastic. A newcomer might have expected the ads on the walls to run to hand-colored photographs of Ovaltine or Libbey's Dairies—even a faded yet still demure Breck Girl wouldn't have seemed amiss.

Rosco had taken a much-shaken Belle to Lawson's time-warped haven in hopes that the abundance of smiling faces would comfort her in some small way. It was one of his favorite haunts in this city, a soothing gathering place where the congenial murmur of conversation was interspersed with boisterous orders to and from the fry-cook and the ever-present jangle of the tarnished tin bell haphazardly affixed above the door. The aromas of grape jelly, underdone toast, rubbery bacon and coffee mingled gleefully in the air.

"But, why?" Belle asked for the second time since they'd entered.

"Lever believes it's armed robbery." Rosco didn't go into his contribution to the theory.

"But that's a mistaken assumption, don't you think?" Belle sat close to him in the booth as if she were suddenly icy cold. "I mean, doesn't it look as if the same person who killed Briephs was trying to murder JaneAlice? As if she knew something that might be incriminating?" Belle shivered violently. "And she was almost unrecognizable?"

Rosco regretted including that particular piece of information, but added, "She'd been badly beaten," as if it might somehow neutralize what he'd seen.

"I should send her some flowers, poor thing."

Rosco didn't answer for a moment. "She's unconscious, Belle. She may not make it."

Belle shivered again. "The scary thing is . . . this person is still out there."

Rosco couldn't dredge up any words of comfort. Deep down, he was as upset as Belle. Briephs' death had been one thing, but the attack on JaneAlice struck closer to home. He'd been talking to her only yesterday morning and now she was on life-support.

"Lever's a good cop," he said as he glanced across the street. "He'll catch whoever did this."

"But he thinks it's just a mugging . . ."

"He'll dust for prints. He'll be thorough."

"Murderers don't leave fingerprints! There aren't going to be any at Windword Islands—that's what you said. And if this was the same person who killed Briephs, there won't be any in the garage either." Belle's large, frightened eyes leveled on Rosco's.

Here was a cop's toughest call: sympathy versus professional detachment. Rosco would have given his eyeteeth to remain hunkered down in the booth with Belle, but he had work to do.

"Look, Belle, Housemann said he'd be willing to give me a few minutes at nine-thirty. If I run across the street, will you wait for me here?"

Belle glanced out the steamy window toward the *Herald's* imposing redbrick presence. Her expression changed visibly, as if she were persuading herself to remain calm and collected. "I'm fine."

"And you'll wait for me here?"

She tried to laugh. "Aye aye, sir."

"You don't have to be brave."

"I am brave, though; that's the odd thing. In fact, I'm beginning to think I'm completely unflappable."

"I won't be long. Housemann reminded me twice how valuable his time is—nicely, though."

"You're still not convinced I'm right, are you?"

Before dodging across the street, Rosco spotted a red-and-white *Herald* vending machine. He dropped in two quarters, slipped out the morning edition and flipped open the pages until he spotted the crossword. Then he folded the paper neatly and scooted back to Belle. "Something to

occupy you. My treat. Oh, and order up some eggs or something. They're great on the homemade hash browns . . .
over-easy, that's my favorite."

"Eggs? I thought I mentioned that I'm broadening my
cuisine."

"Well, waffles or pancakes then . . . They use real maple
syrup here." He pointed at the *Herald*. "There are no answers to yesterday's puzzle in there. I guess I'll just have to
trust you."

"Thanks, Rosco." She looked up at him. "I mean it.
You're a good guy . . . Don't let Housemann push you
around."

Alone with the puzzle, Belle swiveled it to face away from
her. She didn't want to be tempted to fill in the blanks. The
concept of a murderer being revealed in a word game had
begun to seem absurd—as if she were treating Briephs'
death and Rosco's investigation as a joke. JaneAlice's beating seemed to attach a permanent chill to her bones. She
looked out the window and drank her coffee. But gradually
habit overcame her resolve, and she found herself glancing
sideways at the puzzle. The fact that yesterday's answers
were missing had started to intrigue her. "Oh, all right,"
she decided. "Rosco bought the thing. I might as well have
a go at it."

Slowly, she shifted the paper's alignment, scanning the
clues and blank spaces with professional speed. "Wow,"
she murmured. "Another one . . ."

Across

1. Deface
5. Grace, Scot.
10. ___ laugh
14. Other
15. Forgets
16. Old Peruvian
17. San ___ Obispo
18. Striped French cat
19. M.E.'s course
20. This monkey's uncle?
23. Apiece
24. A couple of Scots? Var.
25. Wager
28. Alloy: abbr.
30. Frighten
35. Sound of contentment
36. Radical from acid
38. Indian calico
39. Herald's editor in chief
43. Shellac, e.g.
44. Tied
45. Cyan conclusion
46. Slender as___
47. Jacob's brother
49. No vote
50. Hebrew weight
53. Not con
55. Bad actor?
63. Woodwind
64. ___ Agnew
65. Spanish painter
66. Touts
67. Moon over Greece?
68. Idea
69. Ed. leaves?
70. Not true!
71. Talk up

Down

1. French seasonings
2. It's often under your nose
3. M___ murder
4. Grade "Z" maple syrup?
5. First one on the A train?
6. Arabian knight?
7. Result of a Freddie Kruger evening?
8. The last ___
9. Where Whittier is: abbr.
10. Fibber
11. I, in "The King and I"
12. Look over
13. London gallery
21. It's often black
22. End
25. Iraqi city
26. Consumer
27. "___ are the times that try men's souls"
29. Pain
31. On the ___
32. ___ Delon
33. "Help Me ___," The Beach Boys Today!
34. Gelt
37. Plague
40. Compete
41. Grace
42. What a photographer does
48. Sub ending
51. Henry's daughter Jane
52. "Once Upon a Mattress" soundtrack?
54. Get-up-and-go
55. Scribbles
56. Last words?

PUZZLE #2

57. Wish
58. Robin's home
59. Old-time befores

60. Greasy
61. Ensnare
62. Sharpen

CHAPTER

17

Aᶠᵗᵉʳ ʳᵉᶜᵉⁱᵛⁱⁿᵍ ᵃⁿ impatient "Yes, Miss Holland?"
Steven Housemann's secretary gingerly opened
the inner-office door that led to the editor in chief's
oak-lined haven. There, she motioned for Rosco to step
past her, then eased the door shut behind him, leaving the
two men standing alone—face-to-face. The secretary's hesitant behavior resembled that of an animal trainer tossing
raw meat into an angry leopard's cage.

The walls of Housemann's office were hung with a
gloomy collection of nineteenth-century fox-hunting prints
and ominous marine oils depicting shipwrecks that had occurred along the North Atlantic coast. A brass floor lamp,
a desk lamp, also brass, and two pallid wall sconces completed the seigneurial theme. These fixtures had once
been fitted out for gas rather than electricity; their authentic green glass shades retained a murky aura of old

money mingled with cigar-chomping, backroom deals. The suggestion of intrigue was reinforced by a suite of dark, leather-covered furniture: a Chesterfield sofa placed against one wall and two overstuffed club chairs facing the stony-faced master of the wide mahogany desk.

"I'll give you five minutes," Housemann said as he turned from the desk and walked to a window whose wooden venetian-blind slats were angled to look down upon the world rather than up into the sky. "And that's only because I offered you the time yesterday." As he spoke, Housemann watched Lieutenant Lever's tan sedan emerge from the garage below and nudge its way into Newcastle's morning traffic.

"It's a shame about JaneAlice Miller," Rosco offered carefully gauging Housemann's body language and expression to determine how much he knew about the incident.

"Polycrates, I don't have time for small talk. I've got a newspaper to run. First, I lose my crossword editor, and now his secretary gets knocked unconscious and the week's remaining puzzles are nowhere to be found. Not only that, but prior to her unfortunate . . . *accident*, JaneAlice appears to have lost the answers Briephs must have prepared for the cryptics. God only knows what the woman did with them. Don't waste my time."

"The puzzles aren't in her office? When I spoke to Miss Miller yesterday she mentioned it had been Briephs' custom to be five puzzles ahead."

Housemann turned from the window to square off with Rosco. "That may be true, but there's no telling where the idiot woman put them. We've been through the offices with a flea comb. But that's my concern, not yours. Just what is it you want here?"

Rosco was beginning to see the side of Steven Housemann Belle had warned him about, but, oddly, it made him more comfortable with the situation. He no longer saw a need for the niceties he'd mustered up during their previous conversation. "Here's the situation, Mr. Housemann: Mrs. Briephs has asked me to look into the possibility that her son might not have died of natural causes, i.e., she believes Thompson was murdered."

Again Rosco studied the older man, but his expression and posture remained inscrutable. Rosco continued: "At first I pegged her as a distraught mother overly concerned with her son's death. But I said I'd look into it for her—"

"Oh, I'm sure of that," Housemann interrupted. "I wouldn't expect one of you bloodsuckers to miss out on a chance to hustle a few bucks out of an aging widow."

Rosco smiled. "Well, we do what we need to do. Sort of like those ads for the porno theatres and massage parlors you run in the sports section each day? We all have to put food on the table, don't we?"

"Call a spade a spade." Housemann chuckled. "I'll bet you're a tough man on the squash court. You know how to return a good serve."

"I play a little handball now and then."

"Of course . . . Nothing so trendy as squash for the private dick . . . A brief warning, Polycrates: don't push your luck, I can be an unpleasant adversary." Housemann pulled a ten-inch cigar from a humidor made of some rare and endangered species of wood, and lit it without offering one to his guest or asking if the smoke might annoy him. "As far as I'm concerned, the world is better off without Thompson Briephs and his blueblood bull—the prep school accent and supercilious laugh and those asinine hats he wore with his hair flying out the back . . . I won't deny that his puzzles played a large part in keeping our circulation apace with the *Evening Crier*. And for that, he'll be missed. But let's cut to the chase, if he *was* murdered, and you're standing here because you have some misguided notion that I might have had something to do with it . . . well, it wouldn't be in the *Herald*'s best interest, now, would it?"

Rosco brought his left hand up and scratched lightly at the back of his neck. "That's a good point. But past experience has told me that murderers don't always consider their best interests before they act. Most of the time, it's a case of passion or hatred gaining control of a person's reason."

"You honestly believe I would kill Thompson Briephs?"

"I have no idea. Anything's possible. Your secretary"—Rosco cocked his thumb toward the door—"mentioned that you were out of your office on the afternoon of Briephs' death." Rosco opened a small notepad he'd removed from his coat pocket and scanned it. "She said your wife stopped in around eleven that morning, stayed for only ten minutes and then you left shortly afterward. In a hurry. I was only curious where you might have gone."

Housemann's jaw clenched and the taut muscles turned his face into a mummylike grimace. "Don't stick your nose where it doesn't belong, Polycrates. If you step on my toes

I will use the power of the press to run you out of this town—and I'll do it so fast it'll make your head spin. You can take that as a threat. I don't play games." Housemann returned to his desk, sat with the rigid economy of movement of a man struggling to contain his temper, then reached for the intercom, depressed a red button and spoke to his secretary. "Miss Holland, Mr. Polycrates is finished here. Show him out."

Rosco ambled toward the inter-office door, but before Miss Holland appeared he turned back and said, "The police are going to reopen the Briephs' case and treat it as a homicide. You can count on that. You haven't seen the last of Al Lever . . . or me."

"Get out!"

"One last thing. Who's going to make up the crossword puzzles for tomorrow's paper and the remainder of the week?"

"Are my choices in staff now under your dubious scrutiny as well?"

"I'm just curious. I know you hired Shannon McArthur to replace Briephs—"

"I have nothing more to say, Polycrates—"

"—which seems curious, because JaneAlice mentioned some sort of scandal involving McArthur. Wasn't she working at the *Herald* then?"

"In the future, I'd suggest you refer staffing questions to me rather than some fatuous, lovelorn secretary. That appointment has not been confirmed."

"So, you're not hiring Shannon McArthur?"

Housemann bellowed a louder "Miss Holland!" at the

same moment the woman rushed through the door. She didn't say a word, but Rosco saw her jump to attention.

Dumped unceremoniously in the *Herald*'s suspiciously vacant corridor, Rosco considered Housemann's reaction, then decided there were more ways to skin a cat than by browbeating the *Herald*'s editor in chief. He glanced at his watch and wondered if Belle might still be waiting for him at Lawson's Coffee Shop. The thought of her having left produced a definite sensation of disappointment, but he had a few details to check before he left the building. The missing puzzles had piqued his interest; their whereabouts were bound to be the first question out of Belle's mouth. And, if he'd guessed correctly, it would be impossible for Housemann to let Wednesday's paper go to press without a crossword puzzle.

Rosco moved to the other side of the hallway and tapped on a door marked with the number 404. From within, he heard an irritable male voice call out, "What is it?" It was the kind of tone that reverberated with too many cigarettes, too much coffee and Scotch and too few of the other basic food groups.

Rosco eased the door open. Sitting behind a gray metal desk whose surface had all but disappeared beneath a two-foot-high layer of papers, magazines and rumpled file folders, sat Pat Anderson, the *Herald*'s sportswriter. Rosco had no trouble recognizing him from the picture that accompanied his byline—and his signature handlebar mustache. Beyond his glowering face the office walls were plastered with signed photographs of nearly every man who'd played ball for the Boston Red Sox since World War II.

"What the hell do you want?" An inch of cold cigar hung from the corner of Pat's mouth. As he leaned possessively over his Underwood portable, the dead cigar bobbed up and down like a wine cork lost in a half-full bottle.

Rosco found himself stuttering in the great man's presence. "You're P-Pat Anderson, aren't you?"

"Who the hell are you?"

Rosco could think of nothing he'd like better than to sit in Pat Anderson's office and talk baseball, but he had work to do. "Me? I'm nobody . . . Actually. I was looking for the personnel office."

"Second floor. Now, get the hell outta here."

As Rosco began to withdraw he couldn't resist asking the big question that had been on the minds of most New Englanders all summer long.

"Say, Pat?"

"What?"

"What do you think the Sox are going to do with Billings?"

Pat didn't bother looking up from the Underwood as he muttered, "Trade him. Bad rotator cuff . . . Besides, they need another southpaw like they need a new wall in left field . . . Do me a favor."

"Sure, Pat. Anything you want."

"Get the hell outta here."

"Right."

Rosco closed the door as quietly as possible and returned to the elevator, where he descended to the second floor. At the end of the hall behind an aged and fingerprint-smeared door that might have been emblazoned with the words *All hope abandon, ye who enter here* he found the personnel office. With a quick, deft smile, Rosco entered. There he was confronted by a woman of such impeccable bureaucratic bearing that she might have served as the template for every government agency meting out drivers' licenses, marriage licenses or copies of birth certificates.

"May I help you?"

"Yes. I know this may seem rather crass, so soon after Mr. Briephs' passing, but my mother always told me that if you want something, you can't wait for it to land in your lap. I figured coming in person was the only polite way to handle it."

"Yes?"

"Well, I work as the crossword editor for a Midwest newspaper . . . The *Cincinnati Courier*?"

"I don't know it." This statement was delivered in a manner that would have quashed even a Nobel Laureate.

"It's very small . . . Actually, we only publish one issue weekly . . ." Rosco laughed as if this were a private joke, but the woman didn't join him. "Anyway, Mother and I were vacationing near Newcastle when I heard of Mr. Briephs' untimely demise, and I was wondering if the position might now be open? I hope I'm not being too pushy."

"That position has already been filled." A censorious line bit at the edges of the woman's mouth.

"I see. Anybody I might know . . . taking over for Mr. Briephs, that is?

"Shannon McArthur." The name was accompanied by a grimace of distaste.

"Oh! I think I heard something about her."

The woman didn't respond, but her lips twitched in a quick, spasmodic tic.

"Well, I won't waste your time." Rosco turned as if to leave, then appeared to remember a final question. "You wouldn't know, by any chance, if Shannon McArthur is contributing the rest of this week's puzzles? Because, if not, I have a few I've never published . . . As I said, Mother and I—"

"Mr. Housemann's office has made all necessary arrangements."

CHAPTER

18

W HEN ROSCO STEPPED into Lawson's Coffee Shop
he spotted Belle exactly where he'd left her—in
the window booth, her chin resting in the palm
of her left hand as her right hand drummed the *Herald*'s
crossword puzzle with the tip of a red Bic pen. She was lost
to all thought other than the idiosyncratic groupings of ver-
tical and horizontal letters. Rosco moved to the table and
was tempted to slide into the banquette beside her, but
thought better of it and slipped into the facing seat.

"Rosco!" In her surprise, she nearly yelped the name.
"Look at this puzzle! Just look at it!" She spun the paper
around and pushed it toward Rosco. It had been completed in red ink with no sign of errors or amended answers.

Rosco picked up the paper, glanced at it, then turned it
over as if searching for something else.

"Where did you find the answers?" he eventually asked.

Belle began to laugh, although she sensed the timing was wrong for a smart-aleck remark about his vocabulary. "Sometimes I get lucky and I don't make mistakes. Besides, it's Tuesday. The *Herald* puzzles are usually easier at the beginning of the week."

Rosco smiled. Belle seemed to have worked past the shock of JaneAlice's beating. He studied the paper. "I can't believe you did this in ink and didn't make any mistakes." He pointed to 36-Across. "I mean, what is this? A-C-Y-L? That's a word?"

"ACYL? Sure it's a word. A little rarefied perhaps, but a word nonetheless. It's used in certain laboratories. It's a chemical term . . . a radical derived from an acid . . ." Belle grabbed the paper from Rosco. Excitement floated on her words: "But that's not important. Look at some of these other answers, and tell me I'm crazy."

"You're crazy," he said, trying not to smile too broadly.

"I'm serious. Look at this, 2-Down: CLUE, 12-Down: SCAN, 56-Down: OBIT, and 61-Down: TRAP; perfectly spaced. Don't you see? Briephs is talking to us from the grave. SCAN the puzzle for clues, TRAP the murderer!"

Rosco's smile grew. Belle was definitely fired up.

"I'm going to slap you if you don't take that grin off your face, and I mean it . . . Okay, 34-Down: MONEY; lending more credence to a blackmail theory. 3-Down: *M* AS IN *murder*. You can't ignore that . . . The big one in the center, 7-Down: NIGHTLY OVERKILL. And then Briephs misses something—and I don't think it's an accident. Right here." Belle turned the paper and pointed. "8-Down: *The last* STRAW, and then, LAST *laugh*. In any other puzzle Briephs would have connected those clues—made a pun or some arcane, etymological leap. He loved to play games like that. Why didn't he do it here?"

"I'll bet you have an answer to that question."

"Yes! He was trying to get across two different ideas: *it's* the last straw and *he* will be getting in the last laugh."

"I don't know, Belle. Where does this lead? Even if your theory is right, what do these clues point to? More importantly, *who* do they point to?"

"Wait! Wait! Here's the kicker. Remember I believed that Thompson would name his killer. And I also had a hunch that person would have fifteen letters in their name? The same number of letters that run across a daily puzzle?"

Rosco nodded.

"Well look at this, Mr. Private Detective." She pushed the puzzle over to Rosco. "39-Across: STEVEN HOUSE-MANN, fifteen letters. There's your murderer. Ha ha ha."

Rosco picked up the puzzle and studied it. After a moment he said, "I don't know, Belle . . ."

"Come on, Rosco, this is highly unusual."

Rosco pointed to 20-Across. "SENATOR HAL CRANE?" Then he added with a dose of sarcasm, "Gosh, maybe it was the Senator . . . No, he's in Southeast Asia, dang, can't be him. Wait, wait, look at this—55-Across: JOHN WILKES BOOTH! I'll bet that's our man."

"It may surprise you to learn there really is a John Wilkes Booth right here in Newcastle. I told you, Briephs was backing an experimental musical theatre piece about Mary

Todd Lincoln. Naturally, there's an actor playing Booth. Thompson had invited Garet, my husband—"

"Thank you, I *know* who Garet is."

Rosco's tone surprised him as much as it did Belle, and it brought on a long, uncomfortable silence. Eventually Rosco broke it by looking out the window. "Sorry," he said.

"No-no," Belle stuttered. "I realize you know who Garet is. I'm the one who should be sorry. Anyway, Thompson had invested a great deal of money in this Mary Todd Lincoln show. According to Garet, he had some grandiose ideas about taking it to New York, so it *is* possible."

"What's possible?"

"That if Briephs wasn't killed by Steven Housemann, he might have been killed by John Wilkes Booth."

"Did you get something to eat?"

"Just coffee."

"No wonder you're wired. Booth is no longer among the living, in case you hadn't heard."

Rosco waved to one of the aging waitresses, who hollered, "Be with you in a minute, angel. Hold your horses."

"Angel?" Belle repeated with a raised eyebrow.

"Martha calls *everyone* angel, even parking scofflaws. What would you like to eat?"

"Well, *angel*, it's a little late in the day, but the French toast looks awfully good."

When Martha arrived at their table Rosco ordered French toast for two along with two large glasses of grapefruit juice. After the juice and fresh coffee arrived, Rosco again picked up the completed puzzle, studying Belle's near-perfect handwriting and the fifteen letters that composed Steven Housemann's name. "I don't know," he said, "I suppose it's possible that Housemann killed Briephs, but there seem to be too many other folks who harbored a real dislike for the man—people who might even have wanted to see him out of the way. I'll need to talk to all concerned before pointing fingers. Plus, Housemann's name appearing in this puzzle is hardly enough evidence to warrant an arrest. And, as I said, John Wilkes Booth is dead."

"What about the actor playing the part?"

"Belle, let's be reasonable."

Belle chewed on her lower lip as she pulled the puzzle back to her side of the table. Again, she rested her chin in her upturned left hand while she studied the paper. "You're right, this only confuses the issue." She picked up her red pen and began doodling on the margin of the *Herald*. Rosco remained silent and when she finally brought her eyes up to meet his, she saw a warm smile on his face. "What?" she said.

"Nothing, I was just wondering what the hearts were for."

"What hearts?"

"The one's you're scribbling next to the puzzle."

Belle's face turned as red as the Bic ink. She dropped the pen on the table and sat up straight. "Nothing, I was just doodling. Don't you ever doodle?"

"Powdered sugar and maple syrup?" Martha asked as she stood before them with two orders of French toast.

"Sounds good to me." Rosco smiled, then looked to Belle.

"Please," she said as she glanced down at the eight pieces of French toast before her. "Yikes! I can't eat all this."

Martha placed the syrup and sugar on the table and moved off behind the counter. After she left, Rosco said, "I'm sorry about the puzzle, Belle. In the back of my mind I've been hoping you'd be right."

"I am right," she said after swallowing a mouthful of French toast. "These are only two puzzles. And the answers are ludicrous. Absolutely ludicrous. You don't put the name of your editor in chief in a puzzle. Or your uncle! It just isn't done!" Belle had regained her enthusiasm as quickly as she'd lost it. "I guarantee you this will make sense when I figure out the answers to the other three puzzles. So, hand them over."

"I can't."

"Why not?"

"I didn't get them."

"What! Why not?"

"According to Housemann, the other puzzles have vanished. Apparently, JaneAlice was the only person who knew where they were. Now that she's unconscious, nobody at the *Herald* can find them."

Belle dropped her fork on her plate, brought her hands to her face and slowly shook her head. Then she glanced at the *Herald* building. "So, who do you think has them?" she said.

"No telling."

"This proves I'm right, doesn't it?"

"How do you figure that?"

"Well, whoever killed Briephs recognizes that his—or

her—identity is about to be revealed. JaneAlice was attacked because someone believed she possessed the remaining puzzles. You have to see that, Rosco."

"It's possible."

"Possible? Ha! You won't admit I'm right, that's all." Again, Belle stared across the street. "Whose puzzles is Housemann publishing for the rest of the week?"

"What makes you think I'd know that?"

Belle speared a large corner of French toast and said, "I have confidence in you as an information gatherer. I've seen you in action. So, who is it?" She placed the toast in her mouth and smiled as she bit down.

"Shannon McArthur."

A lightbulb seemed to go off in Belle's head. "You don't think she killed Briephs, do you? Just to get his job? There was a big scandal a year or two ago when Thompson accused her of plagiarizing some of his old puzzles."

"JaneAlice alluded to that. Have you ever met this McArthur woman?"

Belle didn't answer. Instead, she leaned back in the banquette and silently chewed her French toast, keeping her eyes glued to the ceiling. Rosco watched her, almost hypnotized by the concentrated serenity of her thought process. When she returned her gaze to him, his expression made it clear what he'd been thinking.

"I'm married, Rosco" escaped from her mouth before she had time to reconsider. "I mean it's not that I don't—"

"I know," he protested, covering poorly. "I was just . . . I was just wondering about . . . Now I forgot what I asked you."

"Shannon McArthur. No, I've never met her. But this is what I was thinking. Look at this." Belle wrote Shannon's name on the *Herald*, next to the hearts she'd doodled earlier. "There are fifteen letters in her name. We have to find those other puzzles. That's all there is to it."

Rosco shook his head. "Two problems with that. First: If the person who beat up JaneAlice managed to obtain the puzzles, they're long-since destroyed. Second: This person is dangerous. He's killed once—possibly twice, if JaneAlice doesn't make it."

"He—or she."

"Right . . . Anyway, we have to face the fact that those remaining puzzles are gone, which means it's time for you to butt out . . . to put it bluntly. Even if your theory was right, there's no following up on it now. And I can't afford to see you hurt by this person. I'd never forgive myself. I feel bad about getting you involved as much as I have."

In the back of her mind, Belle realized Rosco was correct. Most likely, the puzzles were gone. And from what she knew about Thompson Briephs and his quirky cryptics, the killer's complete identity wouldn't be revealed until all five crosswords had been solved.

She rested her chin in her palm once more and watched Rosco stab his last piece of French toast with his fork and slide it around his plate until he had trapped the remaining drops of maple syrup.

"I'm going to miss you," she said with a gentle smile. "I was beginning to really enjoy playing assistant private eye."

"I'll tell you what, I'll keep you posted on how the case progresses."

"What will you do next?"

"Contact Shannon McArthur. You might be right, she has a lot to gain with Briephs out of the way."

"And John Wilkes Booth? Don't tell me my efforts haven't produced at least one red herring?"

Rosco laughed, raised his hand, looked toward the counter and said, "Martha, check please."

"Coming right up, angel."

CHAPTER

19

BELLE STOOD ON her small porch and watched Rosco maneuver his Jeep down narrow Captain's Walk and out of sight. After that she retrieved the envelopes and magazines from the letterbox hanging beside the front door and walked directly to her office in the rear of the house. She didn't pause for a moment or allow her glance to fall on a single "attractive" artifact or piece of "period" furniture.

Finally ensconced in the comforting world of her office, she sat at her desk, pulled a licorice stick from a glass jar and began perusing the mail that, typically, consisted of three catalogues, a magazine (a copy of *Preservation*) addressed to Garet, the phone bill, two pieces of junk mail, and a postcard from Egypt depicting an unhappy, snarling camel. Belle flipped the card over. It read: "A., Sorry I haven't written. Been busy. Lots going on. Letter to follow.

G." She tossed the card onto her desk, bit into her licorice stick, then sighed without being aware that she'd done so. "Garet," she said aloud, "Garet . . . 'Love is not love which alters when it alteration finds' . . ."

The perfectly stated Shakespearean quote suddenly seemed to represent the dry impersonality of all her relationships: mother, father, husband. Belle sat for ten full minutes slowly drumming her fingers on her desk as she pondered this unhappy revelation. For a split second, she felt almost defeated by a sense of loneliness.

Finally she stood, moved to her filing cabinet and removed a piece of graph paper containing a crossword puzzle she'd created a few weeks earlier. On the top of the page she scrawled a disinterested "Wednesday's Puzzle" with a black marking pen, initialed it BG, then crossed to her fax machine and entered a memorized number at the *Evening Crier* office. "Well, that takes care of that," she muttered. "Now, on to more exciting things."

From the lower drawer of her desk, she removed a beat-up copy of the Yellow Pages, flipped to the theatre section and punched a number into her telephone.

"Plays and Players Theatre. How many I direct your call?"

"Yes," Belle answered. "I was wondering if your Tuesday rehearsals were still open to the public?"

"Indeed, they are. From two to four. This afternoon included. No late arrivals, no early departures, please. And no talking. We have to be very strict on that count. It disturbs the actors. Are you bringing a class?"

"A class?"

"Are you a teacher?"

"No, I'm coming by myself."

"Good. The director doesn't do well with children. Remember, no later than two, or you won't be admitted. Do you have the address?"

"Thank you. Yes."

At one-fifty P.M. Belle slipped into a seat halfway down the aisle to the Plays and Players' small proscenium. The stage manager had handed her a sheet of paper listing the names of the actors and the director. It also explained the scene for that afternoon's rehearsal, "Booth's Final Hour," and reiterated the need for absolute silence from those watching the proceedings. Since *The Trials of Mary Todd*, as the play was known, was due to open the coming weekend, the set had been completed; the scene took place in a dilapidated barn in rural Virginia. The part of John Wilkes Booth was being played by an actor who'd come down from Boston to perform the part. His name was Vance Kelly.

Just before two o'clock the stage manager informed Belle—she was the only visitor—that costumes and lighting had not yet been finalized and that the house lights would not be dimmed. He suggested she use her imagination. "That's what rehearsal's all about, isn't it?"

As if on cue, Eugene Abbott, the director, entered from the rear of the theatre. Moving regally down the aisle and speaking with such extreme British elocution that Belle believed the accent assumed, he addressed the near-empty room as if he were declaiming to an SRO crowd in Covent Garden. "Let's get started, people. It's after the witching-hour. Vance, you're on, love. Pick it up from 'Damn this ankle . . . ' if you would be so kind? Vance, are you there, sweetie?"

Belle watched Vance Kelly lumber onto the stage. He was tall, well over six feet with sandy hair draped across broad shoulders, and muttonchop whiskers appropriate to the Civil War era. The attempt at authenticity was marred, however, by the fact the actor also seemed enamored of bodybuilding. Decked out in high-top basketball sneakers, baggy blue shorts and a tight T-shirt, Vance looked as though he'd just returned from the local gym. "Gene," he complained, "I'm not feeling the ankle thing today. I mean, the ankle's not working for me. Can't we play with something else?"

As instructed, Belle sat silently while the two men spent nearly thirty minutes discussing what scene they intended to rehearse. In the end, the director won, and for the next hour and a half Belle watched as they worked and re-worked a scene where Vance limped across the stage, pistol in hand, raging at invisible Pinkerton detectives, until finally, an imagined bullet struck close to his heart, whereupon he draped himself over a wooden crate, mumbled, "Cowards die many times before their deaths; the valiant never taste of death but once," and then rolled onto the floor, dead.

At four P.M. the director turned a glowing smile upon Belle and said, "Well, love, we usually have a little *Talk Back* after these open jaunts so that you dear audience folk are given a chance to *parlaay vooo* with our actors. But since you're alone and the rest of our merry troop have off until half after four, I suppose you and Vance will have to have a tête-à-tête *à deux*. Don't be too rough on the dear lad. If you'll excuse me, I have to scoot to the little boys' room."

Vance approached the rim of the stage and sat, letting his muscled legs drape the edge. "Why don't you move closer so I can see you?" he said. "I don't have my contacts in. How did you like it? Me, that is?" He spoke in a tone that implied he'd like to know Belle better.

Belle hedged. Actors, she'd heard, tended to be prickly creatures. "Were those truly the last words John Wilkes Booth spoke?"

"Nah. I think the writer made them up." Vance shrugged. "I mean, nobody was with him when he died. So he could've said almost anything. But it's pretty good stuff, don't you think? I mean, you know, for a writer . . ."

Belle opted not to mention the line had been lifted directly from Shakespeare's *Julius Caesar*. She only said, "Yes. It is good stuff." Then she moved to the front row of seats.

"I didn't know Newcastle had such good-looking women," Vance said with an exaggerated wink while Belle found a seat. "Why don't you come to Saturday night's opening. I can get you a ticket. I get two comps a show. There's a party afterward . . ."

"I'm married, actually."

"Do you tell your husband everything?"

"Aren't these *Talk Backs* intended for discussions of the play?"

"Hey, I see a dynamite chick like you and my mind wanders." Vance began to twist and flex his arms in an effort to make his muscles appear even larger.

"I guess the death of one of your backers must have been a setback for the entire company," Belle said.

"Who? Briephs? Yeah. Bummer. Heart attack, you know. You can't be too careful with your body, know what I mean? Actually, Briephs recommended me for the part."

"Really?" Belle looked past Vance, eyeing the set in an attempt to make her questions appear offhand. "So, you knew him before you came down from Boston? It's a wonderful set design, by the way."

"Yeah. He saw me in a production of *Barnum*. I played a lion tamer. It was a great costume. Real stretchy . . . spandex, you know. It showed off my build but good. I got a lot of work from that gig. Commercials mostly. But what the heck, it's money, right? Maybe you saw the one for Advil? I was manning a jackhammer? No shirt?"

"Sorry."

"Too bad. Do you work out? You're in great shape."

"Not really . . . I understand Briephs had an unusual house. Did you ever have the opportunity of going there?" Belle twisted in her seat to study a techie working on the lighting grid suspended from the high ceiling. She appeared to be giving this piece of technical work her full concentration. "How does he do that? It would scare me to death to be up there."

"It's nothing. Those guys do it all the time. That's what they're paid for. Like I get paid to perform."

"So, did you ever see Briephs' house?"

"Yeah. He had a few parties for the cast when we first

went into rehearsal . . . Also, some of the *Barnum* people . . . Weird place. What's all this about, anyway?"

"What do you mean?" Belle asked with a feigned bewilderment.

"All the questions about Briephs. You're not a cop, are you?"

"Me? No . . . What a thought."

Belle again looked around the theatre, avoiding direct eye contact with Vance. The lighting technician had left, leaving her alone with the actor. He hopped off the stage and sat next to her. "Why so nosy, then?"

"N-No reason," she stammered. "I was just making conversation. We can talk about the play if you'd like. That's what these *Talk Backs* are for, I guess. I mean . . . how does it feel to play a murderer? What sort of preparation do you need?"

Vance placed his left arm behind Belle and rested it on her seat, then moved close. The move made her extremely uncomfortable, a fact he seemed to enjoy. "Well, I like to get into these roles. Ideally, if I was to do this thing right, I'd go out and kill someone . . . So I could internalize the feeling. By the way, you never told me your name."

"It's Belle Graham." Out of habit, Belle extended her right hand, which Vance took, planting a soft kiss on her upturned palm.

"That's how we do it in the theatre. We're a very intimate group. One big happy family. So, can I call you Belle, or does it have to be Miss Graham?"

"It's Mrs., remember?"

"Oh yeah, I must have forgot that part."

At that moment, the director reappeared, calling a stagy "All right loves, time to get at it again. I'm afraid I'll have to put an end to this little *Q* and *A*. The rest of our merry troupe has arrived. Mary Todd, where are you, honey-chile?"

"Gene," Vance called back. "Belle here will be attending opening night as my guest; I'll need one of those house seats set aside."

"Yes, love." The director studied Belle. "You don't waste time, do you, love? Watch out for him, though, he's a brute. You may get more than you bargained for." He waved a hand in the air as if chasing away a bothersome housefly. "All right now, off with you. We have our work cut out. But stay away from him until after the opening. I want him rested."

Vance winked at her and said, "I'll see you Saturday."

"Right," she answered.

"Sic semper tyrranis, babe."

"Pardon me?"

"A line from the show . . . something John Wilkes shouted. It's Latin."

"I understood that part." Belle smiled as naively as she could.

" 'Thus always to tyrants,' " the director translated.

Only after Belle was behind the wheel of her car did she begin pondering Vance's closing remark, and his statements regarding his preparation for his role. The actor's facetious tone had made it impossible to know whether the lines had been delivered in jest or not. Besides, there was the matter of the pilfered Shakespeare. No one trained in the theatre, she believed, could have failed to recognize the reference. And were the big muscles and overbearing attitude an act, or was he as dangerous as the director had implied?

Rather than clearing the waters, Belle felt she'd muddied them. And with that realization, she began worrying that she'd mucked things up for Rosco. Darn, she thought. Maybe I should have let him handle this.

She pulled her car out of the parking lot and headed home, wondering whether to tell Rosco what she'd done. After four or five blocks she came to an intersection whose stoplight had failed. A police officer was directing traffic; his blue uniform shone like a large summer bloom against the dusty, dark bark of the heat-parched New England trees. As Belle waited her turn, a strange thought came to her: If Vance believed Briephs died of natural causes why would he ask if she was a cop?

CHAPTER

20

LEAVING BELLE'S HOUSE, Rosco had been beset by a spectrum of contradictory emotions. Because of his concern for her safety, he was happy she'd agreed to relinquish her puzzle theory—although, deep down inside, he'd begun to suspect there might be some truth to it. He reasoned that whoever had killed Thompson Briephs and attacked JaneAlice was no one to be trifled with, and that putting distance between Belle and the case was the wisest course. However, Rosco also found himself inventing scenarios that would force him to consult her again. These scenes invariably ended with the two of them sharing a late dinner, and his thoughts would rotate full circle.

As he drove to Lynchville to meet Shannon McArthur, Briephs' replacement at the *Herald*, Rosco warned himself not to involve Belle further. Then, as if that argument needed additional support, he muttered to himself, "Besides, she's married—she's married. Don't play with fire, Bucko." This dilemma in its various guises lasted all the way to Lynchville and the steps of Shannon McArthur's home.

The *Herald*'s new crossword editor wasn't remotely what Rosco had anticipated. He'd envisioned a bookish woman in her mid-fifties with graying hair and horn-rimmed glasses, but she was closer to his own age—besides being rather attractive in a wholesome, no-nonsense manner. She had athletic shoulders, broad for a woman and well-muscled arms that looked as if they'd handled their share of tennis rackets. A white polo shirt and twill shorts completed the picture, making her appear as if she'd just stepped off the courts. The only discordant note was an abundance of hennaed brown hair. As she led Rosco through her house and into the garden area, the afternoon sun reflected off her curls, turning them an arresting carmine red that didn't match the camp-girl outfit or demeanor.

The back door of Shannon McArthur's house opened onto a wooden deck overlooking a marshy waterway and the ocean beyond. In typical Newcastle fashion, a skiff bobbed lazily at a dock—as did a half-dozen similar vessels at neighboring residences. The impression was that every resident of the city and its surrounding suburbs depended upon boats for transportation. Rosco wondered how he'd avoided this communal maritime fascination. He felt like someone who'd arrived late at a party and missed all the fun.

"Why don't we sit out here, Mr. Polycrates? It's cooler. Would you like something to drink . . . a beer or something?"

"I'm fine, Ms. McArthur. Feel free to call me Rosco, if you'd like."

"Only if you call me Shannon."

"All right."

They sat in wrought-iron chairs alongside a matching circular table shaded by a green, white, and red canvas umbrella advertising an Italian vermouth. A pleasant breeze blew in from the salt marsh, rippling the striped fabric and turning the umbrella's wood pole until it squeaked. Even to Rosco's unschooled mind the sound was definitely nautical.

"I'm sorry if I seem shaky," Shannon said, "but I'm still terribly upset about Thompson's death. And then of course this business with JaneAlice. That is why you called, isn't it? To talk about JaneAlice?"

"Right," Rosco said, perpetuating the tale he'd recited over the phone earlier in the day. "JaneAlice's family feels that the police aren't giving the incident the attention it deserves, so they've asked me to look into it. I appreciate you allowing me this time. You must be under a great deal of pressure to come up with a puzzle for tomorrow's *Herald*."

Shannon pulled a tissue from her shorts' pocket and dabbed at the corner of her right eye, although Rosco saw no indication that any tears had formed.

"Well, I was prepared to start next Monday, so naturally I had some puzzles ready . . . The fact that JaneAlice misplaced Thompson's remaining puzzles only pushed my

schedule ahead by three days. It's not really a problem . . .
You don't think JaneAlice's beating had anything to do with
Thompson's death, do you?"

"It's unlikely they're related. The police feel it was a random mugging, and I'm inclined to agree." Rosco studied
Shannon as she digested this bit of bogus information. A
look of relief settled on her tanned face while her brilliant
red curls bobbed in the breeze. Again, Rosco was struck by
the incongruity of hairdo and attire.

"Well, that's good to hear." As an afterthought she
added, "I mean, it would be terrible to think that someone
was targeting the crossword staff at the *Herald*."

Rosco gave her a look of surprise. "What makes you say
that?"

"I don't know . . ."

"What do you imagine might be a motive? For 'targeting' Briephs and JaneAlice?"

Shannon stood and walked to the deck's rail, staring
across at a neighbor's ten-foot motorboat. "I don't know. It
was only a thought . . ." Rosco heard a tone that seemed almost wistful, but before he had time to categorize it, she
turned back with her Girl Scout smile. "Look, I'm going to
get myself a Coke. All I have is diet . . . Would you like
one?"

"Thanks."

Shannon returned a few minutes later wearing a bikini
top instead of the polo shirt. She handed a Coke to Rosco.
"I thought I'd try to get rid of my farmer's tan."

Rosco looked up; Shannon had no apparent tan line on
either her neck or arms; in fact she looked as if she made

a habit of sunbathing in the buff. "How well did you know JaneAlice?" he asked.

"I only met her a few times. She seemed pleasant enough. Actually, it was Thompson I was close to. We went way back."

"I'd heard there was some confusion about your puzzles a couple of years ago. Briephs had accused you of . . . of *borrowing* them? Is that true?"

"*Plagiarism* is the term he used; you don't have to be afraid of saying it . . . It was an unfortunate misunderstanding. As I said, Thompson and I were very close." She gave Rosco a smile indicating she and Briephs had had an intimate relationship. "We'd worked on those puzzles together . . . When we broke up—well, they became like displaced children in a nasty divorce. We both believed we owned them. I foolishly published them under my name, and Thompson had a fit."

"Some divorces are like that. People find it impossible to forgive a partner's indiscretions."

Shannon responded too quickly. "Oh, not Thompson and I. We got over it in no time. Kiss and make up. That was us. That's why I'm so upset." She pulled another tissue from her pocket.

"The *Herald*'s personnel office said you were hired by Steven Housemann directly. Is that the way it usually works?"

Shannon's eyes squinted into slits. "What's that supposed to mean? I barely know Steve—Mr. Housemann. Besides, what does that have to do with JaneAlice?"

"Nothing. It's just that I'm a crossword puzzle freak,"

Rosco lied. "I was curious about how things work behind the scenes."

She reapplied the tissue to her eyes. "I'm sorry, I didn't mean to snap. I'm just so distraught over Tommy."

"I don't think I've heard anyone call him that . . ." Rosco began.

"I told you, we were close."

"Of course . . . Let's get back to JaneAlice and something you mentioned earlier. If you feel someone may be intent on eliminating the *Herald*'s crossword puzzle staff, aren't you afraid you'll be in danger when you take the job?"

"I thought the police believed it was a random mugging."

Rosco stood and leaned over the deck's railing, gazing at the meandering stream and the marsh grasses and cattails waving above the water. A red-winged blackbird flitted showily among them. "What do you think happened to Briephs' three missing puzzles?"

"How would I know?"

"Do you think a mugger would've taken them? They weren't in JaneAlice's apartment or the *Herald* office."

"I'm afraid I'm not much good at comprehending the criminal mind," Shannon said pointedly. "I also fail to see what role those puzzles play. They're totally useless now."

Rosco straightened and crossed to the other side of the deck. "This is a nice spot. You can't beat a water view. Pricey real estate, but I've always hankered after a place like this."

"I'm fond of it."

THE CROSSWORD MURDER

"What about this crossword woman at the *Evening Crier*?" he asked offhandedly. "What's her name, again?"

"Annabella Graham. What about her?"

"Have you ever met her?"

"No. But to be perfectly honest, I don't think much of her puzzles."

Rosco chuckled. "Do I detect a little professional rivalry?"

Shannon began to laugh. "I suppose so. Okay, I've been entertained by the *Crier's* puzzles . . . every now and then."

"Do you think Ms. Graham was under consideration as Briephs' replacement?"

"Not in a million years."

"You sound awfully positive."

"Look," Shannon said. "What does this have to do with JaneAlice?"

"Well, on the off-chance the attack wasn't random, I have to look at everyone's motives. Someone might have simply disliked her—or someone could have known the missing puzzles would put Housemann in a real bind for tomorrow's *Herald* . . . He's supposed to be a control freak, isn't he? . . . Can't allow his paper to go to bed with anything amiss. A big empty square instead of a crossword puzzle would strike me as something that would make your new boss's blood boil."

Shannon gave another laugh. "You're making me wish I hadn't accepted the position."

Rosco glanced at his watch. "I should be heading back to town. I appreciate your giving me the time . . . and the Coke. Good luck with the new job—and the ogre."

They walked to the front door together, where Shannon gave him another white-toothed smile. "Good luck to you, too . . . I hope JaneAlice pulls through."

Rosco shook her hand and ambled across the street to his Jeep. Shannon waved, then remained in that jovial attitude until he'd disappeared around the corner. After that, she walked into the living room, picked up a black cordless telephone and returned to the deck, where she punched in a number and waited for a man's voice to answer.

"Steven, darling, thank heavens you're still there."

"How did it go, pumpkin pie?"

CHAPTER

21

ON HIS RETURN ride from Lynchville, Rosco mulled over his conversation with Shannon McArthur. JaneAlice had described her as a plagiarizing snake in the grass, and although the woman seemed a trifle touchy regarding Steven Housemann, and somewhat phony with her fake tears, she didn't appear to be the vile creature JaneAlice had described. However, Rosco knew better than to accept a first meeting at face value. People were capable of manipulating the truth, and it often took some detective work to discover their motives. As he stepped into his office, he made a mental note to look a bit deeper into Shannon's relationship with Steven House-mann. There was more there than met the eye.

Rosco strolled across the room, tossed his car keys onto the desk and glanced at his answering machine. The LED readout flashed on and off signaling one message. He reached down, tapped the Play button, then sat, leaning back in his padded "thinking" chair while he put his feet on the desk. As the message played, he returned to an upright position and grinned at the machine. He tapped the Play button once more.

"Rosco, this is Belle. Sorry to bother you. I know you must be busy, but I just discovered some information I think you should have . . . And since I owe you a dinner, I thought we could talk then . . . I spotted this recipe for meat loaf on the top of an oatmeal box and decided to give it a whirl. I can't guarantee anything. It's just an experiment . . . I won't go shopping for vegetables and so forth until I hear from you. Give me a call when you get in."

Rosco immediately picked up the telephone and entered Belle's number. As it rang, he thought: This isn't a good sign; I have the number memorized. She answered on the third ring and asked him to arrive at seven. He offered to bring wine and a dessert, but she seemed quite pleased to have accomplished everything herself, so he said, "Okay, I'll see you later," and hung up.

By six forty-five Belle was fairly well organized, although the meat loaf seemed to require a good deal more chopping, mixing and shaping than the "simple" recipe had at first indicated. At seven on the dot she heard Rosco's knock on her front door. She ran her fingers under the tap, tugged off her apron and used it to dry her hands.

"Right on time," she said with a smile as she opened the door.

"Well, I got myself into a little trouble by being early last time. I try not to make the same mistake twice." Rosco smiled. "Here." He extended the brown paper bag he held in his left hand. "I picked up some stuffed grape leaves on the way. I thought we could have them as a starter course."

Belle peered into the bag. "Oh, I love these things. They're almost as good as deviled eggs."

They walked into the kitchen, where Belle placed the *dolmades* on the butcher-block work island. She retrieved a bottle of white wine from the refrigerator, handed it to Rosco and said, "Is this all right? I'm not much of a wine expert. I tend to go by label and price, and not necessarily in that order."

"A woman after my own heart, although I usually don't waste time with the label. This looks fine to me."

Belle arranged the grape leaves on a fish-shaped platter as Rosco opened the wine and poured two glasses.

"So, what's this mysterious information you referred to in your message?"

"I wouldn't call it mysterious . . . But let me finish my culinary efforts first . . . I'd hate to make a mistake this far into the process."

They crossed to the stove and studied the slab of un-cooked meat loaf. "So, this is it?" Rosco asked. "And those little white things are grains of oatmeal, I gather?"

"That's the idea . . . Basically, the recipe suggests using rolled oats instead of bread crumbs. What do you think?"

"What else is in there? What's all this?" He pointed to some red flecks.

"The recipe called for ground pork, veal and beef—and then chopped red and green peppers, some onion, and spices like sage and dried basil. Salt and pepper, too. The other red ingredient is hot red pepper flakes. I added that on my own. I thought the mixture might need spicing up."

"How much did you put in?"

"Two teaspoons. Actually, almost three . . . You don't think I overdid it, do you?"

"No. No." Rosco coughed. "I'm sure it'll be fine." He brought his wine to his lips to keep from betraying his true assessment.

Belle crossed the kitchen to retrieve the oatmeal box. "The recipe suggests cooking the loaf for an hour and a half at three-fifty . . . Do you want to stick it in the oven for me?"

"Sure."

"Do you know how to turn it on?"

"Actually my kitchen experiences have taken me as far as heating ovens—"

"Wait a minute! Don't put it in yet!" She carried the box to Rosco and pointed to the wording as if displaying a piece of crime evidence. "I didn't notice this earlier. It says we should preheat the oven . . ."

"Check."

"I'm glad you brought the grape leaves. We might have starved while waiting for my experiment to cook." Belle smiled at Rosco and their eyes locked for three or four uncomfortable seconds. Finally, she turned away. "Do you think this is right?" she asked. "Me cooking you dinner?"

"Hey, I'm just a guinea pig, right? I could sign a release form if you want. That way, if I die an agonizing death, you won't be held legally responsible."

Belle let out a quiet sigh and leaned against the kitchen sink. "You know what I mean, Rosco."

"Yeah, I'm afraid I do." He stared into his glass and rolled the wine from side to side. "Okay . . . I'm attracted to you, what can I say? There it is—out in the open. But I'm an adult. I know you're married . . . I can handle myself like a gentleman. We'll have dinner together, and it won't go any further. We can be friends. Why not? It works for a lot of people."

"Thanks, Rosco." Belle didn't offer her assessment on what was happening between them. She'd felt her own attraction, and had pushed it aside more than once. It was dangerous ground, and she was happy he'd managed to sidestep it so gracefully.

"Now, for my news . . ." she said. "I went to the theatre today."

Rosco was relieved to move to safer ground. "What did you see?" he asked before biting down on a stuffed grape leaf.

"I didn't see anything . . . It was a rehearsal at Plays and Players. I figured it would be a good way to meet Vance Kelly without arousing unnecessary suspicion."

"And who might Vance Kelly be?"

"Vance Kelly is playing John Wilkes Booth. He's an actor—the actor in Briephs' puzzle."

Rosco set his wine down on the butcher-block table. "Correct me if I'm wrong; as per our meeting this morning, weren't you supposed to butt out of this investigation?" His tone had turned overly serious.

"Oh, come on, Rosco. It was completely natural for me

to go there. You would have looked out of place—except, perhaps, for your lack of *haberdashery* . . . Anyway, I was able to talk to the actor, the stage manager and the director . . . Just your average Newcastle theatregoer."

"The point is—as I believe I mentioned earlier—whoever killed Briephs is dangerous. How many times do I have to repeat that?"

"Do you want to hear what I learned or not?"

Belle's enthusiasm was too much for him. "Okay, but first we have to make a deal."

"What?"

"Since you seem incapable of staying out of this case—or following simple orders—I want you to promise you will not look into anything else on your own. If you have any further brainy ideas, you have to clear them with me first. A deal?"

Belle let her eyes drift toward the ceiling. "Okay . . . it's a deal."

"Right. I don't believe you for a second, you know." He refilled their wineglasses, returned the bottle to the refrigerator, looked at her long and hard and said, "Well . . . ?"

"Well, what?"

"What did you find out about our friend, John Wilkes Booth?"

Belle knew Rosco's curiosity had been primed, so she opted to make him suffer. She walked to the work island and sat on a stool near the *dolmades*, then picked up one and bit into it. "These are wonderful. I could eat the entire plateful. Where do you get them?"

"A place near my office . . . Well?"

"Oh, hold on—the meat loaf . . . I should put it in the oven or we'll never have dinner." She placed her creation on the oven's center rack while Rosco drummed his fingers on the butcher-block table. "Do you think I should set a timer?" she asked.

"Couldn't hurt."

"How long did the box say?"

"An hour and a half."

Belle depressed the button on the electric timer until it read ninety minutes. "Well, that takes care of that. Now, what were we talking about?"

"I believe it was John Wilkes Booth."

"Oh, right." Belle's enthusiasm wouldn't allow her to stall further. "First off, he's large—and strong, certainly strong enough to handle Briephs. Second, he's been to Briephs' house—more than once—so he knows his way around. Third, he point-blank admitted he thought it would be good preparation for his role to kill someone. And four—this is the best—he asked if I was a cop."

"The best?"

"Of course, don't you see? If he believed Briephs had died of natural causes—and if he hadn't heard anything about JaneAlice, why would the police be on his mind?"

Rosco appeared truly amazed at what she'd discovered. "How did you get all this?"

"People like to talk to me, I suppose. Vance also invited me to the show's opening night on Saturday."

"Vance?" Rosco was unable to disguise the jealousy in his tone.

"I assume he's younger than I am, Rosco. You'd hardly expect me to call him Mr. Kelly, would you?"

"I guess not," Rosco mumbled, then picked up his wineglass and began pacing the kitchen. "But where's the motive? And don't forget Housemann's name also appeared in that puzzle." He turned to face her. "Besides, if your crossword theory is correct, we only have two-fifths of the picture—"

"Wait! I forgot another important part of our conversation: *Sic semper tyrannis*." Belle said this with a definitely gloating tone.

"And that would mean?"

"Literally, 'Thus to tyrants' . . . But I looked it up; it's also the motto of the state of Virginia. In that context, the inference is 'Death to tyrants.'"

"I see." Rosco looked bemused. "And because this 'Vance' spouts Latin, he's now a prime suspect?"

"That was Booth's statement when he assassinated Lincoln."

"I take it then, that your hunky young star was reciting a line from the play. Maybe to impress a bright and attractive woman . . . ?"

Belle looked crestfallen.

"It's okay," Rosco said. "I'll store the information away for later consideration. At the risk of sounding domineering, though, I'd prefer that you not tangle with questionable types. This is a murder case."

"What about Shannon McArthur?" was Belle's quick response. "How did that interview go?"

"Well, she knows more than she's letting on. I'm sure of

it. And it wouldn't surprise me if she and Housemann were linked romantically."

Belle grabbed another grape leaf and gobbled it down. "This is great . . . Housemann and Shannon McArthur . . . and Betsey and Briephs."

Rosco shook his head. "One big happy family."

"That's what Vance said!" She pointed at Rosco, waved her finger and laughed. "He was talking about the theatre, but still . . ."

Rosco pondered this for several moments. Eventually, he said, "I'll go talk to Betsey Housemann tomorrow. See where that leads us."

"Good idea."

"Anyway, there's no point in letting all this spoil your dinner. What else is on the menu besides meat loaf?"

"Salad and parslied potatoes. Is that okay? But it's a bottled dressing. Sorry."

"Sounds great."

"Feel like washing some lettuce? It's in the fridge."

"Sure." He moved toward the refrigerator. Lying on the nearby counter was Garet's postcard from Egypt. Rosco picked it up and laughed. "Why do these camels always look like they want to tear your head off?"

Belle spun around. She could feel tension rising in her voice, but was unable to soften it. "Don't you know it's impolite to read other people's mail?"

"I didn't flip it over. I was just looking at the camel."

"Give me that." Belle yanked the postcard from his hand opening an inch-long paper cut at the base of his thumb.

"Ouch," Rosco muttered as he brought the palm of his hand up to meet his mouth.

Belle ripped the postcard into several pieces and dumped them into the trash basket beneath the sink. She stood quietly for a moment, then said, "Here, let me look at your finger." She took Rosco's hand, but the move only served to rekindle the attraction they'd experienced earlier.

Rosco eased his hand away. "It's all right."

"No. Run it under warm water. I'll get a bandage and some Mercurochrome."

Rosco did as he was told while Belle returned with a first-aid kit. She dabbed disinfectant on the cut, then covered it with a bandage.

"Don't think you've fooled me for a minute," she said when her equanimity had returned. "I recognize this for what it is: a cheap trick to get out of washing the lettuce."

CHAPTER

22

ROSCO'S ALARM SOUNDED at seven A.M. with its habitual twenty seconds of blaring electronic buzz before dutifully switching over to *Imus in the Morning*. He flipped off the chatter, brushed his teeth, threw on his running shorts, T-shirt and sneakers and headed out for a three-mile run along Newcastle's waterfront. The half-hour jog gave him the opportunity to relive his previous night's dinner with Belle. They'd had a good time discussing books and movies and where they'd most like to travel—if they had the money. Throughout, their mutual attraction had remained on the back burner, the only spicy element of the evening being Belle's fiery-hot meat loaf. After helping her clean up, Rosco had returned home at eleven-thirty and gone directly to bed. On the one hand, he was pleased their relationship was stabilizing into friendship; on the other, he felt disappointed they hadn't met ten years earlier.

Following his jog, he showered and headed to the Parthenon, his neighborhood coffee shop, for breakfast. From there he went to his office and arranged an afternoon meeting with Betsey Housemann at her home. She seemed anxious to talk to him, which he found strange but refreshing; it was pleasant to imagine he'd be meeting with someone at least superficially cooperative. Rosco had next planned to call Belle and thank her for dinner, but before he could lift the receiver, the phone rang. He answered with his standard greeting: "Polycrates Agency."

"I'm trying to reach Mr. Polycrates." The voice was that of an older man, decidedly nervous, and colored with a marked British accent.

"This is Rosco Polycrates, how can I help you?"

"Thank goodness you're in. My name is Bartholomew Kerr. I write a column for the *Herald.*"

Rosco remembered JaneAlice's mentioning Kerr's name. However, Steven Housemann had interrupted before she could explain his relationship with Thompson Briephs. "Yes, Mr. Kerr, I recognize your name. I've read your column."

Kerr's voice continued to crackle uneasily. "I need to see you. It's urgent."

"Of course. May I ask how you got my name?"

"Not over the phone. How soon can we meet?"

"Well, if you're at the *Herald*"—Rosco glanced at his watch—"I can be there in ten minutes."

"No. Not here. May I come to your office?"

"If you'd like."

Rosco gave Bartholomew Kerr the necessary directions.

He promised he'd be there within the half hour and hung up.

Rosco considered making a few calls to gather background information on the journalist, but opted to sit tight for the moment. The man was obviously shaken; keeping their meeting confidential seemed a top priority. Rosco would respect his wishes until he discovered what he wanted.

Twenty minutes later, Kerr arrived. He was a tiny man, small-boned and frail and almost totally bald. What little hair he had was an ashy, ancient blond. Owlish gray eyebrows poked out from behind oversized, black-rimmed glasses. The lenses magnified his eyes to an absurd degree, making them appear like those of an insect photographed for *National Geographic*. Besides the too-large glasses, Kerr sported a gold Rolex watch that looked too big for his bony wrist and a diamond pinky ring that, again, seemed to weigh down his miniature frame. Rosco invited him in and pointed to a chair.

"Th-Thank you," he stuttered. Sitting, his movements were precise as if no physical activity were accomplished without prior preparation.

"What's all this about, Mr. Kerr?"

The columnist reached into a slim leather attaché case and removed a folded piece of graph paper. He handed it to Rosco. "This was in my mail slot when I arrived for work this morning."

Rosco unfolded the paper. On it was a hand-drawn crossword puzzle, fifteen letters square, with the clues scrawled along the side in what Rosco surmised was most likely Thompson Briephs' handwriting.

"Did this come by way of the Post Office or did someone drop it in your box personally?" Rosco asked.

"The postal service."

"May I see the envelope?"

"I'm sorry, but I put it through the paper shredder. I know it was stupid. But you must understand, I became quite agitated when I realized what the missive contained. I can tell you the envelope wasn't written in Thompson's hand, though. The style was quite different—shaky, almost, as if the work had been done by a child."

"Why did you bring this to me?" Rosco looked up from the puzzle for the first time.

"Mr. Polycrates, a newspaper is a tight-knit operation. When a man such as yourself begins asking questions, it's only a matter of time before reporters begin making their own inquiries. And when notes are compared . . . Well, let's just say, we have fewer secrets at the *Herald* than you might surmise."

"I see. But why not go to the police with this?" Rosco imagined Al Lever chuckling at the puzzle and tossing it into a file somewhere, but there was no reason to share those suspicions with Kerr.

"Number 34-Across."

Rosco glanced at Briephs' clues and read 34-Across. *"Herald snoopster?"*

"I'm not terribly fond of these cryptics, Mr. Polycrates, but I recognize Thompson's peculiar sense of humor. *Herald snoopster*, containing fifteen letters, can only be one person: myself. It was one of Briephs' favorite gibes."

Rosco decided to play dumb. "And what do think that means? Your name in this puzzle."

"Please don't take me for a fool." Kerr pulled a handkerchief from his jacket pocket and wiped away the moisture that had formed on his upper lip. "We're all aware that these puzzles were stolen from JaneAlice, and we're equally convinced that the police force doesn't possess either the imagination or perspicacity to recognize the connection between the theft and Thompson's death. I bring this puzzle to you in the hopes that it will clear my name of wrongdoing. Since it was mailed to me, I obviously couldn't have stolen it. Also my name appears in the word game. These facts should convince you that I had *no connection* whatsoever with Thompson's demise or JaneAlice's tragic attack."

"Didn't you consider that this document could be dusted for prints?"

"Too late, unfortunately. I'm afraid that in my dismay I've considerably mangled the paper. I fear the only fingerprints that would remain legible would be my own."

Rosco studied the creased and rumpled puzzle. He had to admit Kerr was correct. "May I keep this?" he asked.

"Absolutely. If you make inquiries, I'm sure you'll discover that Thompson and I had . . . shall we say, a *strained* relationship? I was not one of his admirers. However, as I stated, I hope in surrendering this piece of evidence to you, I remove my name from suspicion."

"Suspicion's an interesting thing, Mr. Kerr." Rosco watched the bug eyes roam his face as he spoke. They were intent, less fearful than alert; the impression was that of a predator stalking his prey. "And of course the nature of my business makes me more suspicious than most people." Rosco held the puzzle in the air. "Thank you for bringing this to me; if you should receive another, I'd like to see it. But as for suspicion, I'm afraid I suspect everyone until the truth surfaces."

Kerr stood and offered his hand to Rosco. "Fair enough, Mr. Polycrates. However, with regard to my receiving any more of these cryptics, I am leaving for San Francisco at eleven A.M. today. I will be staying with my nephew until this situation has been resolved. I do not intend to suffer the same fate as JaneAlice Miller."

"I'm not so sure leaving town is the answer. The police may have some questions for you once they learn you've received this puzzle."

"My response to that is, let them find me."

Kerr turned and slipped through the door.

Rosco smiled. Kerr wouldn't be a tough man to locate— even if he was three thousand miles away. He picked up the phone and entered Belle's number before the *Herald snoopster* was halfway out of the building.

"Guess what I've got?" he said when she finally answered.

"I hope it's not food poisoning."

He laughed. "No. I'm sorry, the first thing I meant to do was thank you for dinner. It was excellent. I mean for the first time out of the gate and all, it was really good. Great, I mean. I think it was the oatmeal that did it."

"Don't lay it on too thick."

"Listen to this." Rosco was incapable of hiding the ex-

THE CROSSWORD MURDER

citement in his voice. "I have one of Briephs' other puzzles. It wasn't destroyed."

Belle jumped up from her desk; Rosco could hear her chair scrape the floor and something that sounded like an empty cup overturn. "What! You're kidding! Where did you get it?"

"I'll explain later. But I need you to figure out the answers. There's no way I can do this thing by myself. Can I come over?"

"Yes. Yes. I'm here. I'm at home. Well, of course I'm home. You called me. You'd have to know where I am."

Rosco was there in fifteen minutes. Belle was waiting on the front porch when he arrived.

"Let me see it," she called, then grabbed the puzzle and raced to her office without waiting for his reply. By the time he caught up, she had six answers filled in.

Across

1. Scheme
5. Tries
10. Famous murderer
13. Lovers ___
14. Oklahoma city
15. Eight, prefix
16. Competition?
19. Presidential nickname
20. Wide shoes
21. Bond school
22. Evils
24. Beliefs
25. Chest
26. Trails
28. Famous murder victim
30. Way to one's heart?
31. Dine
34. *Herald* snoopster
38. Work unit
39. Dangers
40. French river
41. Some Native Americans
42. TWA offer
43. It'll knock you out
45. Capital no-nos
49. No longer Siamese
50. It's golden
51. French coin
52. Competition?
56. Call up
57. Hirschfeld lines?
58. Clamp
59. Rocks
60. Inhibits
61. Part of USA

Down

1. "Dead Men Don't Wear ___"
2. With 52-Down, Indian isle
3. Publishing biggie
4. Arts org.
5. It could be bum
6. Bullrushes
7. "___ Well That Ends Well"
8. Scout org.
9. Actor's org.
10. Reason to be blessed
11. Not Ollie's
12. ___ Dawber
15. Witnesses take them
17. "___ there, done that!"
18. Second meltdown?
23. It's golden
24. Major ending
26. Tidal ___
27. "___ and the Man," Shaw play
28. Famous murder victim
29. Stop
30. It's a sin to tell ___
31. It ___ right!
32. Grecian ___
33. Before, prefix
35. "For ___ may be seen . . . murder," Malory
36. Done
37. Put out
41. Chinese general, b. 1873
42. Fox or Rabbit
43. Principle
44. Macbeth, e.g.
45. Colorful bird
46. Bos. campus
47. Wake up
48. More positive
50. K-P filler

PUZZLE #3

52. See 2-Down
53. Switch settings
54. Nada
55. Power proj.

CHAPTER

23

ROSCO PEERED OVER Belle's shoulder as she rapidly inked in the final answer to Briephs' handwritten puzzle: 48-Down: SURER.

"Well, you were right," he said, looking at 52-Across and barely able to contain his laughter, "SHANNON MCARTHUR has fifteen letters in her name . . . of course, so does BARTHOLEMEW KERR, which even I knew, thanks to the man himself . . . Not to mention some other people we all recognize, like 16-Across there." He pointed at ANNABELLA GRAHAM.

Belle glanced up at Rosco. "Well, of course. I always knew my own name stretched perfectly across a puzzle. Obviously, with this we have to throw out my fifteen-letter theory."

"Whoa, whoa. I don't know, not so fast there . . . Maybe I should drag you down to Lieutenant Lever's office for questioning. Where were you on the evening of Briephs' death?"

"Don't get too high-handed—your name also has fifteen letters, in case you've been too dense to notice."

Rosco began counting the letters of his name on his fingers. Belle did her best to ignore him.

"So," she continued, "there must be something else in these puzzles. Briephs' cryptics were never that simple. He isn't giving up the identity of his killer as easily as I'd originally hoped. But it's here, I'm certain of it. Look at 35-Down: HEREIN *may be seen . . . murder*, and 1-Down: 'Dead Men Don't Wear PLAID.' 1-Across: *Scheme* becomes PLAN . . . And 45-Across: MURDERS? All these hints at plots and killings . . . such as 28-Across: ABEL, 28-Down: ABE—another excellent reference to John Wilkes Booth, by the way . . . And 5-Across: STABS . . . 10-Across: ASP."

Rosco sat in the black-and-white deck chair across the desk from Belle and stared into space.

"What?" she asked.

"I'm thinking."

"Obviously you're thinking. But what about?"

"The implausibility of all this. Maybe these names are only intended to arouse suspicion. A list of people who'd be happy to see Briephs out of the way. It's possible he had no idea who wanted to kill him, and he was hoping that whoever it was would become rattled by seeing his, or her, name in print and give themselves away . . . After all, Kerr's skipped town."

A beaming smile spread across Belle's face. She folded

the puzzle into a paper glider and sailed it toward Rosco. It bounced off his chest and landed in his lap. "Don't tell me you think I might be correct after all?"

He unfolded the puzzle, forced himself to take a serious tone and avoided making eye contact with her. "It's possible."

"Thank you, Mr. Generosity."

"The thing is, there's just not enough information. If these puzzles do amount to anything, we definitely need the two we're missing." Rosco studied the creased piece of graph paper. By rights, he knew he should be working on the case in his office, but he was having trouble leaving Belle. "Do you mind if I think out loud?"

"As long as you keep it clean."

Again, Rosco avoided her eyes. "Strictly business," he said while he perused the puzzle. "Okay, the crosswords are one thing; if there *are* clues, they create more questions than answers. One: Who stole them from JaneAlice? Two: Why mail one to Kerr? And why did Kerr shred the envelope? Because now there's no real proof it was sent through the post office in the first place. We only have Kerr's say-so. And why did he fly the coop? Three: Where are the remaining two puzzles? Have they been destroyed? Will they be mailed to Bartholomew? To someone else? And it all comes back to: Why didn't the killer destroy the puzzles in the first place?"

Belle placed her elbows on the desk and leaned forward, resting her face in the palms of her hands. "Do you think you should have taken this to Lever first? To look for fingerprints or whatever the police do?" There was real concern in her voice, as if in her enthusiasm she'd overlooked what she believed was the first rule in any criminal investigation. "Haven't we been tampering with evidence or something?"

"Kerr had already thoroughly compromised the evidence. You saw how mangled the paper was when you took it from me. Besides, I have a fairly good idea what Al would have said if I dragged in a limp piece of graph paper and presented it to him as evidence—and it wouldn't have included words I'd use in mixed company."

Belle stared at the puzzle. Rosco was right; it resembled a discarded paper towel. And though she didn't know Lever, she could guess his response. "I still don't understand why Kerr received this. Why would anyone go to the trouble of stealing the puzzles from JaneAlice—and then turn around and make them public?"

"Maybe Kerr's our man. He seemed awfully anxious to get out of town."

"I've met him, Rosco. And you've met him. Do you think he's capable of killing anything more menacing than a housefly?"

"Over the years I've come to realize murderers come in all shapes and sizes. No . . . the answers lie with JaneAlice." Rosco pulled a small notepad from his pocket and flipped through it. "Do you mind if I use your phone? I'd like to call St. Joseph's Hospital."

Belle turned the phone around to face him. "Be my guest."

Rosco punched in St. Joseph's number and eventually got through to the nurses' station on the floor where

JaneAlice was under observation. He was told that her X rays showed no evidence of permanent damage and a full recovery was possible—although the prognosis remained guarded. As the patient had yet to regain consciousness, there was still cause for concern. Accordingly, she was currently listed in critical condition. After hanging up, Rosco explained the situation to Belle.

"Not much help there," she said. "Now what?"

"Back to the basics. At this point, the puzzles are a dead end. Logic would indicate the murderer recognized something in the first puzzle to warrant an attack on JaneAlice. But then logic flies out the window when you consider he gets the remaining puzzles, and turns around and mails one to Kerr."

"He . . . Or she."

"Right, he or she. I'll have to pick up my investigation where I left off—with Betsey Housemann." Rosco gave Belle a serious look. "I want you to promise you won't go snooping around on your own. At the risk of sounding redundant, we're dealing with a murderer. So please don't do anything without clearing it with me first."

"I appreciate your concern, Rosco, but I'm not a child. I'm not stupid either. I know how to handle myself, and I'm not prone to reckless deeds. Besides, I'm also adept at keeping out of the way."

"I'd hardly call you 'in the way.' "

"Thanks." Belle glanced through the window at her small city garden, and as Rosco's warning started to filter through her brain, she began worrying about his safety as well. She shook her head slightly, smiled at him and said,

"Now I have some advice for you: Be careful with Betsey Housemann. She may not be a man-killer, but she's definitely a man-*eater*."

"Sounds like my kind of gal."

They walked out to his Jeep together and Belle watched as he drove off. His warning seemed incongruous on a day this hot and sunny and obviously summery, a time for beach picnics and lazing in the ocean's languid waves, not lying in a hospital bed hooked up to a monitoring machine. Belle perched on her porch's wicker settee pondering JaneAlice's and Thompson Briephs' dual fates. The crimes created a paradox that didn't jibe with the Newcastle that Belle knew; in fact, she realized that if she hadn't met Rosco she would have had difficulty believing that Briephs' death and JaneAlice's comatose state were interconnected—or that the attacks had even been committed with lethal intent.

"I wonder," she murmured aloud. "I wonder . . ." But the sudden yip of a dog in a neighboring street scrambled further speculation. Belle stirred out of her funk. Captain's Walk looked as serene as ever, the adjacent gardens with their hollyhocks and hostas and cosmos as quaint as they'd always been. Violent death didn't intrude in a place as picturesque as this. Belle stood, lazily locked her front door, stepped off the porch and strolled the brick walk down to the small family-run grocery store a block and a half from her house.

There she exchanged the usual banter with the shop's owners, received their customary jests about her culinary prowess while she paid for a dozen eggs, a small jar of mayonnaise and another jar of capers. Then she ambled slowly home wondering if paprika actually had a discernible flavor. That conundrum led to cogitations on saffron, how rare and precious it once had been, and how, despite the prohibitive cost, the streets of Rome had been sprinkled with saffron when the emperor Nero entered the city. The entire trip—including Belle's roving theories—took less than twenty minutes.

On the porch, she set her bag of groceries on a small wicker table and unlocked the dead bolt on the door, then retrieved the bag and reached for the doorknob. It refused to turn. Belle tried it a second time, but the lock on the knob had been latched as well—something she never did.

Her first thought was that Garet had come home. He was notorious for locking every door and window in the house, even if he was only strolling to the corner for a newspaper. However, Garet wasn't fond of surprises. Surprises bordered on the romantic; Garet did not. For all his intellectual acumen, he'd never been comfortable with creativity. Their house was the quintessential example of that thought process.

Belle shook her head, decided she'd double-locked the door without thinking, and fumbled with her keys until she found the one belonging to the doorknob. She slipped it in, but stopped short of turning it.

She stepped away from the door, and returned the groceries to the table. Her heart was beating rapidly; her lips felt dry; she swallowed and tried to think. A voice in her head said, Keep calm. Don't let yourself get ruffled. There's a simple explanation for everything.

She backed off the porch and headed for the pay phone near the market. Halfway there, she stopped. Rosco was at Betsey Housemann's home; calling his office or car phone would be useless, and dialing 911 seemed not only a tad hysterical but also premature. Perhaps she really had double-locked the door inadvertently. Or perhaps the mechanism had broken. The heat could have caused it to swell or slip—or something.

Belle retraced her steps. When she drew near her home, she regarded it with a critical eye—what she imagined might be a detective's discerning gaze. Nothing appeared out of place. The lace curtains in the front windows remained crisp and undefiled; no sound emanated from the interior; the building looked as tidy and trim and unviolated as always. I'm letting my imagination run away with me, Belle thought. I obviously double-locked the door myself.

She returned to the porch, picked up the groceries, then tried the key again. The door was now completely unlocked. Belle paused; chagrin, apprehension and puzzlement raced through her chest and brain. "Garet?" she called. "Is this some sort of surprise?"

She eased her way through the doorway and stopped. "Garet?" she called again. Behind her, sunlight splayed across her back; ahead of her, the house looked shadowy and almost preternaturally empty. "Garet, if this is your idea of a joke, it isn't funny . . . I don't care what they do on the banks of the Nile . . ." Belle clutched the bag of groceries, listening. A knot had begun to form in her stomach and her hands felt weak and trembly. Half of her wanted to march straight out of the house; the other half argued that a mature, capable woman didn't allow fear to sully her judgment.

"If anyone is here," she said in a loud voice, "I want you to know that I've already phoned the police." The lie was so forceful and seamless it almost felt like truth. "They'll be arriving momentarily."

Belle strode forward into the foyer, then stopped again, thinking, I *should* call the police. If no one's here and I made a mistake, they'll think I'm an idiot—but so what? She took one step backward, then a second while her eyes stared straight ahead. But before she could turn toward the door, it slammed shut with such colossal force and a noise so monstrous that she let out a terrified scream. The paper bag flew from her hands and landed on the hardwood floor in a litter of broken glass and smashed eggshells.

CHAPTER

24

THE MAN-EATER Belle had described greeted Rosco at the door to the Housemann residence at precisely two-thirty that afternoon. She wore four-inch spike heels, stretch tights in an aggressive orange-and-black tiger print, and a sapphire-blue leather halter top that left her entire midsection exposed. Her flame-red hair had been pulled to the back of her head where it fell to her waist in an abundant and voluptuous ponytail; and her makeup had been liberally applied—an obvious attempt to keep her age a well-guarded secret. Rosco pegged her at forty-two, maybe even forty-five. He wondered how much longer she'd be able to keep her husband in tow.

Betsey led the way to a small den, and although alone in the house, she closed the door the moment they entered. The sole piece of furniture was an eight-foot-long black leather couch draped with a zebra skin. A larger, matching skin lay upon the floor. On the opposite wall was a 50-inch television, VCR, and the latest in stereo equipment. The remaining decor consisted of floor-to-ceiling shelves displaying books, small East Indian statuary depicting couples in provocative poses, and video tapes, a good many of which appeared to be X-rated.

"Please have a seat, Rosco. You don't mind if I call you Rosco, do you? I loathe formality. It's so pretentious."

Rosco scanned the room searching for an available chair, found none, and sat at the far end of the leather couch. Betsey also sat. About four feet of African animal hide separated them.

"Rosco's fine, Mrs. Housemann," he said.

She laughed. "Call me Betsey. My husband warned me you might want to speak to me," she said with a throaty gurgle. "He 'strongly' advised me against an interview, which of course made the prospect of meeting you all the more stimulating. I assumed it was only his jealous nature speaking. Now that I see how sexy you are, I understand why he wanted to . . . well, let's say, keep us from getting close. By the way, he doesn't know you're here. I hope I'm not being naughty in hiding the truth?"

"I don't enjoy being on the wrong side of a jealous man. Your husband's not the violent type, is he?"

"All bark and no bite. Besides, you look like you can handle yourself." Betsey seemed to be moving closer.

"Did your husband tell you I was investigating the possibility that Thompson Briephs might be murdered?"

Rosco watched Betsey straighten up. She seemed truly surprised by the information.

"Well, n-no," she stammered. "Steven merely said you were snooping around the *Herald*. He never explained the reason . . . Tommy murdered? You're certain?"

"I think it's possible. I also believe the police have re-classified the cause of death to *suspicious*, rather than natural."

Betsey gave a low, harsh laugh. "Well, isn't that a hoot. I have to tell you, Rosco-honey, that makes my day. I'm glad that son of a gun got his in the end. Who do they think did it?"

"Judging from your reaction, I'd imagine the police might want to place your name on their list of suspects. You don't seen terribly upset."

She continued to laugh in the same guttural growl. Again, Rosco had the impression her body was inching toward his. He told himself it was an illusion produced by tiger stripes meeting zebra stripes.

"How well did you know Briephs?" he asked.

"Well enough to want to kill him sometimes." Betsey grinned when she said this. "But I'll bet that could be said for a great many people. He was an arrogant SOB. Charming, yes. Sexy, often. But the only person who made him drool was himself."

"Let's—just for the fun of it—say you didn't kill him; I assume you can account for your whereabouts at the time of his death?"

"You mean do I have an alibi?"

Rosco only nodded.

"Well, let's see; I saw him in the *Herald*'s parking garage that morning . . . We exchanged a few words, and I continued upstairs to Steven's office. I never saw Tommy again."

"Your husband's secretary said you only remained for ten minutes. Where did you go after that?"

"My goodness, honey, you've certainly done your homework." Betsey uncoiled herself from the couch, crossed over to a control panel beside the TV set and touched a button. A section of shelving slid away to reveal a fully stocked bar. "Can I make you a drink?" she asked. "Anything you like; if we don't have it, they don't make it."

"No, thank you."

He watched as she placed a few ice cubes in a tall crystal glass and covered them with Scotch. She then slinked back toward Rosco and sat beside him.

"You are awfully good-looking, you know," she said as she moved her thigh against his and ran the cool glass across her chest.

Rosco stood and moved to the bookcase. He glanced at some of the video titles. "Some of these tapes seem a trifle racy . . . The police found Briephs tied to his bed with women's stockings, did I mention that . . . ?" He turned to face her. "Let me know if I'm out of line, but you seem like a woman who can handle a question like this: You weren't having an affair with Thompson, by any chance, were you?"

Betsey laughed her throaty laugh, and took a long, slow sip from her drink. "I've had affairs with lots of men, honey. But you'll never get me to admit that outside this room. It might put . . . shall we say . . . a *strain* on my marriage? I could see myself having an affair with you, if you're interested." She stretched out full-length on the leather couch and gave Rosco a leer only an idiot would have misinterpreted.

"Let's stay with the Briephs' situation for the moment. We can discuss the other part later," Rosco said in an attempt to keep her talking. "You didn't answer my question. Were you and Thompson an item?"

"So what if we were? That hardly makes me a murderess."

"Actually, a lover scorned is always a prime suspect. He wasn't trying to end the relationship, was he?"

"Nobody dumps me, Rosco-honey; it's always the other way around." Betsey took another slow sip of Scotch. "I hope that doesn't scare you off?"

"I don't scare easily." He pulled a video cassette of *The Maltese Falcon* from the bookshelf and smiled at the intense photo of Humphrey Bogart on the cover. "Great film. Of course, in any affair there's the possibility of blackmail. Thompson threatens to go to your husband . . . There's only one way to keep him quiet."

"Tommy-Boy hardly needed money."

"Understood. But in his case it could be emotional blackmail. Some men don't react to being dumped any better than . . . well . . . some women do." Rosco watched Betsey closely for a reaction and got it. She slammed her glass onto the coffee table and bolted to her feet. Her pussycat demeanor was transformed into tiger-striped rage.

"Nobody dumped anybody!" she nearly shouted. "And nobody *will* dump me. Nobody."

Taking advantage of her outburst, Rosco pressed for additional information. "On the day Thompson died, where did you go after you saw your husband?"

"To a movie. I don't have to answer these questions."

"What theatre? What movie?"

"*Snow White*. At the Harbor View Theatre. Look it up in the paper if you don't believe me. It's still there. It's been there all summer."

"*Snow White*? You went to see *Snow White*?"

"I like Disney flicks. So sue me."

She crossed back to the coffee table, grabbed her glass and drained the Scotch in one gulp. "I didn't kill Tommy-Boy. I'm not sorry he's gone, but I didn't kill him. And if you mention to anyone—I repeat *anyone*—that I had an affair with him, I'll deny it and sue you for every penny you have."

"One last question?"

"I want you to leave."

"If you didn't kill him—and I almost believe you—who do you think might have?"

"Roth," she muttered, too softly for Rosco to hear.

"Who?"

"John Bulldog Roth. The Senator's hatchet man."

"Why Roth?"

"That's for you to find out, honey lamb."

CHAPTER

25

ROSCO REMAINED AT the Housemann house for another ten minutes in an attempt to extract additional information from Betsey, but she refused to say anything further regarding her suspicions of John Bulldog Roth or his motive in murdering Thompson Briephs. As Rosco returned to his office, he reasoned that her accusation might have been a smoke screen designed to throw him off the trail. However, a talk with Roth seemed the next logical step.

Rosco picked up a container of coffee at the Parthenon luncheonette before proceeding to his office. Once seated at his desk, he peeled off the plastic lid and sailed it across the room like a Frisbee. The lid hooked perfectly and dropped into a wastebasket near the door. After downing half the gray liquid, he reached for his phone and called Al Lever, who informed him that Briephs' death had been reclassified as a homicide, and that he was planning to spend the better part of the evening on Congress Street questioning the men and women who earned their living there.

Hoping to keep the lieutenant occupied as long as possible, Rosco responded that Congress Street would be a reasonable beginning. But ending the conversation, he worried: Al's methods weren't exactly subtle; once the murderer knew the police were on the warpath, he or she would become more difficult to trap.

Rosco paced his office for a hesitant minute or two before dialing Belle's number, but hung up before the call rang through. Then he drummed his fingers on the desk while sipping what remained of his now-cold coffee and flipping through his Rolodex for the Patriot Yacht Club's listing. Still holding the cardboard container in one hand, he set the receiver on the desk, punched in the number, then grabbed up the phone and waited for the receiver at the club to ring.

The expected sound never came; instead he heard quiet breathing on the other end of the line. "Is someone there?"

"Rosco?"

"Belle . . . ? What are you doing at the yacht club?"

"I'm not at the yacht club. I'm home." Her voice cracked.

Rosco glanced at the open Rolodex. "I dialed the yacht club—I think."

"You probably did. I called you. That's why you didn't get through. I was on the line. I heard you pushing in the numbers."

"Are you all right?" His voice echoed with concern. "You sound like you've just run a fast mile."

"No . . . I mean, yes . . . I think someone broke into my house."

"When!? When did this happen?"

"Right after you left." Belle stopped. He heard her inhale a long breath. "I walked to the store . . . When I returned the door was double-locked . . . and then it wasn't."

"I'm coming over."

"No . . . I'm okay. Whoever it is has gone. You don't need to drop what you're doing. It just rattled me, that's all. I thought it was Garet paying a surprise visit, and I—"

"Did you call the police?"

"No. Nothing was stolen. I broke some eggs—"

"You're certain you're okay?"

"And an entire jar of capers. Do you know how much capers cost?"

"I'll be there in fifteen minutes. Why don't you wait outside—in public view where you can be easily seen by the neighbors."

"I can take care of myself, Rosco, really."

"I'll just come over and take a look around."

"Really, I'm okay."

"Do me this favor, Belle."

Rosco noticed the change in her immediately. She was hesitant, definitely shaken but attempting such a reasonable demeanor that he decided it was wiser to follow suit. Burglary victims—or victims of any crime, for that matter—dealt with the emotional impact of their situations very

differently. It wasn't the first time Rosco had witnessed behavior like Belle's. They walked the house together.

" . . . I suppose my return scared the intruder off before
he could grab anything . . . The papers on my desk were rearranged somewhat, and some of the books in Garet's office, but other than those two spots, everything appears
normal."

"Did you see anyone? . . . a shadow? . . . anything?"

"No. And I didn't hear any noise either. That's why I
thought I was probably imagining things . . . And then the
door blew shut . . . and I broke the jar of capers."

"So it could have been a man or a woman." Rosco was
muttering to himself.

"It was a big jar, too."

"We can get you more capers, Belle."

She stopped; the meaning behind Rosco's words finally
penetrated her brain. She seemed about to speak, then appeared to reconsider. Her shoulders straightened and a
look of concentration covered her face. "I'm sure it was
just a neighborhood kid's prank," she said.

Rosco didn't fully agree, although he decided to play
along. "Probably."

His tone soothed her. "After all, it doesn't make any
sense . . . someone breaking in and not taking anything."

"You're right."

"Why would a person illegally enter a home without a
reason?"

"You're right, Belle. It doesn't make sense."

She studied his face as if looking for—or fearing—the
answer they were both avoiding.

"And another thing . . . whoever was in here used my copy machine. The counter was up by three numbers. So that proves it was a kid."

Rosco didn't answer immediately. "Why would a kid do that, do you think?"

"I don't know . . . He—or she—must have been playing with it."

Rosco thought, Kids don't break into houses to toy with copy machines, or without leaving marks on a door or window, but didn't say it. Instead he drummed his fingers on Belle's desk. "Why don't we take a look at that copier."

He carried the desk lamp to the machine and angled it toward the Start button. "No visible prints . . ."

Belle's gray eyes grew enormous. "Does that mean the person was wearing gloves?"

"It's a possibility."

Her lips tightened. "I must have made a mistake with my counting . . ."

"Burglaries happen, Belle. No one's immune . . . And the perpetrators are pros . . . I'll call Lever and have him send a squad car over."

Belle's vehement "No" took Rosco by surprise. She softened her response with a gentler "Garet wouldn't appreciate a police investigation. He has an absolute terror of 'adverse publicity.' "

"But it wouldn't be an investigation . . . just a routine visit . . . Besides, Garet's a long way away, isn't he?"

The statement only made Belle retreat farther into her shell. "This isn't a big deal," she said several times. Then they sat in uneasy silence in her office.

"How about I ask Al Lever for a patrol car to make a regular sweep of the neighborhood?" Rosco finally said. "Your house won't be singled out . . . Besides which, your neighbors are bound to be pleased at the constabulary attention."

Belle, after several long, pensive moments agreed. "That should take care of that," she said when he wrapped up his call to Lever. "Safe and sound."

"Yep," Rosco agreed, although he recognized that this particular felon would have little trouble avoiding police scrutiny. "Safe and sound."

On the porch, he was as loath to leave as she was to see him go.

"So was my description of Betsey correct?" Belle tried resuming a joking tone.

"Right on the money."

"And?"

"And, what?"

"And did she make a pass at you?"

"I wouldn't necessarily call it a pass."

The fact that Belle let this comment slide made Rosco realize how distracted her thoughts still were. "So why were you calling the yacht club?" she asked after another painful pause.

"To ask Peter Kingsworth to ferry me out to Windword after he quits work."

His answer seemed to brighten Belle considerably. "I could take you," she said, then added a genuinely pleased, "I gather you're beginning to see things my way?"

"Meaning . . . ?"

"You're visiting Windword to look for missing puzzles . . . or copies of them?"

Rosco smiled. "You're so sure of yourself?"

"Am I correct?"

"No, you're not, Miss Know-it-all. After talking to Betsey the tiger I've begun to take your blackmail theory seriously. I'm going to the island to poke around for Briephs' bank records—"

"We can hunt for them together, then."

Rosco started to protest, then considered the alternative: leaving Belle alone with a probable felon still at large. "Sure. Sounds good to me."

"Oh, no . . . wait," was her halting response. "I forgot . . . We can't take my boat . . . The last time I started the motor, it began belching billows of white smoke. The public marina's mechanic, Eddie, is 'studying the situation'— But I can call Peter for you. I have a better way with him than you do."

CHAPTER

26

DRIVING TO THE yacht club, Belle's take-charge
spirit began to revive. "What do you mean, Betsey
didn't make a pass at you?" was the first question
she launched at Rosco.

"I said, 'not necessarily.' "

"So she did?"

"Did what?" he asked as if unaware of her true feelings.

"Try to seduce you?" Belle watched Rosco study the
road ahead, a line of spurious concentration wrinkling his
forehead.

"Not really . . ."

Belle laughed. "I hope you're a better liar than that . . .
What a pitiful answer." She continued chuckling to herself.

"Well, she's a flirt, sure. But not my type at all."

Belle was about to ask, And what is your type? But

caught herself and moved to safer ground. "What's your opinion of this 'flirt'?"

Rosco responded in an equally businesslike tone, "An interesting woman. Certainly not above suspicion. What struck me as odd, though, was that she was easily persuaded to view Briephs' death as murder. Before we spoke, she'd been under the impression he'd died of natural causes."

"Then where does blackmail enter the picture?"

"Clearly, Briephs didn't need money, but he seems the type who could have been involved in emotional blackmail—money being a secondary issue—part of the game, as it were . . . Anyway, I'm hoping to discover some unexplained deposits in his bank statements."

"But who would Thompson blackmail?"

"Betsey, for one. Your original idea was correct. They were having, or had been having, an affair . . . My hunch is that one of them had dumped the other when the situation grew too dicey."

Rosco eased the Jeep onto the harbor road, increasing the speed to fifty as he continued talking. "Scenario number one: She ditches him, he blackmails her, she kills him. Scenario number two: He dumps her, but he's sadistic enough to keep toying with her . . . Again she's the killer."

Belle considered Rosco's theory. "What about jealous husband discovers affair and murders evil lover?"

Rosco looked at her and smiled. "I haven't entirely discounted that scenario. Is that what your husband would do?"

"I'm not having an affair." Belle felt her face flush.

"No . . . No . . . Of course you're not. But in most circumstances, a jealous husband—if he's the murderous type—will kill his wife before attacking the man she's involved with . . . That's *most* of the time . . . I believe Steven Housemann is capable of murder, although my gut tells me he's indulged in too many affairs to go after the man. He'd nail Betsey first."

Belle turned her head toward the sea, watching day sailers jockey for position in the deeper offshore waters. Rosco imagined she was pondering the Housemanns' tangled relationship, but she wasn't. She was wondering how Garet would behave if she were having an affair. She suspected his reaction would be far less impassioned than murder.

Rosco's jerky stop at the yacht club's security gate returned her to the present. After informing the guard of their appointment with Peter Kingsworth, they were directed to the refueling dock.

Peter was already aboard when they approached. He greeted them with one of his signature toothy white smiles followed by, "Well, if it isn't Newcastle's most gorgeous newspaper person."

Rosco's jaw tightened discernibly, although he managed a smile of his own. "Watch it there, Peter. The lady's married."

"Hey, how are you, Rosco? I'd already forgotten you were going to the island, too. What is it they say? Two's company, three's a crowd?"

"I think that's the way it goes."

Peter's cheery demeanor and big grin irritated Rosco, but Belle obviously found him refreshing and wholesome. "I don't know what happened to my boat's motor, it was fine the other day . . . It's nice of you to do this for us. I'll make it up to you."

As he pushed off, Peter said, "Any time, the pleasure's mine. Maybe we can have dinner sometime?"

"Or lunch. Evenings usually aren't good for me." Belle looked to Rosco for support, but he merely chortled smugly and watched the waves.

"What takes you back to Windword, anyway?" Peter asked.

"That's confidential," Rosco said too quickly, then added an officious, "Mrs. Briephs asked us to pick up a few of Thompson's personal effects."

"Well, I'm here to help. Mr. Briephs really has been missed around here. He was a true fixture in the marina." Peter headed his Boston Whaler directly into a swell and glanced back to watch Rosco grab the side of the boat and turn a light shade of green. He then looked at Belle and winked. "Yep, a real fixture."

"Were you at the yacht club the day he was killed?" Belle asked.

"Nope. My day off. I came in at noon the next day to find the police launch ferrying all sorts of people out there."

Rosco attempted to say something but clamped his mouth shut as Peter slammed into another swell.

Belle laughed and said, "Who found him?"

"No one really. I think the police said his mother had been trying to reach him all night and then finally called the Coast Guard in the morning. That's who discovered him, the Coast Guard." Peter angled for another wave. After he hit it he said, "How you doing back there, Rosco?"

Rosco was unable to open his mouth, and his eyes seemed to be rolling back into their sockets, so Belle answered for him. "He'll be fine . . . Once we get him over there." She gave Peter a quick smile. "I don't think he likes the water."

Once Belle and Peter had secured the lines to Windword's dock they stepped onto it and turned to help Rosco out of the boat. His knees seemed extremely watery as he moved down the dock toward the house, and he grabbed each piling for support as he passed.

"I'd be happy to come in and give you a hand," Peter said as they reached the front door.

"Thanks, Peter. The police have reclassified this as a homicide." Rosco slid the key into the lock. "They've asked that anyone nonofficial remain outside. In fact, you probably should stay on the dock. Forensics will most likely be looking for footprints in the ground near all the windows and doors."

"Oh, boy."

"What?"

Peter scratched the back of his head as he spoke. "I came out yesterday and looked in the windows. Jeez, I'm sorry—I was just curious, you know?"

This gave Rosco a definite feeling of superiority, which erased the final traces of seasickness. "Well, don't worry about it. If the police come out here, just tell them so they don't spend days trying to find out whose footprints they are."

"Right."

Belle pulled the key from the lock and after they stepped inside, whispered to Rosco, "Is that all true? No one can come in here? And they'll be searching for footprints?"

"Yep. I'm surprised they haven't been out here with the crime tape and roped the place off. But Al said they've been busy and didn't expect to get to it until tomorrow. It'll probably take them all morning. Don't lose that key."

"I won't . . . So, if we find anything, we can't touch it?" Belle asked, not attempting to hide the disappointment in her voice.

"As long as the crime tape hasn't been put up we can play stupid. Well . . . you can play stupid. I've been officially informed by Lever that this is now a crime scene. What you do behind my back . . ." Rosco shrugged. "Well, there's not much I can do about it, is there?"

Belle smiled. "Where do you think his office was?"

"The first day out, I spotted a fax machine near the entrance to this mazelike thing. What did you call it? Daedalus' Labyrinth?"

"Very good."

"Anyway, my guess is, Briephs' office is in one of the rooms that shoot off of this central passage."

They left the entry foyer, traversing the convoluted, spiral-shaped hall until they spotted the electronic equipment Rosco had previously noted. A brief and angled passage led to it, passing beneath a low stone lintel that had clearly been transported from one of the Greek Isles. Belle ran her hand along it. "This is amazing. It's a museum piece . . ." In the dim light, her hand almost disappeared on the stone's worn and pebbly surface. "Modern stonecutters can't duplicate this kind of antiquity . . . It's as if it had been imported whole from the ancient palace at Knossos."

Rosco ducked as he walked into the office. "Here's the fax machine. Why don't we split up? You stay put here and see what you can find. And I'll head off that way." He motioned vaguely toward a nearly hidden room off to the right of the office. "Holler if you find any files. I think these plates are the light switches." Rosco touched a one- by two-inch bronze plaque attached to the wall and the room gradually began to brighten with an eerie replica of sunlight. "Yep. See you later." And he disappeared under a second low stone lintel.

Belle walked to the fax and pressed a button marked Reprint Last Document. The machine hummed for a few seconds before spitting out a handwritten copy of the *Herald*'s past Sunday crossword puzzle. She tore it off, folded it and stuffed it into her jeans pocket, then scanned through several insignificant groups of papers before strolling through a stone archway to her left.

The chamber she entered was windowless and tiny with rough-hewn stone walls and floor and an oppressively low ceiling. Light from the main room cast jagged shadows while consigning clefts in the stone to woolly blackness. Belle began running her fingers along the dusky walls but then thought of spiders lurking in the cracks and kept her hands at her sides.

Except for an ancient wooden chest, the place was barren of furniture. Gingerly, Belle lifted the chest's lid; the interior emitted an aged, musty odor but revealed nothing. Then she passed sequentially through three more windowless rooms, each smaller than the one before although each contained a similar chest arranged at the room's center. Pandora's box, Belle thought as she opened all three and found them as empty as the first. In a fit of daring, she thrust her hand inside the third casket, hoping to find a false bottom, but was rewarded only with a powdery coating of moldy, worm-eaten wood. She began to wonder whether she was still above sea level.

The next room she discovered was twice as large as the the original office. Failing to detect a light plate, she was only barely able to discern a fountain at the room's center cascading around the feet of an incomplete statue she believed to be Athena, the goddess of wisdom. Athena, Belle reflected, patron of Athens, the city-state Theseus left to conquer the Minotaur and to which he returned triumphant but also bearing witness to the tragedy of his king-father's death.

Noise from the fountain reverberated from the stone walls, drowning other sound while beyond it the room appeared to open into three archways that seemed identical to the one through which Belle had entered. They were black holes in the dim light, and she decided to proceed no farther. Instead, she stood gazing at the fountain for another minute until a sudden chill swept over her. For the second time, she wondered if the complex she'd discovered was subterranean.

She decided to retrace her steps, and turned to leave, but before she could proceed, heard the sound of footsteps marching loudly toward her. It was impossible to tell from which direction they came, and she froze, recalling the break-in at her home and the front door slamming shut behind her. The footsteps banged across the stone, growing more insistent by the moment while Belle stared from one entry to another, trying to ascertain which passage would be safe.

Then Rosco walked through the archway to her right. Belle ran to him and he put his arms around her and held her tightly.

"I told you to stay put. What happened?" he asked.

"Something scared me. I don't know what . . . It may sound bizarre, but I almost felt as if I were being watched." She looked up and their eyes locked. An unmistakable energy passed between them; they both tried to shake free, but it was futile. In the darkened room, amid the echoing plash of water, Rosco bent down and brought his lips to meet Belle's.

27

THE KISS LASTED close to thirty seconds. Belle was the first to break it off. She stood back and took Rosco's hands, then, looking at their intertwined fingers, said, "It's no good. We can't let ourselves do this."

"I know. I'm sorry. I wasn't thinking." He turned and walked to the fountain. "I don't know what got into me. It wasn't very professional." An uneasy chuckle followed the admission.

"Forget it."

"Right," he said with a shake of the head.

"How did you get in here, anyway?" she asked, trying to cover her own emotions with a professional tone.

"The rooms are interconnected. When I left you next to the fax machine, the trail looped around to lead me here."

"No bank records, then?"

"Listen, Belle, I'm—"

"Rosco, forget it. I was as much to blame as you." She folded her arms across her chest and pretended to study the ceiling. "Well . . . so . . . did you find the bank records?"

"No. No. Just three rooms that looked like dungeons or something. Shackles and leg irons hanging from the walls. A couple of doors leading into places no bigger than closets. Did you find anything?"

"Shackles?"

"That's what they looked like."

"And leg irons? That's certainly unpleasant . . ."

"Lever said Briephs was into the rough stuff, remember?"

"And you think . . . ? Oh, yuck!" Belle paused. To Rosco it seemed as though she'd retreated into herself; he silently cursed himself for bringing up Briephs' less-than-savory love life, then decided to forge ahead as if the subject hadn't been broached.

"How about you? Find anything?"

"Empty rooms with empty antique caskets. Odd and definitely daunting, but nothing physically harmful . . . The rooms looked almost as if Thompson had wanted to construct a stage set—complete with props. Maybe the shackles and leg irons you discovered were part of the set design . . . or perhaps Briephs' research into the ancient Minoan civilization had led him to believe he was re-creating their artifacts and surroundings . . ."

Rosco didn't answer.

"You disagree?"

"Belle, I see a good deal of unusual, sometimes aberrant behavior in my work. Not much surprises me anymore."

Belle pondered his reply. "I'm glad I wasn't aware of some of the seamier details before today."

Rosco considered asking what she meant, but before he could speak, she turned and gazed at the two remaining archways. "Which one do you want to try next? I'd like to stick together this time, though. This place is beginning to give me the creeps."

"Fine by me."

"How's your sense of direction? We shouldn't lose track of where we started. I told Peter we'd be a half-hour at most."

Rosco looked behind him, and then toward the archway through which Belle had emerged. "Well, the lady in the fountain is facing you, so all we have to do is follow her nose."

"Don't count on it. That fountain's turning. It's moving slowly, but watch closely. She was facing left when you walked in."

Rosco studied the statue for a full minute. "You're right." He reached into his pocket, pulled out a somewhat tarnished dime and placed it at the base of the doorway Belle had used. He then turned and pointed toward the opposite wall. "Let's try that one first."

The first room they entered was totally empty, though again constructed of the same rough stone. They passed through, reaching a second chamber lined with dark oak bookshelves carved into the jagged rock. This time Belle was successful in finding a lighting pad. She depressed it and the area was slowly suffused with a gilded glow. She began glancing at the book titles. Most were foreign-language dictionaries. The rest were encyclopedias and other reference materials.

"We're getting warm," she said.

On the opposite wall were two squat heavy wooden doors whose hinges were fashioned of age-blackened iron. Rosco crossed to the door on the right, which was dead-bolted. He bent down and studied the lock.

Belle moved beside him. "I assume you don't have an ancient skeleton key?"

"No. But there's a modern lock disguised within the older one . . . Piece of cake . . ." He pulled a small pick from his wallet and had the door unlocked in less than ten seconds.

"Wow," she said. "That was impressive."

"Are you being sarcastic? That sounded a little snide to me."

"No. Not at all. I'm impressed. Really."

Rosco pulled open the door and they stepped into what had clearly been Thompson Briephs' private office. Although still adhering to the ancient Attic theme, the room contained an orderly desk, a number of bookcases, two filing cabinets and fifteen or twenty Minoan statuettes and amphorae arranged with museumlike precision and individually lighted, each with a pin spot of its own.

"Why do you think he kept the fax machine all the way back there?" Rosco asked as he cocked his thumb toward the open door.

"I don't know. Perhaps it's more convenient to the rest of the house?"

"Maybe." Rosco walked up to one of the filing cabinets and opened it. "I'll take this one. You can have the other."

It took them fifteen minutes to search both filing cabinets and Briephs' desk drawers. They found nothing unusual and nothing they wanted. There were plenty of crossword puzzles, but all had been previously published; there were no copies of the three puzzles currently in their possession, nor any signs of the two still missing.

"What strikes me as odd," Rosco finally sighed, "is that there are no bank records. No canceled checks. Nothing. Wouldn't you think they'd be here?"

"What did you say?" Belle had been staring at one of the statuettes and obviously not listening.

"Where are his bank records?" Rosco's frustration sharpened his tone.

But Belle's mind was elsewhere. "I've seen this piece before," she murmured. "I don't know where, but I'm certain of it."

Rosco moved closer to her. "I don't know, they all kind of look the same."

"This one I recognize." She pointed to another figurine. "And that woman with the coiled hair? I know I've seen her, too. And there's an amphora that looks quite familiar."

"Well, I'm sure there's dozens of them all over the world. You probably saw something like that in a museum somewhere."

"I don't know . . . I don't believe so . . ."

Rosco studied the statuette of the woman with coiled hair. She was a buxom seminude; serpents were entwined in her tightly curled coif and wrapped around her neck like stray and oily tendrils. "I agree with you. It's a unique piece . . . Not to my liking, however."

"All I can say is that I've seen it before. Right down to that tiny chip on her forehead." Belle glanced at her watch and let out a sigh. "We should go. I hate to make Peter wait any longer."

When they returned to the dock Peter could be seen seated at the far end, legs dangling over the edge and his attention riveted to the music coming from a portable CD player. The vibrations of their footsteps brought him back to earth. He switched off the music with an almost guilty expression. "No luck?"

"Pardon me?" Rosco asked, his thoughts unhappily anticipating the upcoming boat ride.

"Didn't you say you were picking something up for Mrs. Briephs?"

"Oh, right, yes. No, we didn't find it."

"That must be some place in there."

"It's not for the faint of heart," Belle said with a shudder. "Briephs never asked you in for one of his famous parties?"

"Nope. He never mingled with the working stiffs. What were you looking for?"

Without thinking, Belle said, "Puzzles."

"Puzzles?"

Rosco jumped in quickly. "Yeah, puzzles. The place is covered with them. Coffee cups with crossword puzzles, place mats with puzzles, plates, bowls, the works. We've got puzzles coming out of our ears. Actually, what Mrs. Briephs wanted was a small statue she said was her favorite. But we never found it. I hope nobody pinched it . . ."

Belle stared at Rosco as if he'd lost his mind, but decided to keep her mouth shut.

Then the three stepped aboard the launch and headed back to the yacht club. Rosco remained in the stern, hanging on for dear life while Peter ran the larger swells and entertained Belle with a seemingly endless monologue. Occasionally he glanced aft and called out, "How're you making out back there?" while Rosco attempted a sickly smile and a wave that never ventured too far from the gunwale.

Eventually Rosco and Belle found themselves on terra firma and ensconced in the Jeep.

"You've got to develop some sea legs, Rosco. I'm sorry to say it, but you look pretty wimpy out on the briny." If the visit to Briephs' pleasure dome had disturbed Belle, she'd already pushed the memory into the far recesses of her mind. Her smile was absolutely buoyant.

"I know." A greenish tinge still clung to Rosco's cheeks.

"What was all that about, back on the island? All that business with the crossword coffee mugs and so forth? It sounded more like my house."

"You can't count *anybody* out as a suspect. Kingsworth's a big guy. There's no telling what he could do. It's just not a good idea to give up information to the wrong people."

"Peter?" Belle said, unable to control a burst of laughter. "You think . . . Peter? Come on . . . How could someone that wholesome be a murderer?"

"He's a big bozo with a cheesy smile and a boat. A boat that doesn't ride very smoothly, I might add."

Belle laughed so hard she couldn't speak.

"What? What is it? What's so funny?"

"You're just jealous, that's all."

"I'm not jealous of Peter Kingsworth."

Belle continued to laugh while Rosco stared at the windshield. Eventually he loosened his iron grip on the Jeep's steering wheel and placed his hands in his lap. "Well, okay, maybe he *is* harmless. But you don't know who he might talk to. And that's the thing. Everyone in this town owns a boat—"

"Except you."

"Right—except me. Let me finish, please. Everyone owns a boat. Every single club member talks to that smirking oaf of a harbormaster. Of all the people in the world, he should be kept in the dark about what we're doing."

"Okay, okay . . . I see your point. You're right, it's not a good idea to blab, but don't you think you're being a bit juvenile?" Belle contained her mirth for a few seconds, then added another small jab: "Just because Peter's so attractive and charming? Not to mention that breathtaking grin?"

"And he has a boat! Don't forget that. He has a boat!"

The ice broken, they both laughed for the better part of the ride back to Captain's Walk.

CHAPTER

28

W HEN BELLE'S HOUSE came into view, the memory of her mysterious intruder returned. While she gazed thoughtfully at the silent windows, Rosco's expression grew equally perturbed.

"Do you think . . . Just for tonight, I mean . . . ?" he began after they'd entered the house, and he'd scanned the foyer and living room with a quick, appraising eye. "What I mean is, wouldn't it be a good idea for me to stick around . . . Sleep on a couch or something?"

"No," Belle responded too quickly. They'd moved into her office, and she masked her abruptness by shuffling a pile of papers lying on her desk.

Rosco said, "What happened on the island won't happen again. I swear."

"That's not why I'm refusing your offer."

"It was totally unprofessional, and I apologize."

"I'm not sorry it happened, so you needn't apologize."

The awkwardness of the situation held them in place. Belle began toying with a battered Italian dictionary; Rosco found himself gripping the back of the canvas chair.

"I'm not in the habit of stealing other men's wives."

"I know you're not."

"I'm worried about your safety, that's all." The chair rocked under Rosco's heavy grasp.

"I'll be fine . . . I will. Look, I realize I seemed upset earlier, but I'm perfectly capable of taking care of myself. I have been for a long time."

Neither spoke for several weighty moments.

Rosco was the first to break the silence. "Belle, I'm not disagreeing with you . . . It's just that in my line of work I've seen a lot of unpleasant situations."

"Garet made certain this house has almost as many locks as Fort Knox."

"I'd like to take a look-see before I go. Check out possible entrances . . . if that's okay?"

"If it will make you feel better."

"It will."

"And then you'll leave?"

"If that's your decision."

Rosco's search was painstakingly thorough; he opened closet doors and paced through the basement while Belle followed at a distance. She could see him struggling to find an explanation for their kiss, but was relieved he didn't reintroduce the subject.

"I'm an adult, you know," she said when at last he walked out the front door. "I can handle myself . . . Emotionally and physically."

"Will you call me if there's a problem?"

"There's not going to be a problem."

"But you'd call me if there were?"

Belle didn't answer, but when he'd left, she double-locked the door.

Alone, she munched distractedly on leftover meat loaf, then decided to treat herself to a can of anchovies, but neither they nor the four licorice sticks she added for dessert seemed to have any discernible flavor. She deeply regretted the ruined eggs and capers. At eleven, she was in bed and asleep almost immediately.

At one-thirty, the phone rang. For some reason she expected the caller to be Rosco; prepared with a witty retort on her Amazonian powers, she lifted the receiver, but no one responded. Whoever had called simply hung up, and Belle assumed that it was a wrong number and drifted off to sleep again. Half an hour later, the phone rang again. This time she detected breathing on the other end of the line, but again no one spoke.

"Who's there?" she demanded, but the caller hung up without replying.

The phone rang three more times during the night; each time the caller followed the same routine: a few shallow and measured breaths that remained on the line for less than ten seconds. On the final call, however, at five A.M., she was startled by the addition of a low, vindictive laugh. It seemed to pulse through her fingers as she held the receiver, but Belle was unable to discern whether the mysterious voice belonged to a man or a woman.

CHAPTER

29

THE FOLLOWING MORNING Rosco was awakened by *Imus in the Morning*—as usual. He flipped off the radio before the I-Man or his brother Fred tried to sell him something for which he had no use, and sat thinking in bed for a few difficult minutes. His head was filled with images of Belle. He reached for the phone, stared long and hard at the keypad, then dropped the receiver back into its cradle.

"I'm glad she's stronger than I am," he mumbled as he climbed out of bed and headed for the shower. "Besides, she'll call me if anything strange occurs. That's what she said."

As the water doused him, his senses began to clear and he turned his concentration on Thompson Briephs' missing bank records. In reality, Rosco hadn't expected them to reveal much, but the fact that they couldn't be found at

Windword perplexed him. Especially as there had been no evidence of anyone's disturbing Briephs' personal effects.

When Rosco reached his office, blue cardboard container of coffee in hand, he placed a call to Briephs' mother, Sara. After two short rings, a maid answered with a crisp "Mrs. Briephs' residence" before scurrying off to summon the grand lady herself.

"What have you discovered, Mr. Polycrates?" was Sara's succinct greeting.

Rosco took five minutes to bring her up to date—as best he could. Much of what he'd found relied on intuition and instinct, and was substantiated by very little fact. His suspicions, he kept to himself. Rosco concluded by informing Sara that the police had reclassified her son's death as a homicide.

"And, I take it, that reclassification must have been a direct result of your probing?"

"Yes, ma'am, I believe it probably is."

"Well then, young man, I owe you a great deal of gratitude, not to mention a check."

"Thank you. There's no rush on the check, though, Mrs. Briephs. My concern now is finding the individual responsible."

"Of course. And I am confident you will."

"But speaking of checks, I visited your son's house yesterday hunting for his bank records. Sometimes canceled checks are a good lead in determining . . . well, let's say, strained business dealings. At any rate, there were no records of financial transactions in his home office."

"That's because I have them."

Rosco gave the receiver a quizzical look, then returned it to his ear. "You do?"

"Yes. Thompson's accountant brought them to me only yesterday. Apparently he was cross-checking my son's bank statements and other portfolio information at the time of his death, and didn't know who else to give them to. He's a kind man. He was thoughtful enough to freeze Thompson's several accounts and obtain finalized statements for me."

"Would you mind if I came over and picked them up? I'll only need to look through them for a day or two. I can be at your house"—Rosco glanced at his watch—"by eight-thirty and return them by Friday afternoon at the latest."

"Absolutely. Please do. I'll postpone my tennis match with the club's pro. Besides which, I'd very much like to see you again. You'll be a breath of fresh air after a most dreary evening with Mr. Roth. I'll also have a check waiting for you. How much should I make it out for?"

"We can wait on that. Let me see how I progress during the next few days."

"Fine . . . Oh, and Mr. Polycrates, I have something else that might interest you."

"What's that, Mrs. Briephs?"

"I'll show you when you arrive. It may be nothing at all."

Rosco replaced the receiver in its cradle, chugged the remainder of his coffee and darted down to his Jeep. He pulled into Mrs. Briephs' circular drive twenty minutes later and parked near the privet hedge beside her tennis court. A gardener was rolling the dark red clay with a large drum-roller. Rosco waved to the man and walked to the house. The front door was yanked open by John Bulldog Roth before Rosco could reach for the brass knocker.

"Mrs. Briephs has gone to a friend's house to play tennis. I'm afraid you've missed her, Mr. Polycrates."

"Really? She told me she was planning to cancel her match."

Roth pulled a check from his suit pocket and presented it to Rosco. "She asked me to give you this and tell you that your services would no longer be needed. The police will handle the investigation from here on out."

Rosco took the check from Roth. It was issued for a sum of five thousand dollars and drawn on Roth's personal bank account, not Sara's.

"I assume that will be satisfactory, Mr. Polycrates?"

Rosco handed it back to Roth. "'Fraid not, *Bulldog*, Mrs. Briephs and I agreed on a different figure."

"And what might that number be?"

"I suggest you ask her. Where'd she go to play tennis? Maybe the three of us can yak about it together."

"She requested that she not be disturbed."

Rosco smiled and shook his head. He knew he was wasting his breath, but he tried it anyway. "She had some papers for me. I don't suppose she left them with you?"

"She didn't mention anything, no."

"Do you mind if I come in? Get a drink of water?" Rosco looked up into the sun and squinted. "It's kind of hot out here . . . not to mention no AC in the Jeep."

Roth leaned his head back into the house and called a commanding, "Emma, would you be kind enough to bring Mr. Polycrates a glass of iced water?"

"Thanks, sport."

"Any time . . . *sport.*"

Rosco chuckled and glanced down at his shoes. "I had a very interesting chat with a woman by the name of Betsey Housemann yesterday." He looked back at Roth. "You wouldn't happen to know her, would you?"

Roth's jaw tightened noticeably at the mention of Betsey's name. "Yes. I've met her. As you know, Steven Housemann and the *Herald* editorial staff have always been generous supporters of Senator Crane."

"Well—"

"As well as loyal friends to me, I might add."

"Right. Anyway, when I mentioned that the police department was now treating Thompson's death as a homicide, Mrs. Housemann suggested, in a roundabout way, that I might want to talk to you. Why do you think that is?"

"I wouldn't know."

"What was your relationship with Thompson?"

"He's the Senator's nephew. Thompson was invited to most of the Senator's social functions. Other than events that included his uncle, I rarely saw Thompson."

"That's an interesting word: *rarely.* It means *almost* entirely. Like *virtually.* It's a very popular expression among politicians, advertisers and military strategists. What you're really saying is that you also saw Briephs at other times . . . besides the Senator's get-togethers?"

Roth's left eye twitched, but he didn't respond.

"I still have some fact-checking to do," Rosco pressed. "If you have anything you'd like to share with me about your relationship with Thompson, you could save me some legwork. Believe me, it will all come out in the wash sooner or later."

Roth remained silent, studying Rosco.

"Okay, how about this one: What was your relationship to Betsey Housemann?"

"My acquaintance with her is from those same social situations."

"But that *is* where you became such bosom buddies? She seemed to suggest that the two of you were, or had been, more than casual friends."

Rosco was laying the ball all over the court and Roth was having a tough time keeping up. A line of sweat had formed along his brow. He pulled the handkerchief from his suit pocket and dabbed at it. Emma emerged from behind him with the glass of water. She handed it to Rosco and nervously backed into the house.

"I don't have to answer your questions, Polycrates. You have no authority. You've got your water. Leave the glass with the gardener. I've got work to do."

"Busy man."

Roth gritted his teeth. "It may interest you to know that there are more pressing matters in this world of ours than your trying to dig up dirt on decent people. It so happens the Senator's itinerary has been changed. He arrives late this afternoon at Dulles. I'm flying to Washington to meet him. Forgive me for not putting international affairs of State on the back burner to deal with your petty innuendoes."

He began to step back inside but Rosco stopped him.

"Let me give you a bit of advice, there, *Bulldog*: one, I

won't back off until I get to the bottom of Thompson's death. And two, Al Lever and I were partners at one time. I know him like a brother. And if you think he can be bought, or persuaded to cover anything up, you've got another think coming. In the end, I'll put my money on a bloodhound like Al long before I'd put it on a bulldog." Rosco gave Roth a patronizing wink. "Give my best to Senator Crane."

Roth tried to slam the door in his face but he was too late. Rosco had already spun on his heel and headed toward his Jeep. On the way he polished off his water and tossed the ice cubes onto the grass. He then circled the hedge and approached the tennis court. The gardener wasn't in sight. Rosco set the glass on a wrought-iron bench and glanced toward the swimming pool. The gardener was standing in the shade of the pool house and motioning to him. Rosco grabbed the glass and trotted over.

"Mrs. Briephs asked me to give this to you." The man bent down and picked up a small red file box and handed it to Rosco.

"Thank you. Is she really gone, or does Roth have her tied up in the house somewhere?" Rosco opened the box as he talked. It contained Thompson's bank records.

"Roth is a forceful man. He talked her into leaving for the day." The gardener tapped the file box, and a huge smile spread across his face. "But I guess the missus outfoxed the fox, didn't she?"

"Looks that way."

"Oh, she wanted me to give you this, too."

He handed Rosco a business-size envelope. Sara

Briephs' name and address had been scrawled across it in a shaky, almost illegible hand. Inside was one of the two missing crossword puzzles.

"Thanks," Rosco said again. "You've been a big help. When do you expect Mrs. Briephs to return? I'd like to talk to her."

"Probably not until dinner. She's waiting until Mr. Roth leaves for Washington."

Rosco skipped out to his Jeep and tore out of the drive-way. He had Belle's phone number punched into his car phone before he'd left Sara's gate.

"Guess what I've got?" he said the moment she picked up.

Across

1. Fence part
5. Agreement
9. Texas player
14. "Hang 'Em ___," Eastwood film
15. Land measure
16. Hindu gateway
17. To the sheltered side
18. Night light
19. Startle
20. "Art is a jealous ___," Emerson
22. Figure of speech
23. Remove
24. Split, prefix
26. Self-satisfied
28. ___ is me
29. Invites
33. "___ of Glory," Kubrick film
35. Above, poetically
36. Falsehood
37. "Truth will come to ___ be hid long," Shak.: var.
41. Here in Paris
42. Bean of India
43. "___ There," Sellers film
44. Prefix meaning 8-Down
46. Clue
47. NASDAQ figs.
48. Pine for China?
50. Second-century date
51. Locale of 55-Down
53. Cheat catcher?
58. Seething
59. Pound or Stone
60. Slanted type? abbr.
61. More logical
62. Pub offerings
63. Not for
64. Dread
65. "___ in Peace"
66. Cartoonist Thomas

Down

1. Fake
2. Caron film
3. "Rock of ___"
4. "Nothing but ___"
5. Like some windows
6. ___ & eights: Dead man's hand
7. You're doing it!
8. Sawbuck
9. Video giant
10. Anastasio ___
11. "Death ___," Levin play
12. Bring down
13. ___-armed bandit
21. "The ___ Stuff," Harris film
22. Johnny Yuma: abbr.
25. Boys & girls together
26. Flavor
27. Wizardry
30. Jargon
31. Worth a___ransom
32. Prepared
34. Lubricious
37. Top
38. Leon ___
39. Point again?
40. Powell now?
45. Gravures
49. Ready
50. Sea ___
51. Shah's land
52. Space quaff
54. Iron and copper

THE CROSSWORD MURDER

PUZZLE #4

55. Sicillan spouter
56. Turner and Cole
57. Opening

58. Dead ___ doornail
59. Corn unit

THE CONVERSATION AT Belle's end of the phone was a jangle of interruptions and misinterpretation.

"I didn't tell you about my peculiar phone calls because I didn't feel they were important," she said, then added, "So, what did Sara give you?"

But Rosco was too het up about Belle's late-night harassments to reply to the question.

"I did not *say* I'd call you." Belle spoke levelly into the mouthpiece. "You asked me to, but I didn't respond . . . So, was Sara able to provide information about Thompson's bank statements or not?" Interrupted again, Belle's words became a staccato succession of: "He did?"; "But why is he going to Washington now?"; "She what?" and "How did she get them to you?" following which came a buoyant: "In twenty minutes? Of course, I'll be here!"

Belle almost threw the receiver into the cradle. All residual anxiety from the previous night's phone calls vanished. She paced restlessly between her office and kitchen speculating on what new clues the puzzle might contain, and with each pass of the refrigerator, yanked open the door and stared dismally into its vacant interior. I could run down to the store and get some eggs, she thought, then canceled the idea with a quick shake of her head.

On her tenth trek between rooms, she heard the unmistakable sound of footsteps on her porch. She raced to the front door and threw it open, only to find the postman stuffing the daily deliveries into her mailbox.

"Thanks, Victor," she said, then retreated into the house and impatiently leafed through the mail. It contained two catalogues, a copy of *Art on the Move*, the water bill, and a thick letter-sized envelope adorned with four colorful Egyptian postage stamps. It was from Garet.

Back in the kitchen, Belle dropped the mail on the counter. She was tempted to leave Garet's letter there, too, but instead sighed, grabbed a knife from the top drawer and slit open the envelope. The letter read:

Dear Annabella,

Egypt continues to enthrall. The country, or more accurately, these ancient burial *arenas*, if you will, seem to have bewitched my soul. In the evenings, the air becomes redolent with the majestic personae of long-removed royalty. They transport me to a place so far sequestered from the turbulent world we inhabit that I find it difficult to communicate with the mere mortals who labor within this workaday globe.

My news is both stimulating and bittersweet. As the months have passed, I've searched the Egyptian sands for words that will communicate the perplexities with which I live my daily life—the passions and confusions that color my veins—

She sighed aloud; Garet's ponderous prose suddenly seemed stilted and stifling, and she stared at the ensuing pages as if daring any meaningful message to leap out, but the doorbell interrupted her effort. Belle tossed the letter on the counter and darted for the door. When she flung it open, she found Rosco standing before her.

"What took you so long?" she said.

He looked at his watch. "Twenty minutes, that's all."

She glanced at her own wristwatch. "You're right . . . Well, it seemed longer . . . Where's the puzzle?"

"In this file case." He held up the red box. "May I come in?"

"Oh, sure, sorry. Let's go to my office; we can work in there."

"I'm not going to say it again, but I wish you'd called me last night."

"Don't say it again."

"You could've woken me up. I wouldn't have minded."

"I thought you weren't mentioning the subject again."

"I'm not."

"It certainly sounded that way."

Rosco shook his head slowly. "Okay, not another word, I swear."

In Belle's office, he sat in his usual spot, the black-and-white director's chair. Belle settled in behind her desk.

"You don't happen to have have any food in the house, do you?" He patted his stomach for effect. "I skipped breakfast and I'm starved."

Belle glanced up at the ceiling. "I would have had eggs, but they're gone . . . ditto the meat loaf . . . Would you like some licorice?"

"I was thinking of something a trifle more nutritious." Rosco handed her the envelope containing Briephs' fourth crossword puzzle. "Here," he said, "you can figure that thing out while I concentrate on the bank records . . . On second thought, where's that licorice?"

"In the jar on the bookshelf. Behind you." She studied the envelope. "Well, at least this proves it was mailed through the post office. That lets Bartholomew Kerr off the hook, doesn't it?"

"Not necessarily."

"Why not?"

"How do you know he didn't mail it himself?"

"Hmm, I see your point." She pulled the puzzle from the envelope and unfolded it. After glancing through the clues, she said, "This is great, Rosco! Look at this; 37-Across. It's a quotation from Shakespeare that I don't know."

He looked up from Briephs' bank records. "Don't you have one of those books that lists every famous quote?"

"You mean a *Bartlett's*?"

"Right. I mean you, of all people, should have one."

"Of course I own one."

"So, look it up."

"Are you crazy!? Are you out of your mind?" Belle stared, astonished that he could suggest such a heinous act.

"No. I'm not crazy. Look it up. It'll save time."

"Are you absolutely bonkers? I can't look it up."

"Why not?"

"That's cheating . . . I mean, I could in a dire situation . . . but I shouldn't have to . . . I'll work on the Down column until I learn the answer." Belle concentrated on the puzzle, muttering to herself as she worked. "4-Down: *Nothing but* _____ . . . Darn, that's tough . . . 7-Down . . . another long one . . . 21-Down . . . Oh, who doesn't know that! . . . 22-Down: *Johnny Yuma: abbr.* . . . What could that possibly refer to . . . Yuma, Arizona? Yuman language . . . ?"

"Johnny Yuma was *The Rebel* . . . Sixties T.V. My mom loved it."

Rosco smiled at his own brilliance and returned to Briephs' financial statements. After a few minutes he set aside the bank statement and began paging through a money-market folder. He studied it slowly. He knew what he was looking for, and there was more than ample evidence—it didn't take a math whiz to find it. Over the past year there had been a number of unusually high cash withdrawals. Far too high for a man who also seemed accustomed to paying for nearly everything with an American Express card. Rosco picked one of Belle's red pens from a coffee mug and began to mark the withdrawals he deemed suspicious. When he'd finished, he raised his eyes and watched Belle fill in the final few answers on the puzzle. The effort made her face glow. After she'd inked in the last letter, she slammed her red Bic pen onto her desk and shouted, "Hah! Done!"

"And what's the Shakespeare quote?"

" '*Truth will come to* LIGHT; MURDER CAN'T *be hid long*,' from *The Merchant of Venice*." She smiled. " . . . And yes, I double-checked with the Bard . . . It should be *cannot* instead of CAN'T; that's why Briephs placed the *Var.* in here." She pointed at the clue for 37-Across. "And the reason I didn't recognize it."

"Are you saying you have all of Shakespeare at your fingertips?"

Belle flushed scarlet. "Not all . . . far from *all* . . . but when your parents are spouting lines from his plays and sonnets, and you're a child of five or six or seven, well, let's just say, I'm not as adept at quoting Dr. Seuss . . . It's Shakespeare's take on Cervantes' *Murder will out*, by the way." Again, she looked supremely embarrassed.

Rosco nonchalantly took a bite from his licorice stick and leaned back in the director's chair. "If you want to get picky, it's actually the other way around; Cervantes started *Don Quixote* in 1605, about eight years after *The Merchant of Venice* was first performed at the Globe Theatre. So if anybody had a *take* on anybody else, it was Cervantes, not old Bill."

This statement left Belle stuttering. "W-w-what? W-w-where did that come from? Are you sure about that? I mean, those dates? How did you discover that?"

"Look it up. I read *Don Quixote de la Mancha* in college. Maybe one of the only things I *did* read. But I loved it. What else do you want to know? The sky's the limit."

" 'The sky's the limit'?"

"That's a paraphrase from the book. 'No limits but the sky' is the actual wording."

" . . . And fifteen letters, too . . ." Belle counted them off on her fingers. "I'll have to put that into one of my puzzles some day. Amazing." Belle found her eyes glued to Rosco. She suddenly realized there was an entire life she wanted to know more about.

"Well, anyway"—she broke her stare with a slight toss of her head—"it's obviously a message, wouldn't you say?"

"I'm on your side . . . Any more names in it?"

"No, but 20-Across is MISTRESS, which could be pointing the finger at Betsey Housemann . . . Also the clue for 53-Across: *Cheat catcher*? . . . And there's tons of references to death: 14-Across: *Hang 'em* HIGH; 65-Across: REST *in peace*; 6-Down: *Dead man's hand*; ACES *and eights;* 11-Down: *Death* TRAP; 58-down: *dead* AS A *doornail*. There are also a bunch of clues and answers concerning truth. And number 7-down: CROSSWORD PUZZLE."

"Meaning . . . ?"

Belle walked to the licorice jar. "I don't know, Rosco. But it's unusual. I'm convinced we'll find the murderer's identity revealed somewhere in these puzzles."

"Maybe not . . . If it's a tease, and Briephs' intention was to make the killer so nervous he'd trip himself up, the clues may be too cryptic for us to recognize . . . My hunch is that only the murderer might get them."

"He . . . Or she."

"Right . . . Well, there's some rather interesting items in

these financial records. No large deposits, but there are a number of very large withdrawals. Which means some-body may have been blackmailing Briephs, and not the other way around. There's also a bunch of two hundred-dollar withdrawals from a cash machine located at 102 Hawthorne Place—the old customs house."

"The bus station?"

"Yep."

"Why would someone like Thompson Briephs go to the bus terminal? He wasn't the type to take public trans-portation anywhere."

"I don't know. It doesn't make sense." Rosco leaned across Belle's desk and lifted the envelope that had con-tained the puzzle. "This was mailed from downtown, ac-cording to the zip code on the cancellation stamp. The same zip code as the *Herald* office. The bus station is one zip code to the east."

"So . . . ?"

"I'm just thinking out loud; looking for a connection, anything. I mean, who's mailing these? If it's not the killer, why doesn't the person step forward? And again, why would the killer mail them?"

Belle crossed back to her desk. "We need the fifth cross-word. That's all there is to it."

"What we need is to know why Briephs went to the bus station to withdraw cash when there's an ATM a block from his office." Rosco reached for Belle's phone and punched in a memorized number. "Do you mind?"

"Who are you calling?"

"The police. It's time to share some facts."

Belle scooped up the crossword puzzles. "You're not giving these up, are you?"

Rosco held up his hand. Lever was on the line. "Al, it's Rosco. Can you spare a few minutes, in say"—he glanced at his watch—"half an hour . . . ? Thanks, I'll see you then."

He replaced the receiver and looked at Belle. "No, I'm not giving him the puzzles. It would take me a week to convince Lever there was something concrete in them. I'm having enough trouble explaining that to myself. But I need to find out what he's discovered. I'll share our information on the money market account and ATM withdrawals; maybe it will jibe with something he's got." Rosco picked up the red file box and stood.

Belle said, "You know, that fifth puzzle could have been mailed to anyone, and there's no reason on earth they would even think to bring it to you . . . or to me."

"I'm hoping it's been sent to someone with more brains than that. It might've even been sent to Lever. I'll know soon enough."

"Will you call me?"

"If Al has that puzzle, you'll be the first to know. Keep your pencil sharpened . . . sorry . . . pen."

Belle smiled, walked Rosco to the door and watched him drive off. After that, she ambled back into her kitchen and retrieved Garet's letter. Her large gray eyes squinted into a frown as her husband's verbiage grew clearer.

Finished reading, she marched into her office and stuffed both letter and envelope into her paper shredder; then she turned around and looked through the open office door at the quiet perfection of her home. *"Love's Labour's Lost,"* she said.

The phone rang as she spoke.

"Belle Graham," she said into the receiver.

"This is St. Joseph's Hospital. Mr. Polycrates said he could be reached at this number."

"Oh . . . yes . . . of course. He's on the other line at the moment. May I take a message?"

"JaneAlice Miller has regained consciousness. Mr. Polycrates asked to be kept informed."

"Thank you. I'll see that he gets the message." Belle dropped the receiver into its cradle and grabbed her car keys.

CHAPTER

31

WHEN ROSCO STEPPED into Al Lever's office, the lieutenant was just finishing another of his minute-long cigarette smoker's paroxysms. He looked up at Rosco and said, "Dang this cough. Have a seat, Poly—Crates. What have you got?"

"What have you got, Al?"

"Besides these darn allergies, everything I have points to a jealous husband . . . except for one thing."

"What's that?"

"Housemann didn't do it."

"You sound pretty certain."

Lever lit a cigarette and tossed the match into an ashtray already overflowing with fifteen crushed butts. "Carlyle places Briephs' time of death at sometime Friday afternoon—not long after he left the *Herald* offices. He passed through the yacht club gate twenty minutes after he left downtown. Obviously he went straight home."

"Not *quite* straight home. He made a detour to the bus station, where he pulled two hundred bucks out of a cash machine." Rosco handed Lever the bank statement on Briephs' account.

"Where did you get this?"

"A certain lady seems to have taken a shine to me."

Lever studied the paper for a moment. "The two hundred wasn't there when we found the body. There was only a twenty-dollar bill in the house. Sitting near the silver tray on the bureau. Right out in the open—along with his Rolex. That's why we ruled out robbery so quick. The killer didn't bother to look for the stuff."

"Makes sense . . . Here, look at these." Rosco handed Lever two more bank statements. "He'd been pulling a couple of hundred dollars out of that same machine on a regular basis. My guess is he was using the money on the spot. Either he was seeing a hooker, or we're looking at some form of small-time blackmail. I go with blackmail." He handed the lieutenant Briephs' money market balance sheet and pointed to the places he'd marked with Belle's red pen. "Look at these cash withdrawals. Eleven hundred three weeks ago, five hundred before that. Go back four months . . . There's one for three grand. Erratic, to say the least."

"Not to mention the bus station withdrawals. Why two bills? Why there?"

"Right. There aren't any professionals working the bus

station now. Besides, if Briephs made it to the yacht club in twenty minutes, he wouldn't have had any time for hanky-panky elsewhere."

Lever scratched the back of his head and tossed the bank statements onto his desk. "Thanks, Rosco, I appreciate your help . . . I think. Okay, here's what I have: Pay attention, it gets seamy. Housemann couldn't have killed Briephs, because he was off for a little 'love in the afternoon' with Shannon McArthur. My sources are tight on that, so it clears them both."

"Bartholomew Kerr?"

"He didn't leave the *Herald* offices until seven-thirty Friday night, then went straight to the Ludlow Gallery for an 'installation'-artist's opening—some guy who 'refocuses televisions while wearing only boxer shorts'—as an audience watches, natch. Don't ask. Anyway, Kerr took Housemann's secretary with him. They spent the night together. One big happy family over at the *Herald*."

Rosco folded his arms over his chest, leaned back in the chair and placed his feet on the corner of Lever's desk. The lieutenant put his feet on the opposite corner. They sat quietly for a minute. Then Lever said, "Your blackmail theory is nice, Rosco, but it's only a sideshow. Briephs obviously made his two-bill drop and went home. If anything, it only clears the blackmailer of murder. Why kill the goose that lays the golden egg? No, I'm pointing the finger at Betsey Housemann. I think Briephs dumped her and she went to the island for revenge. It's as simple as that."

"You'll never prove it, Al." Rosco stood and collected Briephs' bank records into a neat pile. "I told Mrs. Briephs

I'd return these, but after giving them the once-over I think you should hang onto them. She'll understand. She wants this solved as much as we do." He crossed to Lever's door. "Oh, one other thing, Al."

"What's that?"

"Do you know any feds over at customs?"

"A few. What's up?"

"A guy by the name of Garet Kaine Burke. Could they check with the passport boys and see if he's still in Egypt? Or if he's reentered the States?"

Lever's loud laugh quickly worked its way into another coughing fit. It ended with, "Rosco, you're a dog, you know that?"

"Yeah, well, you can't be too careful with these things." As he spoke, Rosco found himself mentally counting the number of letters in Garet's name. "I'll keep you posted if I find anything else."

About three minutes after Rosco left, a police sergeant entered the same door without knocking. "Oh, sorry, Lieutenant, I didn't see you come back from the briefing room." He handed Lever a pink message slip. "This came in fifteen minutes ago. JaneAlice Miller has regained consciousness."

CHAPTER

32

HURRYING TO ST. Joseph's Hospital, Belle decided to make a quick detour. Stopping at Robertson's Flower Shop, she purchased a dozen long-stemmed yellow roses, and asked to have them wrapped in especially cheery paper. After a nurse ushered her into JaneAlice's room, the roses formed an instantaneous bond between the two women. Belle decided she was the first person to have given flowers to Thompson Briephs' secretary.

"They smell wonderful," JaneAlice managed despite her swollen, purple jaw.

"Everyone was worried sick about you," Belle said with an encouraging smile, "both at the *Herald* and the *Crier*. This whole thing has shocked Newcastle to the bone. How are you feeling?"

"Pretty bruised and sore, and I'm not allowed to eat solid

food yet. Just sip out of straws . . . I'm surprised I'm not hungrier than I am . . . Do the police have any idea who murdered poor Mr. Briephs?"

Belle was on the alert in an instant. "How did you know he'd been murdered?"

JaneAlice's eyes stared back out of her battered face. "That's what I was told . . . The nurses, you know . . . As soon as I came to . . . I guess I'm kind of a celebrity . . . On account of being involved . . ."

Belle considered this response, trying to decide whether or not it removed JaneAlice from the list of suspects, and then wondering how Rosco would proceed. She opted for caution masked in honesty for her reply.

"No . . . They don't seem to have any concrete leads as yet . . . I guess they're hoping you can describe the person who attacked you and stole Thompson's puzzles . . . that there might be a connection . . . Actually, I'm surprised Lieutenant Lever hasn't arrived yet. The nursing station said he was called half an hour ago."

"Stole the puzzles?" JaneAlice murmured weakly.

Another jolt of disbelief flashed through Belle's brain. "Thompson's last three puzzles . . . Your assailant must have stolen them from you. No one at the *Herald* has been able to find them."

A nurse entered with a large vase, handed it silently to Belle and left. Belle filled the container with water and began arranging roses; as she worked, she continued what she hoped JaneAlice would mistake for casual conversation. "Actually two of the crosswords have shown up in the mail . . ."

"Two? I mailed all three of them."

Belle dropped the remaining roses on the windowsill and turned to face JaneAlice. "*You* mailed them?"

"I was afraid to keep them. He said he'd kill me if I didn't hand them over, but I couldn't tolerate the thought of his destroying them. They were Mr. Briephs' final accomplishment. His epitaph, as it turned out." Through the patient's bruised and swollen lips came the unmistakable sound of crying, but Belle decided to pursue her interrogation.

"*Him?* You were attacked by a man?"

"Oh, yes."

"Did you recognize him?"

"No. I'd never seen him before in my life."

Belle began counting the men JaneAlice might have recognized: Steven Housemann, Bartholomew Kerr, Pat Anderson—the entire *Herald* staff.

"JaneAlice . . . dear . . . there's an actor playing the part of John Wilkes Booth down at—"

"Oh, Vance, he's such a lovely young thing. A close friend of Mr. Briephs. No, it wasn't Vance. Vance wouldn't hurt a fly. He's very handsome . . . like a young Sylvester Stallone, don't you think?"

"In a bovine sort of way," Belle muttered while she continued fussing with the roses. After a moment, she resumed her disinterested tone. "So, you mailed those puzzles yourself?"

"Yes."

"Who did you mail them to?"

JaneAlice didn't answer. Instead, she waited for Belle to turn and face her. "I don't know . . ."

"You don't know?"

"No, I mean, I don't know if I should tell you. I'm afraid you'll get mad at me."

"Oh, JaneAlice, I'd never get mad. Why would I do a thing like that?"

A guilty grin twisted across JaneAlice's unhappy face. "Well, Mrs. Graham—"

"Call me Belle, please."

"Well, Belle, this person called me. Threatened me. The voice made me think of that Clint Eastwood movie, *Play Misty for Me*. Have you ever seen it?"

"No."

"It's awfully scary. Jessica Walter co-stars as a woman obsessed . . . Anyway, I guess I had Mr. Eastwood on my mind because I decided the puzzles should go to *The Good, the Bad, and the Ugly*. After that nasty telephone call, I was convinced they revealed the name of Mr. Briephs' murderer; that's why the killer wanted them so badly . . . But I'm not very good at cryptics—despite working for Mr. Briephs for so many years—and he left no answers to the clues . . . I guess what I hoped was that one of the three people would become sufficiently intrigued . . ."

Belle was beginning to lose her patience, but she retained her warm smile. "And who were the *three* people, JaneAlice?"

"You don't know? They didn't get them?"

"JaneAlice!" Belle snapped, then caught herself and pasted another smile on her face. "As I said, dear; *two* have been received. The *third* is still missing."

"Well, the *Ugly* is Mr. Kerr. Anyone could have told you

that. The way he snoops around the *Herald* offices . . . Always burrowing around looking for dirt and unpleasantness . . . And he's not a real gentleman . . . No matter how much he tries to act the part. I remember one time—"

"Yes," Belle interrupted, "I'm sure . . . Who else did you mail the puzzles to, *dear*?"

"Well, the *Good* of course is Mr. Briephs' mother. Some people find her gruff, but she's always been more than cordial with me . . . even when Mr. Briephs was in one of his *moods*, and threatened to fire me. Mrs. Briephs could always be counted on to calm her son, and make him understand how important a good secretary can be. She really is a good person, you know. How is she, by the way?"

"Just fine." Belle could feel her teeth grinding into one another and tension spreading through her jaw. "And who might the *Bad* be, JaneAlice?"

"Oh, I thought you would have guessed by now."

"I suppose not."

JaneAlice missed the sarcasm in Belle's response; instead she began laughing softly. "I can't believe you haven't."

"No . . . I haven't guessed, JaneAlice."

"But it's you. *You're* the Bad. Because you work for that other newspaper. I hope you're not cross with me."

"You mailed it to me? But I never received it! Are you sure you had the correct address?"

"You live on Captain's Walk, don't you?"

"Yes."

"I thought if the other two weren't sufficiently interested in solving the puzzles, you would be. Oh, well, I guess it must be lost in the mail. It happens all the time, you know."

"But, JaneAlice, we need that last puzzle to find out who killed Mr. Briephs. Did you make copies?"

"Oh my, no. I didn't want them anywhere near me . . . Oh, I do hope I did the right thing—"

Belle walked to the window, picked up the three remaining roses and stuffed them into the vase. Then she balled up the wrapping paper and jammed it into the trash basket; the activity only partially relieved her mounting frustration. How does Rosco tolerate this interrogation business? she wondered. Then her previous suspicions returned full-bore. Perhaps the simpering secretary routine was merely an act. Maybe JaneAlice wasn't as dumb—or as docile—as she seemed. Or could she and her mysterious assailant have been partners who'd plotted Briephs' murder and subsequently argued? Or had the mugging merely been a random act of violence unconnected to the murder? Belle glued a polite smile to her lips. "I'm sorry I can't stay longer, JaneAlice, but I have a deadline. I'm sure you know what that's like."

"Oh, yes. Deadlines used to be torture for Mr. Briephs."

Belle walked to the door, opened it, but turned back to the room with a final question. "JaneAlice, dear, have you ever met Mr. Briephs' uncle, Senator Hal Crane?"

"Oh, yes, he's a lovely man. Did you know he's in Southeast Asia right now? He sent us a postcard from Hue."

"Yes, I know. Actually he's returning today. Anyway, there's a man who works for the Senator. His name is John Bulldog Roth. Have you ever seen or met him?"

"No, I don't think so . . . Is he good-looking?"

"If your taste runs to attack dogs."

"Is he married?"

"I doubt it."

"Well, don't worry about the puzzle, Belle, *The Postman Always Rings Twice.*" JaneAlice tried to laugh at her little joke, but a sharp pain in her side quickly erased any evidence of a smile.

Before Belle left the hospital, she phoned the post office and asked to speak with a supervisor. She was told it would be almost impossible to locate a missing letter—and that she should wait. If it didn't turn up in three months, they would "attempt" to put a trace on it. When the supervisor was informed the letter had neither been registered nor dispatched by overnight service, Belle was greeted by an annoyed sigh and a curt, "Well, we can't be held responsible for every insignificant piece of paper that passes through the system."

"Thank you," Belle responded. "You've been most helpful."

Her sarcasm was wholly lost on her listener.

The drive back to her house seemed to take forever. She was tempted to speed, but then realized there was nothing waiting for her. Even if the puzzle had been only slightly delayed, there wouldn't be another delivery until the next morning. Nonetheless, she checked her mailbox before opening the front door. It was empty. She walked into the kitchen and opened the refrigerator before remembering that it, too, was empty. She then sat on a stool, placed her elbows on the counter, rested her face in the palms of her hands and sighed.

Out of boredom, she reached for Garet's latest copy of *Art on the Move* and began leafing through it, back to front. The last few pages of the glossy magazine were filled with classified ads for various pieces of artwork, as well as outrageously priced real estate properties in North Carolina and Connecticut. The next section was dedicated to a listing of curators who had changed positions or moved to different museums. After that, Belle came to the only portion of the magazine she found remotely interesting: photographs of stolen artwork which the editors believed all collectors and curators should be apprised of.

She flipped slowly through the pages and on the third spotted a small and somewhat blurred photo of an amphora executed in a red-and-black design. She tried to go on to the next page but her eyes kept returning to the one picture. The caption beneath the photo explained the piece's provenance; it also stated that it had been stolen from a museum in Istanbul six months before. Present whereabouts unknown.

"Not anymore," Belle murmured; she was convinced it was one of the pieces she'd seen in Thompson Briephs' home the previous morning. She tossed the magazine onto the kitchen counter and darted into Garet's home office where she began tearing through previous issues of *Art on the Move*. In almost half the magazines she discovered a piece she recognized from Windword Islands.

"It's all stolen!" she exclaimed. "Rosco's not going to believe this!" She hurried toward her own office, but as she passed through the kitchen she noticed the latest copy of *Art on the Move* had fallen to the floor. She stooped to pick

it up, and as she did so, a business-size envelope slipped
from the pages and slid beneath the stove.

"Oh, darn." Belle pulled a large knife from a drawer, got
down on her hands and knees and extracted the envelope.
It was addressed to her. The handwriting was the same
shaky scrawl that had been scribbled across Sara Briephs'
envelope. Belle tore it open. Inside was the fifth crossword.

Across

1. Pendleton, maybe?
6. Deadly one
9. Jester
14. Walk-on
15. Nucleic acid
16. Shortwave
17. Error's partner
18. Gullet
19. Correct
20. Elvis said it best
23. Duct
24. Center
25. 100 yrs.
26. It's a trap!
27. Certain Nicaraguan
30. French for 42-Across
33. Own, Scottish
34. Scrap
36. Senator's bagman
41. Marlins' home: abbr.
42. So long!
43. Classic lover?
44. I was one!
47. Swedish import
49. Gun grp.
50. 50%
51. It's often enclosed: abbr.
54. Porky Pig said it best
57. "I have ___ eye, Uncle," Shak.
59. L.A. time
60. Elis and Tigers
61. Where to dump hot stuff?
62. Resident of, suffix
63. Pawnee home
64. Travels
65. ___Beatty
66. No longer the Shah's?

Down

1. You won't find 43-Across here
2. Magna ___
3. Something's ___
4. Average
5. Pony gang?
6. Gun locker
7. It's a trap!
8. Where to dump hot stuff? slang
9. Cowardly
10. Mourn
11. German river
12. "Heads, I ___!"
13. Doze
21. Court
22. Rental car class: abbr.
26. Murderer's retirement home?
27. "El ___," Heston film
28. Space
29. "The ___ of Rhetorique," Wilson
30. Indy inits.
31. Hand-out
32. "If ___ a Hammer"
33. Tankard filling
35. In spite of, informal
37. WW II craft
38. Songlike: abbr.
39. Wall flowers?
40. Steal
45. Owe
46. Baseball deals
47. Like some nuts
48. "Death closes___," Tennyson
50. Waste maker
51. ___ Mickey to: drug

PUZZLE #5

52. "___ intelligent mind,"
Aristophanes
53. Curves
54. Chime
55. ___ control
56. "It's all ___," Cosell
57. Rear
58. ECM member

CHAPTER

33

AFTER BELLE FINISHED inking in the answers to the final puzzle, she grabbed the telephone and punched in Rosco's office number, then smiled to herself and thought, This is a good sign, I have the number memorized. The phone rang four times and was picked up by an answering machine. She left no message, instead hanging up and trying his car phone. There was no response there, either. Belle returned her attention to Briephs' puzzle, hunkered down in her chair and studied the words and clues. All at once, everything seemed to fall into place.

She'd been certain the killer's name would contain fifteen letters, and there it was, revealed in stark black and white—36-Across: JOHN BULLDOG ROTH. The other two long answers—20-Across: IT'S NOW OR NEVER, and 54-Across: THAT'S ALL FOLKS, served to further convince her that every mysterious link had been solved in this final puzzle. She began thinking out loud.

"56-Down: *It's all* OVER; 48-Down: *Death closes* ALL; 57-Across: *I have* A GOOD *eye, Uncle*, and 12-Down: *Heads I* WIN. Again Briephs mentions himself, but this time employing the past tense—44-Across: EDITOR. He *was* an editor. The entrapment clues are also repeated—26-Across: PLOY; 7-Down: SNARE."

Without taking her eyes off the crossword, Belle carried it to her bookcase and pulled a licorice stick from the jar. She continued talking to herself while she chewed the candy. "All the references to the stolen artwork are here too . . . Roth simply *must* have been involved . . . 40-Down: ROB; 61-Across: FENCE; 8-Down: PAWN—three words with multiple definitions, yet Thompson maintained a thievery motif."

Once more, Belle tried Rosco's office; when his machine answered, she hung up without leaving a message, then called his car phone, but again failed to reach him. She returned to Garet's office and methodically searched through copies of *Art on the Move*, looking for photographs of stolen artwork she believed might have attracted Briephs, then tore out the relevant pages, tossing aside the butchered magazines. After she'd collected eight pages, she hurried back to her office, scooped up the five crossword puzzles and placed everything in a manila envelope. I need concrete evidence, she decided as she opened the phone book and located the number for the harbormaster. Peter Kingsworth answered her call on the second ring.

"Oh, Peter, I'm so glad you're in." Belle laid on a heavy dose of charm. "Could you do me the *biggest* favor? I need to make another trip to Windword Islands, and the mechanic hasn't finished repairing my boat yet. Is it at all possible for you to motor me out in half an hour? I won't be long—"

"Well, I'm working right now . . ."

"You could drop me off and return for me at your convenience . . ."

There was a long pause before he agreed. "Sure . . . why not? I'll need to rearrange a few things first, though. Is half an hour okay?"

"Thank you, Peter. You're a peach."

"A peach!" was his startled response.

"How about: 'You're terrific'?"

"I like that description better," she heard him reply. "You should wear a bathing suit. It's beautiful out here today."

After hanging up, Belle grabbed her manila envelope and headed for the door, but stopped short of opening it. She stood for a moment, crossed to the living room phone, then tried Rosco's office once more. Again, his machine answered; this time she left a message.

"You're not going to believe this, Rosco; I have the fifth puzzle, and it's Roth! He's *in* the puzzle—his *name* is there! Spelled out in capital letters. Roth killed Briephs! The murder involves stolen artwork . . . I don't have full details yet, but I'm on top of the situation . . . I'll call you later. Don't worry, though . . . I won't do anything to hinder your investigation or compromise evidence . . . But I need to confirm my suspicions before Roth returns from Washington."

CHAPTER

34

PETER KINGSWORTH WAS all smiles as Belle walked down the pier. Reaching out with a muscular hand, he helped her down onto the launch's aft deck.

"It's good to see you again, Belle. I thought you were going to wear your swimsuit?"

"No, this is a business trip."

"Crossword business?" Peter joked. "You know the police have put yellow crime-scene tape up all around the house? I don't think you're supposed to cross it . . . Sorry, no pun intended . . . Besides, the house is locked."

Belle reached into her pocket and pulled out the key to Windword, which she'd forgotten to return to Rosco after their previous visit. She showed it to Peter, but kept the explanation to herself.

Peter revved the launch's engine and headed for Windword Islands. The day was humid and airless, but as the boat gained speed, a breeze lifted Belle's hair and spread it out behind her like a pale gold cloud.

"I have to patrol the harbor," Peter shouted over the engine's throb, "but I'll drop you off and pick you up in about half an hour. How's that?"

"That's great. I really appreciate your help."

"No problem . . . I don't know how to say this, but—" Peter turned and looked into Belle's eyes.

"What?"

"The police have asked me to keep an eye on Briephs' place. You know, let them know if anyone tries to do some snooping around . . ."

"The police know I'm visiting, Peter. They were the ones who gave me the key."

"You're going out on police business?"

Belle began wishing that Rosco was there with her; he was far better at deception than she. "Well . . . actually . . ." she faltered. "What I . . ."

"You have to speak up. I can't hear you."

"Well—" Belle raised her voice, "I lost my reading glasses, and . . . and I think I must have dropped them in Briephs' house somewhere. I can't work without them. The police said they were all finished . . . at the island, that is. So they allowed me to borrow the key. I have to give it right back."

"Oh—" Peter shrugged. "You'd think they would've taken down the tape if they were done."

"I think they intend to remove it tomorrow."

Peter brought his face back into the wind and adjusted his course slightly. They traveled the remainder of the way in silence, although Belle had the distinct feeling he was sneaking glances at her. After he'd eased the launch close to Briephs' dock, Peter offered Belle his hand and helped her off the boat.

"I wish you'd worn a bathing suit," he said. "I'll bet you look great in one."

Belle gave him a big smile.

Peter returned it, displaying nearly every tooth in his mouth. "I'll be back in a half hour, forty-five minutes max. Don't get lost." He laughed good-naturedly and angled the launch toward the marina's perimeter.

Belle hurried down the dock, ducked under the yellow crime-scene tape, opened the front door and stepped inside. The foyer showed no signs of the police having been there. She found her way to the kitchen, where she discovered the detectives hadn't been quite so tidy. A number of water glasses sat on the counter, along with a dirty ashtray. Five or six empty packages of Polaroid film lay beside it.

Belle entered the living room, then circled back toward the labyrinth she and Rosco had discovered the previous day. She passed beneath the ancient stone lintel, paying particular attention to a faint but discernible relief carved on its underside. She wondered if the architectural element was also registered on some "missing artwork" list. After that, she stared at the doorway she and Rosco had exited—the one leading to the four cell-like rooms containing the empty caskets. Feeling the same strange chill she'd experienced previously, she glanced at the doorway Rosco had taken, shrugged her shoulders and thought, Why not? A change of scenery will do me good.

The rooms Belle traversed were precisely what Rosco had described: dungeonlike cubicles with leg irons and shackles attached to the walls. Reluctant as she was to look at these instruments of torture, she found her eyes drawn irresistibly toward them.

What Thompson did was no affair of hers, she decided, then forced herself forward. Like Rosco, Belle began opening doors that led into closet-sized rooms. In the increasing gloom, she wished she'd brought a flashlight. She found herself turning in circles, futilely slapping the rough stone in hopes of finding the light pads hidden in the shadows. Finally she heard the faint sound of water splashing into a pool. Clutching her manila envelope, she charged blindly toward the noise. After what seemed an interminable search, she entered the room containing the fountain and the statue of Athena.

Belle groped for the light pad; when she finally succeeded in finding it, she squinted as artificial daylight slowly filled the area. She focused her glance in an attempt to get her bearings, but the four archways and four walls were identical. She was no longer able to discern which one had been her point of entry.

"No matter," she mumbled. "I wouldn't follow that trail again if my life depended on it."

She watched the fountain slowly turning, then looked down at her envelope. She'd been clutching it so tightly she'd all but crumpled it. "Get a grip, Belle," she whispered aloud to give herself courage. "Briephs' office is only two rooms away. If you don't find it, you can turn back and try another route."

She followed her own advice and marched through the archway on her left, entering an empty corridor she believed she recognized. She jogged its length, expecting to find Briephs' outer office. But it wasn't there. The room in which she found herself was entirely different in appearance. It was a round cavern—a design appropriate to Minoan sacred sites, although in place of bas-reliefs depicting youths and bulls, the curved walls were covered with floor-to-ceiling smoked mirrors that garishly reflected and refracted the chamber's sole furnishing—what appeared to be an ancient altar, a perfectly square block adorned with four carved crossed axes. Reflexively, Belle took note, recalling the emblem as representing the vanished civilization. "Sacrifices to the half-man half-bull," she murmured. Large red and black leather pillows were scattered at the base of the walls. Four video cameras hung from the domed ceiling; in the pale incandescent light, they looked like sleeping fruit bats. Below each camera was a narrow arch leading into deeper darkness.

"Oh, yuck," Belle managed to whisper. She had no idea what use Briephs had made of the room, but her imagination was beginning to picture more than a few unpleasant scenarios. She retreated as she'd entered until she nearly fell into the chamber containing the fountain.

"Clockwise," she muttered. "I'll go clockwise."

She turned to her right and passed beneath the next archway. The palms of her hands were sweating heavily and the envelope had begun to stick to her fingertips. She eased her way through another corridorlike room, eventually reaching the other end—and an area wholly immersed in darkness. Not even the faint shape of the doorway was visible; she fumbled for the light pad, then stopped and turned. She had the feeling she wasn't alone.

"Rosco?" she said softly. "How did you know I was here?"

There was no answer.

Belle stood listening for a long, tense moment; she heard nothing.

It's just my imagination, she thought, trying to laugh as she ran her hand along the black walls, groping for the light pad. When at last she found it, the murky chamber sprang to life. She'd stumbled upon the room lined with bookcases. At the opposite end was the wooden door whose lock Rosco had picked.

"Thank goodness," Belle sighed aloud as she tugged the door open and tapped the light pad illuminating Briephs' hidden office. Everything was exactly as she and Rosco had left it. She pulled the eight *Art on the Move* photographs from the envelope. As she did, the five puzzles dropped to the floor.

"Darn."

She retrieved the puzzles, tossed them onto the desk and started comparing the photos to the statuary and amphorae. She had been correct about every single photo; each matched a piece in Briephs' collection.

So, where does Roth fit in? she wondered. Why did he kill Thompson? Belle began pushing the puzzles around the desk, half expecting the answers to those questions to jump out at her. She shuffled them around, placing one puzzle next to another, angling them upside down and sideways. Her eye kept returning to the middle puzzle, the third one. The word MURDERS was the key. She was sure of it. She circled the word with Thompson's pen.

"Maybe it wasn't Roth, after all," she muttered, now studying the fourth and fifth puzzles. She took the fourth puzzle and circled CROSSWORD PUZZLE. Then she moved to the fifth puzzle and circled EDITOR. She then put the words together.

"Somebody—MURDERS CROSSWORD PUZZLE EDITOR!" Belle nearly shouted. In a quieter tone she continued. "But if that's true, then the murderer's name *has* to appear in the first two puzzles and not in the fifth. Roth's name doesn't show up until the last crossword . . ." She pondered this supposition. "As Rosco said, whoever attacked JaneAlice had to have noticed a word or phrase that triggered a reaction. It had to come from the very first puzzle . . ."

Belle picked up the two crosswords that had appeared in the *Herald*. Again she held them upside down and sideways, murmuring as she did so: "No names except Thompson's in the first puzzle . . . the second has SENATOR HAL CRANE, STEVEN HOUSEMANN and JOHN WILKES BOOTH . . . all of whom profess airtight alibis . . ."

She shuffled the first two puzzles once more. Okay, she said, thinking aloud, "Let's settle down and figure this thing out." She sat behind Briephs' desk, picked up his pen and studied the *Herald*'s Monday crossword. "The first puzzle should have the killer's first name. That would make sense, right? What do we have here . . . ALDO? No. We don't know any Aldos in Newcastle . . . ASTA? Nope, no Astas.

SLIM? No . . . RAE? Nope. DOODLE?" Belle chuckled and waved the pen in the air. " 'Yankee Doodle came to town, riding on a pony, he stuck a feather in his hat, and called it macaroni!' "

She continued chortling as she brought her eyes back to the puzzle. "I sincerely doubt if Yankee Doodle Dandy killed Thompson Briephs." She let out a weary sigh, rubbed her eyes and resumed her pensive monologue. "Okay, so, what else do we have . . . ? Let's see . . . PUMPKIN? No. I know no one named Pumpkin in Newcastle . . ." She laughed again and unconsciously began reciting a nursery rhyme. " 'Peter, Peter Pumpkin-Eater.' "

As soon as the words were out of her mouth, Belle sat up straight in Briephs' chair. Her eyes raced back to the word PUMPKIN. Another icy chill swept her. She lifted the pen. Her hand trembled as she circled PUMPKIN. She grabbed the second puzzle and scanned it. The word EATER leapt from the page. She circled it, murmuring, "PUMPKIN EATER MURDERS CROSSWORD PUZZLE EDITOR."

Belle put her face in her hands. No wonder he figured it out so quickly, she decided. I should have realized the main clue had to be within the first puzzle. Rosco even mentioned it. Aloud, she whispered, " 'Peter, Peter, Pumpkin-Eater—' "

"Had a wife and couldn't keep her."

Belle jerked her head up to see Peter Kingsworth's large frame filling the doorway. His charm and bright smile had vanished; instead, his face had assumed a wolfish, sinister stare.

"I'm surprised," he said. "I expected you to guess my identity sooner. 'Peter, Peter, Pumpkin-Eater. Had a wife and couldn't keep her.' Sorry about this, Belle. I don't think I can keep you either."

CHAPTER

35

"I'M AFRAID YOU'RE a little too smart for your own good," Peter said. "Who would have guessed anyone as pretty as you would have brains?" The muscles in his neck and jaw were stretched tight and the tension in his face forced his eyes into a vicious squint. "I thought my phone calls last night might have put a scare in you. Obviously I was wrong . . . You couldn't leave well enough alone, could you?"

Belle pushed the chair away from the desk, putting as much distance as possible between herself and Peter. "I don't know what you're talking about," she managed in a voice that cracked with fear. "These puzzles don't prove a single fact . . . We should forget the entire matter . . ."

"Peter, Peter, Pumpkin-Eater . . . ? Tommy-Boy loved that stupid phrase. Every time he saw me he used it. He thought he was so witty—as if he was the only person in the whole world to have ever said it to me. Ha! I've been listening to that idiotic nursery rhyme ever since I can remember. Tommy shortened it over the years; pared it down to plain 'Pumpkin.' You have no idea how annoying something like that can become."

"Listen, Peter, I don't want these crossword puzzles. You can keep them. I only came here to study Briephs' artwork. I believe some of the pieces are stolen. Mrs. Briephs wishes them returned to their rightful owners."

Peter laughed slowly and shook his head from side to side. "Oh, they're stolen, that's for sure. That much of it you've got right. But I sincerely doubt the old lady knows anything about it—let alone wants them returned. In fact, I doubt anyone even knows you're here."

"That's not true," Belle bluffed. "I told you, the police gave me the key. They're expecting it back this afternoon. If I don't return it, they'll come looking, I'm sure."

Again Peter laughed at Belle's attempted lie. "That's about as far from the truth as you can get. I radioed the police. They asked me to look out after the place, remember? Lever told me no one was expected for several days. I offered to remove the crime-scene tape, but he said the investigation wasn't finished."

Peter lifted his right hand. In it he held a four-foot length of heavy nylon rope. "I would be following police orders if I had to use extreme measures to stop a *burglary* in progress." He jerked the rope between his hands. "But there would be too many questions to answer if I did that . . . No, I think the only solution is to send you to the bottom of the ocean. Then, I'll be home free."

Belle began searching her brain for a way to stall for time and find an escape route. She glanced around the room. Peter took a step toward her, and she blurted out, "How did you discover that these pieces were stolen?"

He stopped advancing. "Everyone thinks I'm nothing but a big, brawny sea dog . . . that I don't understand anything . . . don't see things . . . But I caught the two of them, Roth and Tom-Boy, right in the marina parking lot. They looked like a couple of low-rent double agents out of a cheesy spy movie. Rather than just handing this package to Tommy, Roth has to throw his coat over it like he's some kind of *Get Smart* agent. I played dumb; made it look like I hadn't seen anything. But it didn't take a genius to figure out the two of them were up to something shady. And a couple of times I even ferried Roth out to Windword with packages. He held them like they contained eggs. Afraid to set them down in my boat. Any dope could have guessed what they were."

"Bulldog Roth swiped these pieces?"

"No. Someone as slick as Roth would never steal them himself. He's just a high-class fence. He brought them back to the U.S. under diplomatic immunity. No one searches his bags. He can bring anything he wants into the country. These guys get away with murder."

"I don't understand," Belle said, avoiding eye contact with Peter for fear it would incite him to action. "I mean, what did Roth get out of it?"

"I think Tommy had something on the Bulldog, and was blackmailing him into bringing the stuff back for him . . . That's where I got my own clever idea." There was a hint of pride in Peter's voice when he said this.

"What idea was that?"

"My little blackmail scam. I guess there's no harm in telling you about it. You won't be around much longer . . . See, I figured, what's good for the goose is good for the gander. If Briephs was blackmailing Roth, why shouldn't I do the same to Tommy-Boy? He antes up, or I go to the customs people and tell them about the hot artwork. Pretty much everything here came in from Turkey or Lebanon. I checked that out on my own—looked it up in a book."

"So that's why he was withdrawing that two hundred dollars on a regular basis. Why the bus depot?"

"That's where my drop was; in the lockers on the lower level. He didn't know it was me who was threatening to expose him. I was pretty clever about that. I made a bunch of notes from torn-up puzzles that looked like a real dummy had created them . . . and then kept changing the amounts from a few grand to five hundred to two hundred bucks to keep the creep guessing . . . My scheme would have lasted a long time if Tommy hadn't stiffed me last Friday. He broke the rules . . ."

Without thinking, Belle blurted, "But he made an ATM withdrawal just before he died."

"So he said. But I went to the usual drop and came away empty-handed. That's when I decided to up the ante and confront the cretin. I thought Tom-Boy would be real surprised, but he told me he'd already guessed my identity . . . said he had put my name in his puzzles . . . like a form of life insurance in case something 'ugly' happened. I didn't believe him."

"Until PUMPKIN showed up in Monday's newspaper."

The word made Peter's head jerk back. "Pumpkin!" he spat out. "Exactly! That's when I figured old Tom-Boy'd been telling the truth. I knew I had to get rid of the other puzzles, but that stupid JaneAlice outsmarted me."

Belle continued to glance surreptitiously around the room. Peter stood directly between her and the only exit. "JaneAlice has regained consciousness, Peter. If you don't believe me, call St. Joseph's. You know she'll identify you, don't you? Lieutenant Lever was on his way to interview her when I left the hospital."

"Don't you worry about old Miss Miller. Besides, Lever didn't mention anything about her describing her assailant." He tugged at the rope again. "I thought I'd finished her off in the garage. I'll be more careful next time."

Belle stood and started to work her way out from behind the desk.

"Where do you think you're going?" Peter demanded with a flick of the rope.

"Just over here." She pointed to the far corner of the room and the stone carving of a griffin. "I think I saw this piece in a museum in Cyprus three or four years ago . . . It's a sacred griffin, very rare . . ." She casually crossed the office and picked up the mythical beast. It weighed close to fifteen pounds, but Belle juggled it back and forth in her hands in an attempt to make it seem lighter. "So, what kind of dirt do you think Thompson had on Roth?"

"I don't know, but it must have been good."

Belle continued to play with the stone griffin. "Why did you kill him, Peter?"

"Who? Tommy? Like I said, because he stiffed me. I

went to the bus depot as usual, opened the locker we always used and came up empty."

"Maybe someone found the key and beat you to it?"

Peter slapped the nylon rope across the desk and shouted, "That's not my problem! It was Briephs' responsibility to see that the money was there! That's why I came looking for him." He twisted the rope tightly around his hands, making the veins in his forearms pop out from beneath his leathery skin. "Look at all this stuff! He could afford to cough up a lot more than he did. What's three thousand dollars to a guy like Thompson Briephs? I mean, just look at this . . . this weird house . . . that car of his . . . He has all these expensive things and what do I have? Nothing!"

"But he wouldn't pay last Friday, would he?"

"No! He refused . . . threatened to expose me as a black-mailer, said he'd tell people what I do down on Congress Street . . . I couldn't let him . . . I'd be ruined here at the yacht club."

Belle stared at the floor and shook her head as though in sympathy while Peter began walking toward her.

"And now it's you," he said. "You're the one who's got to go. Why didn't you stay away?"

Peter pulled the rope taut between his clenched hands and continued to approach Belle. When he was within two feet he raised the rope to chest level. "I hate to do this," he said. "You're so pretty."

Belle pulled the griffin close to her chest and waited for Peter to take his final step toward her. At the exact moment he had the rope behind her neck, Belle flung the statue at his foot.

Peter howled in pain and dropped the rope. His facial muscles contorted as he reached for his injured foot, which she was pretty sure was broken. Belle jabbed his shoulder with her fist sending him toppling to the floor. She jumped over his prone body and raced for the door. Peter reached out with one long arm to grab her ankle, just missing. She could almost feel his fingers pawing the air.

In the outer office, Belle slammed the door shut and frantically tried to lock it. Failing that, she grabbed a free-standing bookcase and sent it tumbling to the floor, kicking the books in an attempt to form a wedge but soon realizing it would offer little resistance to someone of Peter's size. She could hear him struggling to his feet. He began shouting obscenities, finally calling out, "You can run but you can't hide. I know this place like the back of my hand. I came to all of Tommy's little parties!"

Belle ran into the next room and down the corridor. Behind her she could hear Peter bashing his shoulder against the office door. She continued into the fountain room and watched the statue of Athena slowly turning in place. "Which way? Which door do I take?" she cried as she glanced around the room and the three remaining archways. "Which one? How do I get out of here?"

Belle began turning in a circle. "Clockwise, I traveled clockwise." She stood still and remained perfectly quiet. She could no longer remember through which door she'd entered. The sound of water dripping into the pool seemed to grow louder and louder until her ears ached. She tried to attune her hearing to any noise Peter might make, but she heard nothing outside of the dripping water.

"You can't hide from me!" Peter's voice suddenly echoed from the stone walls. It was impossible to tell from which direction the words came. Belle could hear his footsteps, a discordant clip-clop as he hobbled on his broken foot, and then a slapping sound, as he whipped his nylon rope against the damp walls. "You can't run far!" he cried. This was followed with a ringing laugh.

Peter was getting closer, but Belle was unable to determine through which archway he'd emerge. She pointed her finger around the room. "One potato, two potato, three potato, four." She dropped her hand and raced through the last archway she'd pointed to, but she found herself in another long and empty corridor. "Oh, no," she groaned. She knew she was either headed back toward Peter, or toward the stone altar she'd found earlier. Again, she listened intently. Peter's footsteps were definitely behind her. It was too late to turn back.

Belle ran the length of the corridor and through the arched doorway at the far end. As expected, she emerged staring at the ancient stone altar. "This time I keep my bearings," she murmured. There was an exit in each corner of the room. Belle had entered from one. She studied the other three and opted for the one directly opposite. She scurried around the altar and through the opening. The room before her was dimly lit, but she immediately realized there was no way out—other than going back to the altar chamber.

"So you've decided to visit Tommy's sacred site?" Somewhere behind her, Peter's voice reverberated off the wall while his hobbling footsteps grew ever louder.

Belle rubbed her palms together. They were dripping with sweat. Five seconds later Peter entered the altar room and froze, listening for Belle. She could feel her heart pounding in her chest and tried to limit her breathing for fear the sound would give her away.

"One potato, two potato? That's how you made up your mind, wasn't it? Sound travels for miles in here." Peter laughed. "I'm a man of the sea, Belle. I can't be so care-free. I set my course based on knowledge because my life depends upon it." Again he laughed. "If I have to find a lost boat, I speculate on how the navigator made his decision. You? You create word games. Your decisions will be based on linear thinking. Across and down. Horizontal and verti-cal. That's why you've been so easy to follow . . . I know ex-actly what choices you'll make."

Peter fell silent. Belle could hear him breathing. She re-mained motionless; pressing her hand against her heart in an attempt to silence it.

"The pain in my foot is pretty bad, Belle. I'm going to have to hurt you, too, when I catch you. It's only fair, don't you think? . . . But let's return to your predictability. We can discuss pain later . . . Now, I have a choice of three archways. The average man wouldn't know where to start, but I do. I look at the across and down and I tell myself Annabella Graham doesn't sneak out sideways, does she? No. She goes straight across."

Belle nearly screamed when she heard Peter's decision, but terror had frozen her vocal chords. She stood and lis-tened as Peter's irregular footsteps began their final approach. Get your bearings, she thought. Calm down, get your bearings and run. You can outrun him!

She darted back into the altar room. Peter took a swipe at her with his hank of rope as she passed, but she was too quick for him. She worked her way around the altar, keeping Peter on the opposite side. They were now separated by a six-foot square block of stone.

"Well done, Belle. But it does no good. Twice around this altar and I guarantee you'll have no idea which arch is the actual exit." He began circling counterclockwise forcing Belle to do the same. "The other three archways lead to dead-end rooms . . . and I do mean *dead*." Peter rested his rope on the stone. "An appropriate place to die, don't you think? A sacrificial altar?"

Belle mustered all her strength and squared off against him. "You're wrong, Peter," she declared. "I know a lot more than you think." She kept her eyes glued to his. "For instance, I can tell you precisely which museums Briephs' stolen pieces came from, and I can tell you where this altar came from . . . That rope of yours? I can list fifty different synonyms for it. Tell me when to stop: lasso, cord, riata, lanyard, jute, leash, painter, line, guy, lariat, cordelle, longe, strand, ratline, string, vang, hemp, bola, noose—"

"What's that prove?" A look of confusion swept over Peter's face. "What does that have to do with anything?"

Belle kept her eyes locked onto his. "Nothing. I'm just explaining I know more than you think. Another example: three-letter Hawaiian words: *lei, hoi, ava, hee, hui, koa, aku, imu, poi*. I could go on with about ten or fifteen more, but I'd hate to bore you."

"Who cares about this stuff?"

"Lots of people. Here's another one: four-letter Greek gods and goddesses: Ares, Hera, Leda, Cora, Nike, Hebe, Zeus, Eros, Gaia, Eris, and Leto. As you see, I have many facts at my fingertips. Like for instance"—she watched Peter's eyes closely—"I know exactly which of these doors leads back to the fountain."

Peter's gaze inadvertently shot to the archway on his left. Belle smiled. "Thank you, you've been a big help." She dashed through the opening, down another corridor and reemerged at the fountain.

"Very good, Belle," Peter bellowed in pursuit, "but you'll never find your way out of that room alive!"

"Don't count on it." Belle ran from archway to archway studying the floor. At the third entrance she saw what she was looking for: the dime Rosco had placed there. She grabbed it, then tore through the arch, past the four empty chambers until she came to the room containing Briephs' fax machine. She snatched up the receiver to call the police, but realized there wasn't enough time. She had to leave the house as quickly as possible. Hopefully, she'd be able to flag a passing motorboat.

Belle ran back to Windword's entry, reached for the door but stopped short of opening it. Through an almost invisible glass side panel she could see a moving shadow. He was waiting outside. Belle threw the dead bolt on the door just as he lowered his shoulder and plowed his full weight into the carved mahogany. The wooden doorjamb splintered and flew across the entryway while the entire door rocked on its hinges. Belle stood motionless as he stepped toward her and enfolded her in his arms.

"It's all over," Rosco said.

CHAPTER

36

R OSCO HELD BELLE in his bear hug for a full
minute, long enough for her to stop trembling.
Eventually she lifted her face from his shoulder
and looked at him.

"Where is he?" Rosco asked.

"I don't know." She dropped her head back into his
chest. "I thought it was Peter coming through the door.
You don't know how happy I am to see you." She clutched
him tightly.

"I'm happy to see you, too . . . in one piece. You're not
very good at following orders, are you?"

Belle stepped back and gave Rosco a wan smile. "I have
something to tell you, Rosco . . . I got a letter from Garet.
He said—"

"Is he armed?"

"Garet?"

"No. Peter."

"Oh . . . He has a rope, but I think that's the extent of it."

"We're in a certain amount of danger until we have Mister Peter, Peter Pumpkin-Eater under wraps," Rosco said in an understated tone. "You can fill me in on this letter business later."

"So you figured out the PUMPKIN-EATER clue?"

"Uh-huh. Then I checked with the mechanic at the marina. He said someone had dumped sugar in your tank—thus explaining the billowing white smoke. Peter must have gained access to your boat. It was a good way for him to keep tabs on us. We had to phone him every time we wanted to come out here."

Rosco pulled a .32 caliber semiautomatic pistol from a holster attached to the back of his belt. He took Belle's hand and led her to the far side of the foyer. "I want you to stay with me. Do not, I repeat, *do not*, wander off."

"That's not likely to happen. Peter probably knows this place better than Briephs did." Belle pointed to the hallway leading toward the fax machine. "You can't go down there, Rosco. He could be hiding anywhere. The place has more doors than a high-school locker room."

Rosco glanced down the corridor, then lowered his voice. "Well, he'll do one of two things—stand and fight or run for the hills."

"He's not running anywhere. His foot is broken."

"How did that happen?"

"Something fell on it."

"Tough luck . . . Well, he's not going to come after both of us with a broken foot. My guess is he'll try to return to his boat and vacate the island as soon as he can." Rosco squeezed Belle's fingers. "Let's give him a few minutes."

Belle was shocked. "You're not going to let him get away, are you?!"

Rosco released Belle's hand and reached into his pocket, pulling out a small green wire. "I may not be a yachtsman, but I do know how to disable an engine. It's not much different than a car. A spark-plug wire's a spark-plug wire, on land or sea. Peter's not going anywhere without this baby; and he'll be a lot easier to handle if he's trapped on the end of the dock."

"Speaking of your prowess on the high seas, how did you get out here?"

"Hitchhiked. On a lobster boat."

Belle shook her head and chuckled softly.

"It wasn't much fun for me or the lobsterman. The combination of the smell, the waves and the bucket of fish guts he was using for bait was a little too much for me. I was hanging over the side the entire way out."

Belle continued to smile until Rosco moved his finger to his lips, indicating that they should remain quiet. A faint sound of footsteps could be heard trudging unevenly outside; they were headed away from the house and toward the dock. "I think our friend is making his move," Rosco whispered, then eased his way to the shattered entry and looked out in the direction of the pier. "Yep . . . As soon as he steps into the boat, I'm going to take him." Rosco turned back to face Belle. "I want you to stay here, okay?"

"Aye aye, sir."

After a minute he said, "Okay. He's trying to start the engine. I'll be back."

Rosco slid silently through the broken door frame and Belle quickly positioned herself beside it. She watched him approach the dock, then slow his pace to a casual stride while Peter, suddenly aware that he'd been cornered, began frenetically twisting and turning the key in the ignition.

When the engine didn't kick over, Peter jammed the shift-handle back and forth in the gearbox, then tried the ignition once more. The motor refused to respond. Peter began pounding on the gauges, to no avail, then grabbed a long gaffing hook and heaved it at Rosco. It sliced the air like a harpoon, but Rosco sidestepped the weapon and moved closer to the launch. When he was alongside, he pulled the green wire from his pocket, then held it aloft in his left hand while his right kept a firm grip on his pistol.

"You're not going anywhere without this, Peter."

Peter looked up at Rosco and seemed to deflate. He slouched down into the pilot's seat and dropped his head in his hands. Then he began to weep. "He had so much. It's not fair. It's just not fair. I have nothing."

"I'm taking you back to Newcastle, Peter. You can explain your motives to the police. Now, move to the bow of the boat. Slowly."

As if he'd received the order from an otherworldly source, Peter stood and shuffled to the launch's bow. Then he slumped down on the bright orange cushions that doubled as flotation devices.

"Now, I'm not much of a boat person, Peter, so I'm going

to have Belle motor us back to the mainland." Rosco pulled a pair of handcuffs from behind his back. "And just to make certain we don't have any problems during the trip, I want you to put one end of these around your right wrist, and attach the other end to that front railing there." Rosco pointed with his .32. "You can handle that, can't you? I don't want to use this pistol, but I will if I have to. You can believe that."

Peter looked up at Rosco and nodded. Rosco tossed the cuffs to him and watched while Peter did as he was told.

"Okay, I'm going to get Belle. Sit tight."

Rosco replaced his pistol in its holster and returned to the house.

"So, how did it go?" Belle asked from the doorway.

"As if you weren't watching the entire thing?"

"What do you have, eyes in the back of your head?"

Rosco laughed. "No. I just think I'm getting to know you too well."

"How did you discover it was Peter who killed Briephs?" Belle asked.

"I didn't suspect him at first . . . Actually, I had a strong hunch it was Roth. Only a gut feeling . . . I had nothing to base it on—other than the fact that he was throwing every obstacle in the world in my path. So, after I talked to Lever, I caught Roth at the airport. He knew the entire case was about to break wide open, with regard to bad press, that is. Lever had already informed him of that. Roth's real loyalty is to the Senator, if nothing else. His concern was that the situation be kept from the media— that it not endanger the Senator's chance for reelection."

"Briephs was blackmailing Roth, did you know that?"

"How did you come to that conclusion?"

"I have my sources." Belle smiled smugly. "Roth was smuggling stolen artwork into the country for Briephs."

Rosco shook his head. "You seem to know everything."

"What I don't understand is, what could Briephs possibly have had on Roth?"

"Try nothing."

"Nothing! What do you mean, nothing?" Belle looked at Rosco as if he'd lost his mind. He merely shrugged his shoulders. "Why would Roth risk going to jail?" she demanded. "There must have been something . . ."

"He laid it all out for me. He's an arrogant turkey, I'll give him that much. He hand-fed me every lurid detail: museums, middlemen, the works, then basically dared me to do anything with the information—and threatened to sue if I leaked any of his disclosures to the press. The plus side was that my visit eliminated him as a suspect . . . which made me reexamine the entire investigation. And that's how I came up with the Pumpkin idea and phoned the mechanic at the marina. Whoever beat JaneAlice had to be tipped off by the very first puzzle."

Belle took his hand. "Great minds think alike . . . So, what was Roth's story?"

"He and Briephs went to Yale together. They rented a house when they were seniors."

"You're certain?"

"Straight from the horse's mouth. They've known each other for over thirty-seven years. Briephs got Roth his first job—with his uncle, the Senator, when he was still a member of the House."

"But why didn't Sara explain the relationship when you met her?"

"Because Roth never left her house the day Thompson died. She knew he hadn't murdered her son; consequently, she never imagined there would be a reason to suspect him. I don't think she knew how close their friendship had grown; otherwise I'm sure she would have suggested I speak with Roth from the beginning."

"I can't believe Roth would risk his career like that."

"First of all, Ol' Bulldog has a passion for this stuff that's just as strong as Thompson's was. He visited Windword at every opportunity. He told me so himself . . . And it wasn't simply to see his old friend. He only came out to sit and sur-round himself with the artwork . . . And according to Thompson's will, Roth gets it all. The house and everything in it."

"You're kidding."

"Nope . . . And really, when you look at it from his stand-point, smuggling the stuff was a no-risk situation. He was doing his old Yale roomie a favor. Paying him back for past help and getting his own private museum in the bargain. There was no possible way he could have been caught. He knew that . . . Plus, there's always the thrill of getting away with an illegal activity. You'd be surprised how many crim-inals spring into action for that reason alone . . . And, as Roth so willingly explained, in the long run there's no way to obtain actual proof of his involvement—especially now that Briephs is dead."

"And he gets to keep it all?"

"Not anymore . . . That's the other thing that eliminated

Roth as a suspect, but explained his desire to conceal the crime. If Briephs is murdered—which he was—investigators enter the house. They discover the stolen pieces and return them to their rightful owners. Roth doesn't go to jail, but he loses his museum."

Belle thought for a moment and then shouted, "Yes! There's still a way to get Roth! Peter witnessed Roth giving Briephs 'a package.' This happened in the yacht club parking lot. According to Peter, the two appeared incredibly suspicious. Plus, he said he brought Roth out here cradling packages in his arms as if the contents were extremely fragile."

"You're certain about this?"

Belle's excitement colored her words. "Peter told me! He watched the exchange!"

Rosco stood thinking. After a moment he said, "I don't know . . . At this point, Peter's a murderer. And unless he can positively identify a specific item, it's going to be difficult to convince a jury that an aide to a senior U.S. Senator was smuggling stolen artwork into the country—and exchanging it in public . . . We'll supply Lever with the information when we deliver Peter. It'll be up to the police and the D.A.'s office to pursue it . . . We can push them, but they might not be willing to plea-bargain on murder one, and that's the only way a defense lawyer would allow Peter to cooperate . . ."

Rosco stepped into the sunshine. He put his hands in his pockets and stared out at the water. The case was over; as he glanced back at Belle, he felt a definite sense of loss. He'd miss spending time with her. That fact had become painfully obvious. Why are all the good ones taken? he found himself wondering again. Aloud he said, "We should be heading back, I guess . . . You don't mind driving, do you? Or skippering . . . or whatever they call it?"

"Not at all." Belle smiled and placed her hands around his waist. She moved her lips toward his, but Rosco stopped her.

"I'm not going to do this, Belle," he said. "I'm not cut out to fool around with a married woman. I'm sorry. That's the way it has to be."

"But, that's what I've been trying to tell you . . . I got a letter from Garet. He's not coming back from Egypt."

"Ever? As in permanently?"

"Well, not for a few years, at any rate. He's found someone else. A 'soul mate' is the term he used. He wrote that if I wanted a divorce, he'd understand . . . In his convoluted way, he was saying that he'd prefer to end our relationship . . . I think he was hinting that I should instigate the action."

"So, it seems the ball's in your court?"

"It looks that way."

This time Rosco pulled her close. "Well, no matter how you look at it, I'd say you were separated."

"By about eight thousand miles."

Across

1. "The ___," Uris novel
4. Test
8. Light at sea?
13. Where Castro keeps a convertible
14. List
15. Shoot for
16. Sign
17. Old Staubach stat.
18. Burke: ___ by strangulation
19. Principle character?
21. A Nice farewell
23. Sounds of contentment
25. "___ Hur"
26. Tick ___
30. Mud tossers
32. To be in Paris?
33. Congreve lady
34. 18-Across, e.g.
35. He
39. Gaelic
40. It escapes at a crime scene
41. Flower part
42. Easy touch
44. ___ Garr
45. Undefined: abbr.
46. 9-Down's kids grp.
47. Pretty Spanish girl?
49. The Emperor and Blanc
53. Tests
56. Flapjack home: abbr.
59. "If, after I depart this ___," Mencken
60. New
61. Church part
62. Tied
63. Trap
64. Give off
65. Thing in law

Down

1. ___ Cronyn
2. Aid
3. Gal Friday?
4. Down under bird
5. Housemann has many
6. She
7. Cain's crime
8. Vanish
9. Al, formally
10. Carlyle's org.
11. Squeal
12. Bib. verb ending
13. 9-Down, e.g.
20. Black or white
22. Immigration grp.
24. Break
27. Dorothy's dog: pig-Latin
28. Mean
29. Views
30. Back-talker
31. Day ___
33. Puzzles for Belle, e.g.
35. Break
36. Old Staubach stats.
37. Cut off
38. Start the coals again?
42. Outlaw
43. It's good in a scrape
48. Man, e.g.
50. What Vance is after?
51. Cheers from 47-Across
52. Hal Crane, e.g.: abbr.
53. Switch positions?
54. ___ Howard
55. One of Frank's
57. Egg: comb. form
58. Favorite

THE CROSSWORD MURDER

POSTSCRIPT PUZZLE

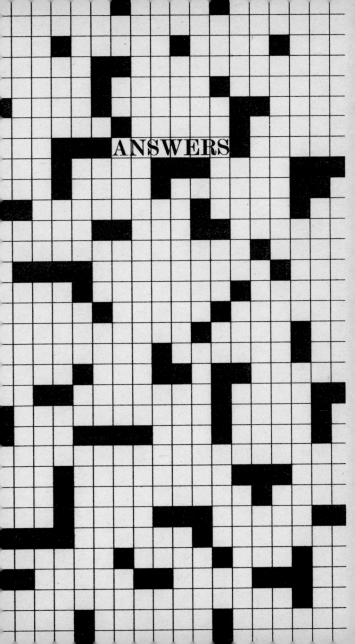
ANSWERS

THE CROSSWORD MURDER

PUZZLE #1

¹A	²G	³A	⁴L	■	⁵U	⁶S	⁷P	⁸S	■	⁹O	¹⁰B	¹¹E	¹²A	¹³H
¹⁴S	I	R	E		¹⁵S	L	A	P		¹⁶E	L	R	I	O
¹⁷T	R	I	M	T	H	E	Y	A	¹⁸R	D	A	R	M	S
¹⁹A	L	D	O	²⁰E	D	S		H		C				E
		²¹N	²²P	R		²³B	E	A	²⁴K			²⁵W		³⁰X
²⁶A	²⁷P	L	U	S		²⁸T	R	A	P		²⁹W	A		X
³¹S	L	I	M		³²D	U	I		³³R	³⁴A	I	S	E	
³⁵T	H	O	M	P	S	O	N	B	R	I	E	P	H	S
³⁶K	O	P	E	K		³⁷R	A	E		³⁸C	R	E	E	
³⁹O	R	S		⁴⁰I	⁴¹S	M	S		⁴²D	O	O	R	S	
	E		⁴³A	N	T	S		⁴⁴O	T	S				
⁴⁵M		P		U		⁴⁶F	⁴⁷A	O		⁴⁸P	⁴⁹A	⁵⁰S	⁵¹E	
⁵²A	⁵³F	⁵⁴T	⁵⁵E	R	⁵⁶N	O	O	N	D	E	A	T	H	S
⁵⁷I	L	O	R	O		⁵⁸R	O	I	L		⁵⁹C	O	O	N
⁶⁰L	O	O	S	E		⁶¹E	L	L	E		⁶²E	P	E	E

PUZZLE #2

S¹	C²	A³	R⁴		M⁵	E⁶	N⁷	S⁸	E⁹		L¹⁰	A¹¹	S¹²	T¹³
E¹⁴	L	S	E		O¹⁵	M	I	T	S		I¹⁶	N	C	A
L¹⁷	U	I	S		T¹⁸	I	G	R	E		A¹⁹	N	A	T
S²⁰	E	N	A	T²¹	O	R	H	A	L	C²²	R	A	N	E
			P²³	E	R		T²⁴	W	A	E				
B²⁵	E²⁶	T²⁷		A²⁸	M	A²⁹	L			A³⁰	L³¹	A³²	R³³	M³⁴
A³⁵	A	H		A³⁶	C	Y	L³⁷		S³⁸	A	L	O	O	
S³⁹	T	E	V⁴⁰	N⁴¹	H	O	U	S⁴²	E	M	A	N	N	
R⁴³	E	S	I	N		E⁴⁴	V	E	N		I⁴⁵	D	E	
A⁴⁶	R	E	E	D			E⁴⁷	S	A	U⁴⁸	N⁴⁹	A	Y	
			O⁵⁰	M⁵¹	E⁵²	R		P⁵³	R	O⁵⁴				
J⁵⁵	O⁵⁶	H⁵⁷	N⁵⁸	W	I	L	K⁵⁹	E	S	B	O⁶⁰	O⁶¹	T⁶²	H
O⁶³	B	O	E		S⁶⁴	P	I	R	O		M⁶⁵	I	R	O
T⁶⁶	I	P	S		S⁶⁷	E	L	E	N		P⁶⁸	L	A	N
S⁶⁹	T	E	T		F⁷⁰	A	L	S	E		H⁷¹	Y	P	E

PUZZLE #3

¹P	²L	³A	⁴N		⁵S	⁶T	⁷A	⁸B	⁹S		¹⁰A	¹¹S	¹²P
¹³L	A	N	E		¹⁴T	U	L	S	A		¹⁵O	C	T	A
¹⁶A	N	N	A	¹⁷B	E	L	L	A	G	¹⁸R	A	H	A	M
¹⁹I	K	E		²⁰E	E	E	S		²¹E	T	O	N
²²D	A	N	²³G	E	R	S		²⁴E	T	H	O	S
		²⁵B	I	N		²⁶P	²⁷A	T	H	S	
²⁸A	²⁹B	E	L		³⁰A	O	R	T	A		³¹S	³²U	³³P
³⁴B	A	R	T	³⁵H	³⁶O	L	O	M	E	W	³⁷K	E	R	R
³⁸E	R	G		³⁹E	V	I	L	S		⁴⁰O	R	N	E
	⁴¹C	R	E	E	S		⁴²B	E	V	
	⁴³E	⁴⁴T	H	E	R		⁴⁵M	⁴⁶U	R	D	E	⁴⁷R	⁴⁸S
	⁴⁹T	H	A	I		⁵⁰L	A	M	E		⁵¹S	O	U
⁵²S	H	A	N	N	⁵³O	⁵⁴N	M	C	A	R	⁵⁵T	H	U	R
⁵⁶R	I	N	G		⁵⁷N	I	N	A	S		⁵⁸V	I	S	E
⁵⁹I	C	E		⁶⁰S	L	O	W	S		⁶¹A	M	E	R

PUZZLE #4

S¹	L²	A³	T⁴		P⁵	A⁶	C⁷	T⁸		A⁹	S¹⁰	T¹¹	R¹²	O¹³
H¹⁴	I	G	H		A¹⁵	C	R	E		T¹⁶	O	R	A	N
A¹⁷	L	E	E		N¹⁸	E	O	N		A¹⁹	M	A	Z	E
M²⁰	I	S	T	R²¹	E	S	S		T²²	R	O	P	E	
			R²³	I	D		S²⁴	C²⁵	H	I	Z			
	S²⁶	M²⁷	U	G		W²⁸	O	E		A²⁹	S³⁰	K³¹	S³²	
	P³³	A	T	H	S		S³⁴	O³⁵	E	R		L³⁶	I	E
L³⁷	I	G	H	T	M	U³⁸	R	D	E	R³⁹	C⁴⁰	A	N	T
I⁴¹	C	I			U⁴²	R	D		B⁴³	E	I	N	G	
D⁴⁴	E	C	I⁴⁵		T⁴⁶	I	P		A⁴⁷	V	G	S		
		M⁴⁸	A⁴⁹	T	S	U		C⁵⁰	I	I				
	I⁵¹	T⁵²	A	L	Y		Z⁵³	O⁵⁴	O	M	L	E⁵⁵	N⁵⁶	S⁵⁷
A⁵⁸	R	A	G	E		E⁵⁹	Z	R	A		I⁶⁰	T	A	L
S⁶¹	A	N	E	R		A⁶²	L	E	S		A⁶³	N	T	I
A⁶⁴	N	G	S	T		R⁶⁵	E	S	T		N⁶⁶	A	S	T

PUZZLE #5

1 A	2 C	3 A	4 M	5 P		6 A	7 S	8 P		9 C	10 L	11 O	12 W	13 N
14 C	A	M	E	O		15 R	N	A		16 R	A	D	I	O
17 T	R	I	A	L		18 M	A	W		19 A	M	E	N	D
20 I	T	S	N	O	21 W	O	R	N	22 E	V	E	R		
23 V	A	S		24 C	O	R	E		25 C	E	N			
	26 P	L	O	Y		27 C	O	N	T	R	28 A	29 A		
30 A	31 D	32 I	E	U		33 A	I	N		34 O	R	35 T		
36 J	O	H	N	B	37 U	38 L	L	D	O	G	39 G	40 R	O	T	H
41 F	L	A		42 B	Y	E		43 R	O	M	E	O		
	44 E	45 D	46 I	T	O	R		47 S	48 A	A	B			
	49 N	R	A		50 H	A	L	F		51 S	52 A	53 E		
54 T	H	A	T	55 S	A	L	L	56 F	O	L	K	S		
57 A	58 G	O	O	D		59 P	S	T		60 I	V	I	E	S
61 F	E	N	C	E		62 I	T	E		63 T	E	P	E	E
64 T	R	E	K	S		65 N	E	D		66 I	R	A	N	S

POSTSCRIPT PUZZLE

	H¹	A²	J³		E⁴	X⁵	A⁶	M⁷		F⁸	L⁹	A¹⁰	R¹¹	E¹²
C¹³	U	B	A		M¹⁴	E	N	U		A¹⁵	I	M	A	T
O¹⁶	M	E	N		U¹⁷	S	N	R		D¹⁸	E	A	T	H
P¹⁹	E	T	E	R²⁰			A²¹	D	I²²	E	U			
		A²³	H	S²⁴		B²⁵	E	N			T²⁶	O²⁷	C²⁸	K²⁹
	S³⁰	L	I	N	G³¹	E	R	S			E³²	T	R	E
	F³³	A	I	N	A	L	L				N³⁴	O	U	N
R³⁵	O	S	C	O	P	O	L	Y	C³⁶	R³⁷	A³⁸	T	E	S
E³⁹	R	S	E			A⁴⁰	D	R	E	N	A	L		
S⁴¹	T	E	M		B⁴²	I⁴³	G	S	O	F	T	Y		
T⁴⁴	E	R	I		A⁴⁵	O	R		P⁴⁶	A	L			
		L⁴⁷	I⁴⁸	N	D	A			N⁴⁹	E	R⁵⁰	O⁵¹	S⁵²	
O⁵³	R⁵⁴	A⁵⁵	L	S		I⁵⁶	H	O	P⁵⁷		V⁵⁹	A	L	E
N⁶⁰	O	V	E	L		N⁶¹	A	V	E		E⁶²	V	E	N
S⁶³	N	A	R	E		E⁶⁴	M	I	T		R⁶⁵	E	S	

MARGARET COEL

THE EAGLE CATCHER

When tribal chairman Harvey Castle of the Arapahos is found murdered, the evidence points to his own nephew. But Father John O'Malley doesn't believe the young man is a killer. And in his quest for truth, O'Malley gets a rare glimpse into the Arapaho life few outsiders ever see—and a crime fewer could imagine...

❏ 0-425-15463-7/$6.50

THE GHOST WALKER

Father John O'Malley comes across a corpse lying in a ditch beside the highway. When he returns with the police, it is gone. Together, an Arapaho lawyer and Father John must draw upon ancient Arapaho traditions to stop a killer, explain the inexplicable, and put a ghost to rest...

❏ 0-425-15961-2/$6.50

THE DREAM STALKER

Father John O'Malley and Arapaho attorney Vicky Holden return to face a brutal crime of greed, false promises, and shattered dreams...

❏ 0-425-16533-7/$5.99

THE STORY TELLER

When the Arapaho storyteller discovers that a sacred tribal artifact is missing from a local museum, Holden and O'Malley begin a deadly search for the sacred treasure.

❏ 0-425-17025-X/$6.50